P9-CES-027

Disorderly Attachments

Jennifer L. Jordan

Spinsters Ink
2006

Copyright© 2006 by Jennifer L. Jordan

Spinsters Ink, Inc.
P.O. Box 242
Midway, Florida 32343

All rights reserved. No part of this book may be reproduced or transmitted in any form or by any means, electronic or mechanical, including photocopying, without permission in writing from the publisher.

Printed in the United States of America on acid-free paper
First Edition

Editor: Christi Cassidy
Cover designer: LA Callaghan

ISBN-10: 1-883523-74-5
ISBN-13: 978-1-8883523-74-9

For those who aren't afraid to believe

About the Author

Jennifer L. Jordan, a Lambda Literary Award finalist, is the author of *A Safe Place To Sleep, Existing Solutions, Commitment To Die* and *Unbearable Losses*, all mysteries in the Kristin Ashe series. For more information or to read excerpts of her books, visit her Web site at www.JenniferLJordan.com.

PROLOGUE

Some people, it takes time to despise.

Not Carolyn O'Keefe.

She made me wary the minute she walked into my office twenty-nine days ago. Something in her mannerisms gave me pause—her smug arrogance, her detachment, her false relaxation. While I couldn't define my fears, I nonetheless decided to turn her away.

Yet before the end of our first appointment, she had uttered two words that guaranteed I would do as she asked.

Words that could never be taken back or forgotten.

My temper started to crack the second I agreed to do her bidding, and the fissure widened over the days that followed. I suppose I could have accepted help or sought intervention, but I was on a path that could not be corrected.

Each decision I made from this boiler of anger has led me to where I am today.

I can see that now as I lie in wait for Carolyn O'Keefe, but I remain certain in my convictions.

Especially one.

When she comes into sight, I will kill her.

CHAPTER 1

"I have thirty days to decide whether to have an affair."

Those were the exact words Carolyn O'Keefe used, over the phone, to secure an appointment on a Tuesday morning in late July. She would identify herself only as Lynn, but she promised to stop by my office within the hour.

By the time she walked through the door four hours later, I was fuming, an emotion that disintegrated when she placed a rubber-banded bundle of cash on my desk.

"I assume you're Kristin Ashe," she said in an authoritative voice.

I nodded.

"Thirty days, that's the deadline. I'll pay you ten thousand dollars to retrieve information to aid in my decision."

I offered her a seat, but she declined.

This put me at a disadvantage when I lowered myself into the leather swivel chair behind my desk, but I had to bear it. I couldn't very well take notes standing up, and sitting put me closer to the cash.

Ten grand.

I smiled inside. That would pay a lot of overhead for a lot of months.

"Tell me more about the affair," I said noncommittally.

"I'm in a long-term partnership, but recently, I've become uncontrollably attracted to someone else."

"A woman?"

"Yes." In her mid-fifties, my prospective client wore a designer tan pantsuit and heavy jewelry, large rings and bracelets with rainbow-colored stones. Reading glasses rested on top of tiger-colored hair that swooped up in a girlish, straight style, and thin eyebrows, plucked to perfection, set apart wide eyes and drew attention to a high forehead, which was now wrinkled.

"You're afraid this will threaten your relationship with your partner?"

"That's the least of my worries. We have an open agreement that's tolerated a number of trysts. My concern is that in becoming intimate with this much younger person, I might create a messy entanglement."

"How did you meet, you and the younger woman?" I said as my gut tightened.

"I can't disclose the exact circumstances, but let's just say in a professional context," she replied, her eyes never leaving mine.

Since she arrived, her stare hadn't wavered.

Nothing on my desk would have distracted her, because I kept it stark, no personal photos or mementos. Only a blank blotter, a digital clock, a laptop and two empty in/out baskets. But the items on my colleague's desk—the pinwheels and kaleidoscopes, gumball machine, tabletop Zen garden with pen-size rake and dozens of framed snowboarding photos—something should have elicited a reaction.

Unable to tolerate her gaze, I pushed back from the desk, held a legal pad close to my chest, and concentrated on taking notes. "What happens in thirty days?"

"I have the opportunity to go away for the weekend with her, without varying my routine or arousing suspicion."

"This woman you have your eye on, does she share your feelings?"

"She does."

"You know this because . . . ?"

"I know," she said harshly, then her voice softened, almost disappearing. "We've fallen deeply in love, without words or touch."

I raised an eyebrow. "You haven't said anything or made a pass?"

"No."

"She hasn't made a move on you?"

"I believe she has, but not in a provable manner. For example, there have been quite a few lingering touches."

"Meaning?"

"When we shake hands, when our knees touch below the conference table, subtle overtures."

I fastened my gaze on the wad of cash. "What do you expect me to do?"

"I want you to follow her, around the clock."

"I have a full caseload," I said, stretching the truth by three-quarters of a caseload.

She said briskly, "I'll purchase as many hours as you can spare. I want you to make this your highest priority. I must know where she goes, what she does, who she knows. You'll be with her in the morning when she leaves her house and at night when she pulls into the driveway. I'm paying you to interview her coworkers, her neighbors, her associates. You need to get inside her and find out everything there is to know."

"Background checks? I can run a civil check, a criminal check and a credit history. I could have those reports to you within twenty-four hours."

"Those are fine, but you'll have to go further. I want to make sure she's emotionally stable. You'll bring me information on her character, her values, her likes, her dislikes, what she eats, what makes her laugh, why she cries, what scares her, what delights her."

"Wouldn't it be easier for you to uncover those yourself, er, naturally, as the relationship unfolds?"

"You have no idea who I am, which we'll leave at that, but I hold a position of extreme trust. My career is in the public eye, scrutinized at every turn. I can't afford a dirty breakup, or blackmail or, worse, a widespread outing. I've been burned in the past, very badly. I must act with more caution."

"If you're so concerned, why risk an affair at all?" I said neutrally.

"She's the most beautiful woman I've ever met. I won't squander the opportunity."

"If you don't mind my asking, what are you attracted to in her?"

Lynn/Carolyn stood perfectly still, hands clasped loosely in front of her, and remained expressionless. "Where do I begin? The curve of her smile, the sound of her laugh. The way she dresses, the glow of her skin, the jewelry she wears." She checked herself, before continuing in a carefully controlled tone. "I could live in the light shining off her golden hair or lose myself in her green eyes, tender pools made radiant by the sun. Her touch is electric, and she smells fresh, of oranges and flowers."

I suppressed a cough. "Is this woman in a relationship?"

"Discovering that is your first order of business. I don't enjoy competition, but if I must fight for her, I'll win."

Honestly, the whole scenario gave me the creeps, but the tower of bills beckoned.

"How can I contact you?" I said, stalling.

"You can't. I'll call for updates, but we mustn't meet again."

"I'd like to know your last name, for my records. And a phone number, in case of emergency."

"Absolutely not."

"I have a standard contract that clarifies and protects your interests and mine," I said, opening a drawer to retrieve the one-page document.

"No. These are my conditions."

I slammed the drawer. "You trust me with the money, but not your name?"

"The money is replaceable. My reputation isn't. I can't afford to jeopardize it in the event of a misstep."

"I rarely make mistakes," I said, tense.

"I'm aware of that, or I wouldn't have hired you."

"How did you hear about me? Do we have a mutual acquaintance?"

"We certainly do, but I'm not foolish enough to reveal her name."

"Fair enough," I said with an easy smile as I fingered the money.

"You'll do as I ask?"

I had no intention of working for this woman, but I did pose one more question, out of idle curiosity. "What's her name, the object of your lust? I assume you can reveal that."

She measured me before saying, "Don't mock me."

I pushed away the money, back toward her, almost off the desk, when she uttered two words that suspended my movements.

Two words that I'd heard and screamed and whispered a thousand times.

Two words that jump-started my rage.

"Destiny Greaves."

CHAPTER 2

Destiny Greaves.

Follow my own lover?

I laughed nervously at the mention of Destiny's name, but my bemusement turned to cold fear when I saw the look on her face.

She wasn't kidding, which made me feel sick to the core.

If this woman was interested in Destiny, Destiny must have given her a signal.

I couldn't think of anything to say.

She filled in the gap. "Is there a problem?"

Outside, a squeal preceded the sound of a collision. I didn't flinch, because that particular noise from the busy one-way street penetrated my psyche at least twice a week, but she didn't jump either.

Instead, she stared at me impassively, almost looking through me, never moving from the corner of the room.

"No, no," I stammered. "Not at all." I pushed the money into my top desk drawer and lowered my shaking hands to my lap.

"As director of the Lesbian Community Center, I believe Destiny Greaves is well-known."

"Very."

"Is she an acquaintance of yours?"

I froze with indecision.

I had three options. I could turn down her proposal, but what if she hired someone else? I could tell her I lived with Destiny, but that would prevent me from finding out more about her motives. Or I could lie, hoping to discover the truth as soon as possible.

"We've never met," I said calmly, denying the existence of my three-year love affair with Destiny, the best days of my life.

"Splendid," she said, turning to leave. "I'll be in touch."

• • •

My head felt like it could explode, and all of my calm had evaporated by the time Fran Green joined me at the office.

She must have responded to the panic in my summons, because when she sprinted through the door, her short, gray hair lay lifeless, absent its usual combing. She wore the same shirt as I'd seen the day before, inside out, making it hard but not impossible to read, "Just Say No To Faux."

Never one to hide her feelings, Fran often broadcast them across her flat chest. The look worked with her compact, five-foot frame, drawing attention away from her belly, complementing her crew cut and lack of makeup. Typically, she rounded out the outfits with sweats or jeans in the winter, cargo shorts in the summer. On a good day, at the end of the summer, her legs displayed a shade of color, but on this afternoon, only strands of red and purple veins broke the monotony of white skin.

Concern registered in every crevice on her 67-year-old face, and the worry deepened as I paced back and forth, gesturing wildly and ranting.

"Slow down, Kris. Gotta stop spouting gibberish. Destiny okay? She been in some kind of accident?"

I gulped for breath and shook my head. "Someone's trying to have an affair with her."

Fran's features relaxed. "That's it?"

"That's it?" I cried. "This woman loves Destiny's smell and her shiny hair. I bought that citrus shampoo. Remember the hairdresser who loaded me up on product? I gave it all to Destiny."

"Pipe down, kiddo."

My voice rose. "The way she dresses! This woman loves that? I've picked out half her wardrobe. Remember how she used to wear everything oversized, never tucked in? I changed that! Me!"

Fran nodded. "Certainly helped accentuate her fine figure."

"Her jewelry. I gave her those diamond earrings for our second anniversary."

"Stunners."

"Her eyes. This woman had the gall to call them 'radiant pools.' She wouldn't have seen them in sunlight if I didn't nag Destiny to take off her sunglasses. How dare this Lynn person try to have an affair with my lover." I screamed.

"Okay, Kris," Fran said soothingly. She lowered herself to the wooden chair behind her desk, pulled out a bottom drawer and propped her feet on its edges. Pointing to the Zen garden, she bent an eyebrow. I shook my head, resisting the offer, and Fran absentmindedly began to move sand. "Gotta know that happens a fair amount at the Center. Women approach your squeeze all the time. Can't be helped, doesn't mean anything."

"They do? Don't they respect our relationship?" I said plaintively.

"Some don't know about it, some don't care. Speaking of smell, what's that odor?" Fran bent toward the floor and flared her nostrils. "You clean the carpets this morning?"

"That's Lynn's perfume," I spat. "I've been airing out since she left, but I can still taste it."

"Surprised the woman could smell Destiny through this cloud. Someone needs to tell her fragrances are best smelled in a nuzzle, not from a bus stop away."

"Fran," I said irritably, "could you please focus?"

"Where was I? Oh, yeah. You know Destiny wouldn't encourage a dalliance. Wears that commitment ring of yours proudly. Never seen her twist it, much less take it off. Girl has a narrow range, only sees you. Everyone else disappears. But that doesn't stop the fan mail. Is that what happened? You found out about one of the letters?" Fran said, gesturing at me with the miniature rake.

"Fan mail?"

"Comes to the Center as often as hate mail. Nothing to it. Destiny's a role model, one of the few lesbians out there in the papers and on TV. Good-looking and friendly. Some gals might cross a boundary to get at her."

"How do you know about this fan mail?" I said indignantly.

"She tells me about it. Destiny and me, we're tight."

"Why don't I know?"

With the rake, Fran scratched an eyebrow until its hairs stood on end. "Doesn't want to worry you. Unpleasant part of the job. No sense bringing it home, dumping it on the hearth. Adulation bothers her as much as hatred. Best you forget about it."

"This isn't a letter. This woman knows Destiny personally, or at least says she does. There's something about her . . ."

"What gives? How'd you get wind of the crush?"

"She tried to hire me." I stopped striding long enough to retrieve the money from my desk drawer. I dropped it into Fran's lap with a heavy thud.

"Holy smackers! Must be a couple thou here."

"Try ten. Lynn wants me to follow Destiny for the next thirty days."

Fran's face lost all color. "We've got a problem."

She tossed the money to the floor, stood and began to march, military style, a straight path across the carpet, hitting the rake into the palm of her hand in a steady drumming.

Afraid we'd collide, I plopped onto the couch across the room and massaged my forehead, but the touch did nothing to ease my searing headache.

"I've been trying to tell you," I said, hysteria nipping at the edges of my voice.

"Cripes!"

"I'm supposed to report back on Destiny's character, so this bitch can decide whether to have an affair with her. Destiny Greaves, my partner. The most important person in my life. The woman I made love with last night. The one who lights up every time she sees me." My words came out faster and louder until they dissolved into an incoherent muddle.

Fran joined me on the couch, grabbed me by the shoulders and held me tightly until I stopped shaking.

Holding my hand—as much to prevent me from bolting as to provide comfort—she said, "Better start from the beginning."

The determined look in her eyes momentarily quieted my dread, and I began a calm summary.

"What should I have done?" I said after concluding.

"Taken the case," Fran replied bluntly. "No other choice."

"What am I supposed to do now?"

"Leave it to me."

"What will you do?"

"Soon as possible, get a line on her, turn the tables." Fran started pacing again. She paused only long enough to stand next to the edge of her desk and furiously rake the Zen garden, sending sand in every direction. "Everything that broad wants to know about Destiny, we'll find out about her. When I'm done, we'll know how many times a day she takes a crap. You pretend to tail your lover, and I'll stalk the stalker."

I sighed in relief. If anyone could help me through this, Fran Green could.

She'd spent most of her adult life in the convent and, in that time, dealt with addiction, suicide, child abuse and rape. She'd also set up programs for pregnant teens, women in prison and seniors, and while many of her efforts had won as much criticism as awards, she'd never backed down. Three years earlier, shortly after she ended her service to the Catholic Church, we met during an investigation and began a friendship.

I looked at Fran eagerly. "Where will you start?"

She stabbed the rake into the Zen garden and brushed off her hands. "For starters, track down her identity. Smoke her out."

"I have her address." Fortunately, some of my brain cells had continued to function after Lynn left my office.

"Came by it how?"

"I had Beth follow her."

"Young thing next door, at the florist's?"

I nodded. "As soon as Lynn left through the front, I ran out back, caught Beth and asked her to help. She took off after Lynn in the delivery van and stayed with her for about six miles to thirty-one hundred South Oneida Street. I gave Beth twenty bucks, and she was thrilled, but don't say anything to her mom. She's not supposed to drive the van."

"Too many tickets?"

"Too many accidents."

Fran ran to the seat behind her desk. "Let's hop online and search property records."

"I already did. Shirley Bassett owns the house."

She pulled up abruptly. "Shirley Bassett? You sure?"

"Positive."

Fran said stoutly, "Can't be accurate."

"You know a Shirley Bassett?"

"Yep, and can't be her. Upstanding woman. Oozes integrity. Your woman short, petite with black-burgundy hair? Big mole on her right cheek, early fifties, glasses with no frames?"

I conveyed my discouragement with a loud exhale. "It's not the same person. The woman I met was tall, slightly heavyset, tiger-colored hair, reading glasses. Only their ages match, more or less."

Fran frowned and muttered to herself, "Lynn, Lynn, Lynn."

I interrupted her mental scrolling of an imaginary Rolodex. "Fran, you can't know every woman in Denver."

"I sure as hell know Shirley Bassett," she retorted, pride injured.

"You've met her?"

"Many a time. Press her flesh every month. Been telling you, you should get out more, join me in the old girls' networking."

"She comes to your meetings?"

"Never misses one. Don't know what it all means, what association she'd harbor with someone chasing after your honey, but you've landed yourself right in it. Pulled up the address of the most influential businesswoman of the past decade. Says so herself every chance she gets, boasting about some nomination she landed in the last century."

"What does she do?"

"Owns a boutique investment firm. Wants to get her hands on my nest egg, but the business is a lark. Her true calling is the Denver Women's Chamber of Commerce. Largest women's chamber in the country. Built it up to twenty-two hundred individual members, including yours truly, and a few hundred corporations. Multimillion-dollar annual budget."

"Is she a lesbian?"

"Always thought so, but she does her best to convey the opposite. Shows up at every fancy function with a gentleman."

"The same one?"

"Rotating. Always makes it a point to dance a few slow ones, groin to groin, with whatever stooge she brings."

"Does she volunteer for the women's chamber? Don't tell me she's on the board."

"Founder and president," Fran said, not smiling. "Built it from scratch five years ago."

This revelation caused me to lie back down, with a pillow smashed against my head. I had to block out the jabs of fluorescent light, or I was afraid the throbbing in my brain would leak out my ears.

Fran cautiously peeked under the fabric. "You okay?"

I groaned. "What am I supposed to tell Destiny?"

"Not a thing. That girl's got enough to worry about without telling her a middle-aged crackpot's on her path. Might break her concentration with that big deal she's working on with the schools. Don't go grilling her, either. Two questions into it, and she'll zoom to red alert. Trust me to fix this, and we'll bring your sweetheart into the loop when it's all over."

This was only the beginning of Fran's lecture.

She spent the next hour delivering ice packs from the freezer for my headache and convincing me not to say a word to Destiny.

Everything she said made sense, and before she bolted out the door for a date she'd almost forgotten, she extracted a promise of silence.

CHAPTER 3

Too bad I broke my word before the day's end.

In my defense, I had no idea how hard it would be to keep my mouth shut until I saw Destiny, and somehow, she sensed a shift in me before I could say a word.

Maybe I shouldn't have hugged her for so long when she came home at eight with takeout Mexican food, but I couldn't help myself.

"That was nice," she said at the end of our embrace, which progressed into an even longer kiss. "What brought this on outside the bedroom?"

I pushed a clump of shoulder-length blond hair away from her eyes. "I'm glad to see you."

She backed away and held me at arm's length. "Are you okay? You look terrible. You slept well last night, didn't you? I only heard you get up once."

"I'm not tired," I said truthfully. With the adrenaline coursing through me, I could have pulled a month's worth of all-nighters. "I had a long day at work."

"That new case, that woman who called this morning?"

I nodded feebly, thankful I hadn't shared anything more during our phone call earlier in the day. I'd told Destiny I had a new client coming in, but not who or why.

"Do you want to talk about it?"

"Not tonight, thanks."

She slid food from Styrofoam containers onto plates, and we carried it outside, along with two tall glasses of lemonade, to our four-tiered deck. I lit the lantern on the table, and we sat, side by side, on matching chairs.

"Why don't you tell me about your day," I offered, which made her brighten.

Between bites of burrito and chips and salsa, Destiny filled me in on her current project. Her vision included services for gay, lesbian, bisexual and transgendered adolescents, provided through the Metro Denver Public Schools system. Slowly but surely, she'd initiated contact with the diverse factions that influenced education: the school board, administration, teachers union, parent-teacher associations and student councils. I'd never seen such passion in her, and it appeared as if she'd set aside everything else in favor of this agenda, one which she claimed could make a lasting difference in the lives of GLBT youth.

"I can't believe I've secured the tentative approval of the superintendent of schools. Her opinion carries weight with all the groups. A parent from the PTA introduced us a few weeks back, and we've had a series of productive meetings. I think I've brought her around, made her see that we need to give these kids a safe environment to express themselves. If we can do that, we can prevent them from dropping out, from running away from home, from committing suicide. I feel like it's going to happen," Destiny said excitedly.

"I'm sure it is," I agreed, my headache beginning to reappear.

"Do you know what a breakthrough this could be, Kris? We'll begin with a pilot program of social clubs for the kids, but can you imagine how far we could take this? We could introduce speakers' bureaus, outreach, crisis intervention, one-on-one mentorships. There's no end to the possibilities. We could set an example for the nation."

She went on to outline successful programs, on smaller scales, that had been introduced in Boston and San Francisco and recited setbacks in Toledo and Dallas, but my mind began to wander.

Back to Lynn, the mysterious woman who had set her sights on my lover.

"Not to change the subject," I said, after Destiny returned from the kitchen with servings of rhubarb cobbler, "but do women still approach you?"

"Approach me for what?" she said lightly, but my plate crashed to the table when she let go.

"You know, put the moves on you?"

"Sometimes," she said cautiously, still standing. "Why?"

"Fran mentioned today that you get a lot of fan mail. Why haven't you said anything to me about it?"

Destiny grabbed the arms of her deck chair and cocked it away from me before dropping into it. "I wouldn't call it a lot, and most of it's harmless. You and I don't need to talk about every woman who writes to me because she doesn't know any other lesbians."

"Has anyone done anything inappropriate with you lately, said something, touched you?"

"Not that I'm aware of, but where's this coming from, Kris? Don't you trust me?"

The night deteriorated from there, capping off one of the worst days of my life.

The dirty dishes stayed outside as we moved our heated discussion inside, an argument that stretched without resolution late into the night. The main themes revolved around trust, autonomy and the difference between emotional and sexual monogamy.

I had begun the evening desperately needing reassurance that Destiny would never become involved with another woman, on any level.

I ended it more confused and suspicious than ever.

• • •

The next morning, a vein in Fran's forehead bulged.

"Only a lesbian would bring a date on a date."

"Huh?" I said absently. I'd only been half-listening as I played a game of solitaire and fought off drowsiness.

"I take a woman to Cuisine Couture, top five restaurant in Denver. Not exactly a buddy bistro. Linen tablecloths, hundred smackers for a bottle of wine. Where's she think the relationship is headed?"

"This is Mary Ann?" I said, proud to have remembered the name. I moved two cards and jerked my concentration away from the computer screen.

"One and the same. How's she respond? Invites me to a Rockies game. Tells me friends from Kansas coming in. Peachy, I tell myself. Making progress. Gal's bringing me into her circle of friends."

"The date didn't go well last night?"

"Understatement of the year. I had to pay for my own ticket, and picture me sitting in the back of her SUV, between the two friends."

I grimaced sympathetically. "Who was in front?"

"Floozy named Molly. Two of them birds held hands across the stickshift. Rude. Dangerous, too. What am I, chopped liver? Ground my teeth to a nub making conversation about the drought with those Kansas farmhands."

"No need to get nasty," I said mildly.

"No offense intended. Ursula and Rita own a farm near Topeka. Nice enough couple. Felt bad not saying good-bye."

"You left that abruptly?"

"Quick as I could. Soon as we got to the stadium, left my seat to get a brat with kraut. Mary Ann followed and asked what I thought of Molly, her date. I said, 'You serious?' She nodded, and I gave her a good look at my backside and left. Caught a cab home."

"Don't be discouraged," I said, responding to Fran's forlorn expression.

Ever since her 33-year relationship with Ruth had ended the previous winter, Fran had been on a slew of first dates, but not many seconds.

"I've got a friend e-mailing everyone in her address book, trying to land me a date. Wants me to write a physical description of myself. Pluses and minuses. Can you believe that?"

"What's wrong with describing yourself?"

"I ain't no steer at auction."

"You know people care about physical features."

"You try it."

My voice rose an octave. "Me?"

"Never mind. I'll do it for you, see how you like it. Pluses: nice teeth, even and white. Cute nose and ears. Sparkling eyes. Well-sculpted calves. Trim legs and narrow hips. Good-sized chest. Physically fit. Average height and weight. Look a little younger than your age, thirty-seven, but not much."

"Okay, okay," I said, uncomfortable.

"Not done. Minuses: Short fingernails. Posture not as erect as it could be (blame it on the boobs). Too many freckles. Dry skin, need to use more moisturizer."

"I notice you didn't mention my hair."

"Asset and liability."

"Thanks," I said, acknowledging Fran's rare display of diplomacy.

It was bad enough that I'd been born bald and remained hairless for years, my wispy locks combed up in early J.C. Penney portraits, but my adult surplus had developed into an even greater disadvantage. In nine months, I'd gone through five hairdressers as I searched for one to style, rather than hack, my thick, brown hair. My second crown in the back, or cowlick, or whatever, apparently didn't help. Leave those hairs too long, and they formed an ugly helmet. Cut them short, and they stuck straight out the back of my head, like a makeshift shelf. Hairdresser number one? I'd tolerated mediocrity for years but had to fire her when she labeled the unruly section "dog hair." Number two I loved, but she retired before our second appointment. Number three moved to Crested Butte, a half-day's commute away. Number four worked at a salon in lower downtown, with snooty clientele and no parking. Number five's cut was too ordinary to justify the sixty-dollar price tag.

Number six I hadn't met but needed to urgently.

"Do you want me to list your features?" I offered.

"No need. Going to check out speed-dating, let the girls see for themselves. Can't beat it. Meet five women, spend ten minutes talking to each, move to the next seat. At least all the participants know this ain't no chum club."

"How odd."

"Latest rage, Kris. Have to go with the times."

"Who arranges these?"

"Sponsored by the Grays."

"The social group for lesbians over fifty?"

"That's it! Didn't know you were up on the community."

"Destiny mentioned them the other day. They called to rent office space from the Lesbian Community Center."

"She have room?"

"She will. The incest survivors group is moving out."

"Can't go wrong renting to the Grays."

"In this speed-dating setup, what do you do after you've met all the women?"

"End of the night, everyone fills out a slip listing the names of the ladies who caught her eye. Any crossover, organizer e-mails both parties, puts 'em in touch."

"What if no one chooses you?"

Fran guffawed. "Doubt that'll be a problem, but them's the breaks. Go back another week, fresh crop of gals. Graze the Grays, catch my drift."

I smiled. "You believe you can orchestrate love like this?"

"Random approach ain't working. Have to dedicate myself to the hunt, focus my efforts."

"Okay."

"You ain't convinced?"

"Not really."

"That's because you have someone in your nest. Bully for you, but I'm babeless. To correct that situation, I'll need luck and timing. What if a dame's attracted to me, but no sparks here? Or what if I go loopy, but nothing there? How about if we both feel comfortable, but no fireworks? Flames, but no contentment? More complicated than it seems. Only way to beat the odds. Volume."

I sighed. "How about a cat?"

"No can do. Not until they breed one that meets my requirements."

"Which are?"

"No shedding, no shredding."

I laughed, a hollow sound. The more I tried to concentrate on Fran's woes, the more my own interrupted.

Fran looked at me carefully. "Everything go okay with Destiny last night? Didn't say anything, did you?"

"No." I changed the subject before she could sniff out deceit. "Are you ready for Roberta Franklin?" I asked, referring to a new client who was scheduled to walk through the door in two minutes.

"You betcha. But I need to run something by you."

"About Destiny?" I said, instantly alarmed.

"About us. Better postpone the new business arrangement. You be the primary on this one."

"What made you change your mind?"

"Roberta's a sharp cookie, with an intricate dilemma. Best leave it to you, the expert. I'll cut my teeth on something with less at stake."

"You're trying to distract me, aren't you, hoping I'll forget about the threat of Destiny's affair?"

"Who me?" she said, throwing up her hands to underscore her innocence.

Although Fran Green and Roberta Franklin had traveled in the same social circles for years, their paths never intersected until the week before, when they shared a table at a community function. Fran came back from the dinner with Roberta's card and told me that she'd found another client, which brought us to a crossroads in our professional relationship. For several years, Fran had sent clients my way and helped out as needed but consistently refused compensation or recognition. While we sometimes experienced power struggles, the loose-knit agreement generally had worked.

With this case, however, she'd asked if she could be the primary, with me assisting. I agreed immediately but insisted she take half the paycheck. We fought about that for hours, but I held my ground, and Fran eventually capitulated. We hadn't put the new arrangement into action, but I liked it, because in many ways it provided a more honest framework.

Six months ago, in order to focus exclusively on private investigation, I'd sold the marketing business I started at the age of nineteen. My comfortable office and steady source of income had gone to my sister, but I'd never looked back.

Almost never, anyway.

I didn't miss the payroll or deadlines, but I did miss my six employees.

Fran must have sensed this, because over the past few months, she'd moved more and more of her possessions into my one-story office on Sixth Avenue. The migration started with her favorite stapler, then an old computer from home, followed by a bulletin board, a two-drawer filing cabinet and a spare phone. Add weekly trips to the office supply store and the delivery of an oak desk and chair, and one day, it dawned on me as I shut off her brass lamp and unplugged her humidifier, that she was more at home in my office than I was.

With this new comprehension, I felt slightly tricked, but I also realized that Fran Green understood, perhaps better than anyone, the way to my heart.

Little by little, without pressure of commitment.

Once struck, our verbal partnership agreement made me feel less beholden, but I harbored a thread of fear that Fran's new position and power would change her.

In a way, they already had, at least in how she dressed. She'd arrived that day wearing pressed khakis and a starched white, short-sleeved shirt, an outfit I would have chosen myself except for the elastic waistband and breast pocket. She'd exchanged her customary sneakers for a pair of clogs, and while her walk was wobbly, I credited her with trying.

I couldn't let Fran throw away her first opportunity so readily. "This was important to you. You wanted more responsibility."

"Consider I've got it, on the Greaves case. Primary on that one. You don't lift a finger without my A-OK."

"Never," I agreed.

A lie.

I had no intention of sitting by idly. In fact, I'd spent sleepless hours the night before coming up with a plan.

As I lay next to Destiny, in a hyper-alert state, listening to the rhythm of her sleep, I'd made a few decisions. First, I would spend every moment I could wrench from Fran's scrutiny tracking Lynn's movements.

I had to stay one step ahead of her.

If Destiny was a victim of Lynn's delusions, I would fight for her.

Next, I would examine every one of Destiny's words, gestures and actions. I would split each breath she took to see what gave it life, and I would slice her days into minutes.

At the first proof of betrayal, physical or emotional, I would leave in the middle of the night, without explanation or fight.

For my own sanity, I'd promised myself that our relationship, nurtured through three years of struggle and ecstasy, could end in an instant.

CHAPTER 4

Apparently, Fran caught my faraway look, because she looked at me shrewdly. "No meddling from you with Lynn or Destiny?"

"None, but what about the cash? We can't keep ten thousand dollars. I'd rather work at McDonald's than keep her money."

"Worry about that later." Fran wiped sweat from her brow, checked her armpits for dampness and opened the front door. "Tell you what, any money comes into this joint ought to go toward central air. Hotter than a convection oven in here."

"You get used to it."

"Better upgrade the furnace, too. Colder than a meat locker last winter."

"We're not going to renovate this place when we're only leasing. You have to take half the Roberta money for yourself."

Before I could lasso Fran's agreement, a booming voice interrupted.

"Are you two wrangling over my fee?" Roberta Franklin said, softening the accusation with a hearty laugh.

"I'm sorry—"

Roberta extended her hand to cut short my apology. "Don't be. I didn't expect charity, although I suspect Fran Green's done a bit of pro bono in her day."

I almost gulped with surprise when I saw the look Roberta shot Fran, one of open admiration and lust. This coming from someone who, to put it delicately, had been eligible for senior discounts for some time.

Roberta Franklin's slight stoop gave away her age, as did hundreds of wrinkles, which no amount of makeup could have concealed. Her face was a canvas of marks, artistic grooves that reminded me of the New Mexico desert. Bright pink lipstick and strawberry-blond hair, which fell in loose curls and cradled her face, softened an otherwise stern look. She wore a dark blue, short-sleeved mock turtleneck, white slacks and black flats, and her short frame could have held ten more pounds and still been considered slight.

Fran seemed taken aback by Roberta's overture, because I detected a hint of fluster as she offered Roberta the most comfortable chair in the office and dashed into the back to fetch refreshments.

Once we settled in, Fran and I at our adjoining desks and Roberta in front of the oscillating fan, Roberta began to speak. "There's no sense in beating around the bush. I have a chance to make a small fortune on a real estate deal, and I intend to use the profits from it as seed money for my dream development."

"Bert wants to build a retirement community for lesbians. First of its kind in the U.S. of A."

Roberta nodded. "The whole nine yards for folks who are getting on in years. All levels of care on one campus, built around a neighborhood center. I've waited twenty years for someone to bring this concept to the market, but no one has. Lesbians represent the ideal demographic. Most of us are childless and can't fool ourselves into thinking offspring will serve as caretakers. We have no children, which means—"

Fran jumped in, as if on cue, "No one's expecting an inheritance."

"The women with ample means, when they pass on, will leave a portion of their assets to the community. This, in turn, will allow us to provide housing and care for elderly or disabled lesbians in every income bracket."

I raised one eyebrow. "A massive sliding scale?"

"Exactly," Roberta and Fran agreed, in unison.

"Count me in fifty years from now, but what's the deal that's the means to the end?"

Roberta sighed. "I've had my eye on a project on the corner of Twelfth Avenue and Pennsylvania Street. I fell in love with this building fifty years ago. When I had my first job at a law office downtown, I'd take walks on my lunch hour, and I always made it a point to stroll by the Fielder mansion. No other building has captivated me in such a way."

"You've got the fever," Fran said.

"More than you might imagine. I've had crushes in my day," Roberta said, flashing a look at Fran, "but none that has lasted this long. Over the years, the gutters have detached, the wooden pillars have rotted, and the masonry has crumbled in spots. Notwithstanding those factors, it's a remarkable piece of architecture, with a wonderful wraparound veranda and a mosaic driveway. You'll have to see it to appreciate it."

"You want to buy the mansion?"

"Possibly. I've offered half a million, which might be generous, given my contractor's bid of a million or more for renovation."

Fran let out a sharp whistle. "A million large?"

"That's what the contractor says it will cost to make repairs and convert the building into eleven luxury condos, flats such as one would have found at the turn of the century. I've paid to have an architectural firm perform an assessment, and despite its appearance, the building is sound. Its mechanical and structural systems are intact. Nonetheless, if I don't act soon, the building might not be worth saving. I've been told that, as with all vacant buildings, the roof could start leaking. If that happens, the decay and deterioration will accelerate rapidly, reaching a point where it becomes steeply more expensive to restore."

"I assume you've put in a contract," I said.

"A letter of intent. I've deposited twenty-five thousand in earnest money with the family who owns it, and I have thirty days to reach a conclusion. However, before I take the leap, I need more information, facts I'd rather not retrieve on my own."

"Say it, we'll do it," Fran offered.

"I have five concerns that demand your expertise. To begin, I would like to know the complete history of the house."

"Easy enough. Trip to the downtown library'll scratch that itch. Could do it yourself, save some dough."

"I appreciate your concern for my pocketbook, Frances, but I spend enough time crouched over books in a library. I prefer to rely on your knowledge. You know the history of the area—"

Fran chortled. "Heck, I am the history."

"I'll count on Kris to synthesize the facts and summarize them in a quaint story. I'll want to include a brief history of the Fielder mansion in my marketing materials and sales presentations."

"Kris can do that, hands down," Fran boasted.

"Please, Fran," I protested, but secretly I was excited at the chance.

"I imagine she can," Roberta said. "The other assignments are a bit more challenging."

"Can't wait! Bigger the ballbusters, the better."

I shot Fran a sideways glance, which she ignored as she stared at Roberta, enthralled.

"I have two potential rivals who could scuttle the deal. One is a real estate developer, Philip Bazi, who plans to tear down the house and build a high-rise. He's already acquired six lots to the south and paid premium prices. I want to know more about him."

"Bazi, the one who rebuilt the performing arts complex?" Fran asked.

"The same. Apparently, on average, in the past twenty years, not a month has passed in which the family hasn't been contacted by someone who wanted to buy, lease, partner, consult, invest in or do something with the house. Philip Bazi is a man of great influence in the development community, a formidable foe."

"Your other competitor?" I prodded.

"Elvira Robinson, and she, too, is a force in her own right. She's the head of the historic organization, Save Our Denver, SOD. Her group has come to the conclusion that the best, highest use of the landmark is for it to be refurbished as a single-family home."

"You disagree?"

"The risk is too great for the slim profit margin, and the market for buyers of a single-family home of that size and quality doesn't exist. Anyone with three million dollars will move into Cherry Creek North and buy a new home with high-tech wiring, a great room, gas fireplaces, jetted tubs and walk-in closets."

"No big deal for you to include those," Fran pointed out.

"No, but I can't very well clean up the blocks surrounding the mansion that are rife with drug-dealing, vandalism and graffiti. I envision the flats selling to adventurous urban dwellers who feel comfortable paying two hundred to four hundred thousand dollars, with the carriage house commanding five hundred."

Fran paused in her meticulous note-taking and glanced up. "Check out Philip and Elvira. Got it. What else can we do to pleasure you?"

"This may be overstepping my bounds, but I'm concerned for the owner, the matriarch of the family. Hazel Middleton's ninety-one, and she lives alone in the carriage house. Through discreet inquiries, I'd like to ascertain if her daughter Nell is acting against her wishes."

"Railroading the old coot?"

I flashed Fran a sharp look, a warning to ease up on the jokes, but Roberta Franklin didn't seem to find the remarks inappropriate. In fact, she laughed louder with each one, as if tipsy from Fran's influence.

Roberta said with a half-smile, "The mother has signed over power of attorney to her daughter, a prudent move at her age and one that gives me no legal standing to interfere. Nevertheless, I would feel more comfortable with the owner's blessing."

"Fair enough," Fran said, slapping her notebook closed. "We'll get right on this. Got the contract, Kris?"

"Hold on," I said, scanning the tasks I'd recorded on a legal pad. "You'd like us to research the history of the building, investigate the opposition of Philip Bazi and Elvira Robinson and obtain assurance the elderly owner approves of the sale. That's four lines of query. What's the fifth?"

Roberta viewed me with increased respect. "She's as sharp as promised, Frances."

"Told you, Bert," Fran agreed, but with the reddening of her cheeks, I could tell she felt chagrin at having missed the tally.

"My last request calls for extreme caution and delicacy."

"Caution's our motto, delicacy our tagline."

"I'm almost embarrassed to bring it up. Normally, I don't respond to rumors of this nature."

"I'm sure whatever it is, we can address it," I said mildly.

Roberta hesitated. "Usually, I'm more concrete in my thinking."

"Spit it out, Bert!" Fran exclaimed.

"I need you to find out—"

"If there's a ghost in the house," Fran interrupted with a gale of laughter, and I joined in, certain the chorus would include Roberta.

It didn't.

Lips turned downward, Roberta Franklin frowned deeply and said in a somber whisper, "I need you to ascertain, beyond a reasonable doubt, if the house is haunted."

CHAPTER 5

Several seconds passed before anyone spoke.

The open door, the blowing fan and the slight breeze rolling through the office couldn't account for the sensation on the back of my neck.

I felt as if I'd been touched by dead air.

The haunted house revelation provoked an even more startling result in Fran Green, silence.

Roberta was the first to speak. "I saw a program on PBS, on paranormal phenomenon. As I understand it, spirits trapped for a period of time are difficult to move. Change and upset can turn the most docile inhabitant into a violent, evil presence."

Fran's eyes bulged. "You believe in ghosts, Bert?"

"I've been trained as a lawyer to think analytically, but I can't afford not to believe in them. Too much is on the line for this project to encounter obstacles, surreal or otherwise. Does the prospect frighten you?"

"Me?" Fran's voice cracked. "Bring it on. I ain't afraid of anything in this world or the next. I put in enough time at the altar to assure that. How about you, Kris?"

In a steady voice, I said simply, "I'd like to take the case."

I pulled out a contract and filled in the blanks while Fran freshened our drinks. We signed it, Roberta wrote a retainer check, and we toasted the agreement with two ice waters and a Diet Coke.

Nothing unnatural about that!

• • •

After Roberta left, Fran could barely contain her excitement. "Can you believe that beauty's the other side of eighty?"

"You didn't know she was eighty-one?"

"At our age, never discuss age. Would have put her within a year or two of me, maybe younger."

"Does Roberta still practice law?"

"Part-time. Marvel in the courtroom. Riveting. Lowers that melodious voice, struts back and forth in front of the jury and judge, sweet justice in motion."

"You've seen her at trial?"

"Just imagining."

"She has a crush on you."

"Get out!" Fran said, blushing. "Woman's old enough to be my mother."

"Not quite. Not unless she had you when she was fourteen."

"Could happen. Younger girls give birth all the time." Fran shot me a sly glance. "You really think Roberta has the hots for me?"

"Yes," I said patiently. "Was the feeling mutual?"

"Maybe. But I'd hate to date a client. Don't want to ruin pleasure with business."

"Technically, Roberta Franklin is my client."

A smile spread across Fran's face. "True enough."

• • •

Fran spent the balance of the afternoon dragging the subject back to Roberta Franklin.

I'd never seen her in such an altered state, and frankly, it wore me out.

I left the office before six, and by eight, Destiny and I were in front of the television, sharing a white pizza with gorgonzola cheese, figs and spinach.

As Destiny flipped through channels at her customary speed, I caught a glimpse of a woman's face and almost choked on crust.

Before I could ask Destiny to return to the public access channel, she hit the button. "There she is, Kris. That's the woman I told you about!"

My heart stopped for a dozen beats. "Which woman?"

"The superintendent of Metro Denver Public Schools," she said, almost giddy. "She's my advocate, the one who supports the gay and lesbian youth programs."

"What's her name?" I said, my voice hoarse with horror.

For there, filling our 58-inch screen, stood Lynn, the woman who had hired me to investigate Destiny, the one who wanted to have an affair with her.

"Dr. Carolyn O'Keefe. Doesn't she look powerful?"

I couldn't speak.

• • •

I was up all night.

As soon as Destiny fell asleep, I crept out of bed and returned to the living room. I watched Channel 8, catching repeats of Denver City Council meetings, postings of men who had solicited prostitutes, endless versions of neighborhood forums, but no Dr. Carolyn O'Keefe.

At dawn, I returned to Destiny's side and slept until nine o'clock, a fitful three hours.

When I arrived at the office at ten and found it empty, I hopped back in my Honda Accord and drove to Fran Green's house.

In the morning light, Fran's yard in Congress Park looked immaculate. Her lawn was a deep green, thick and without weeds, edged to perfection. In fact, the entire expanse looked as if it had been trimmed with scissors. The mulch, which she replaced twice a year, glistened, and every flower in the small garden was in full bloom.

Within days of moving into the house, Fran had become friends with most of the residents on the block, including her next-door neighbors. Both were named Sherry, and Fran had resorted to calling one "Uphill Sherry" and the other "Downhill Sherry," a designation neither seemed to mind.

On this day, I spent a few minutes chatting with Downhill Sherry, an emergency room nurse returning home from her shift.

Evidently, Fran overheard our conversation, because she opened the door before I could knock and escorted me into the sunroom, off the back of the house. Through floor-to-ceiling windows, I viewed Fran's latest creation, a water feature. Near completion, this was no dinky prefab fountain. Fran had contoured a multilevel waterfall, a ten-foot stream and a pond with a footbridge, all designed to look as if they fit naturally in the Colorado mountains. To enhance the illusion, she'd planted aspens and evergreens around the rock beds.

I took a seat on a white wicker lounger, and Fran pushed aside the newspaper and returned to her seat in a white wicker rocking chair. Inside the house, everything was white. White walls, ceilings, floors, cabinets, furniture and furnishings. When Fran had vacated the apartment she and Ruth shared, she'd given away all her possessions. "Smelled like smoke and reminded me of decay," she said, before we spent weeks shopping for furniture and accessories. The fresh start had chiseled away all of my patience but paid off in a streamlined, clutter-free zone.

Before I could tell Fran about my discovery, she trumped me, speaking with a mouth full of toast. "Carolyn O'Keefe, she's the one chasing Destiny."

"I know."

"Superintendent of a hundred-school system ought to know better," she said, taking a sip of coffee before doing a double take that led to a coughing jag. "How'd you get her name?"

"We saw her on television last night. Destiny said they'd had three meetings."

"About what? Don't tell me. Betcha it's the youth programs."

I nodded.

"Destiny's behavior suspicious when she talked about her?"

"I guess not," I said despondently.

"Didn't spill the beans, did you?"

"No."

"Caught her on Channel Eight, didn't you?"

"Yes, Fran," I said wearily, not nearly as impressed with her detection skills as she was.

"Love that government access channel, better than a soap."

"How did you find out Carolyn's identity?"

"Piece of cake. Last night, tracked her from Shirley Bassett's house to another abode, near Evans and Holly. Searched property records. Name floored me. Read about her in the papers, but never seen a photo or I might have matched it to your description."

"Where does she live?"

"About a mile from Bassett. Keeping the house as a front. O'Keefe stopped by to look around the yard and run the sprinklers. Must be making mortgage payments for appearances. Shacked up tight with that hound, Bassett."

"What should I do now?"

"You? Nothing." Fran leaned forward and spoke earnestly. "We know where she lives, a small victory. Better still, know who she is and where she works. Makes it a cinch to tail her. Power's on our side, but stick to the game plan. Have to control yourself. Don't follow her, don't think about her. Whatever you do, don't mention her to Destiny."

I started biting my fingernails. "But—"

"No buts. You let this come between you, shaves away trust. That happens, you may as well call it quits. Thanks to your stubbornness, this O'Keister will have achieved part of her goal. Earned herself a clear path to an unattached Destiny. You want that?"

"O'Keefe," I corrected. "No, but—"

"I mean it, kiddo. You chase the ghosts. Let me nail this evil spirit."

"Really?" I said grudgingly.

"I'd lay my life on the line for you and Destiny. You know that."

The hardness that washed over Fran's face seemed out of place in the serene setting of that morning, but the resolve in her eyes and clenching of her fists made me believe her.

I had to, because I couldn't allow myself to consider the alternative.

Life without Destiny, that could not happen.

Not ever.

CHAPTER 6

Funny how the mind works.

Every waking minute of the next four days, I waited for contact from Carolyn O'Keefe. I anticipated and dreaded each ring of the phone, even when I was home, where I knew she couldn't reach me.

Yet, on another plane, I managed to put the threat out of my consciousness, in a distant compartment that allowed me to function, to believe life was still good. I enjoyed a relaxing weekend with Destiny, one full of tennis and movies and yardwork.

Whenever doubt seeped in, I remembered that Fran was in charge and changed the subject in my head.

That charade worked until Monday morning, when the knowing and the denying collided in a phone call at eleven o'clock.

Carolyn O'Keefe didn't bother with niceties. "What can you tell me?"

I couldn't think.

My brain cells had stopped functioning.

I barely managed, in a slightly shaking voice, "Just a second, Carolyn. I have a UPS delivery. I'll be right back."

I hit mute and tried to get a grip. What advice had Fran given me? After ten deep breaths, Fran's words came back in a rush.

"First time O'Keefe contacts you, give her harmless info, stuff that doesn't violate Destiny's privacy. Keep it brief. Closer the lie is to the truth, easier to remember. On second thought, don't make up anything. Stick with facts."

Recalling Fran's pacifying voice restored my equilibrium. I picked up the receiver. "Sorry about that."

No reply.

"Are you still there?"

"Very clever. You know my name," she said in an icy retort.

Momentarily disconcerted by the slip, I somehow remained coolheaded. "I couldn't work under the circumstances you proposed. I have procedures to follow, for my own protection."

I waited for an explosion, but Carolyn said dispassionately, "I suppose you wouldn't have been worth the money if you couldn't figure out that simple fact. If you know my name, you've discovered my job title. With that, I assume you can appreciate the delicacy of my situation. It goes without saying you'll keep this in the strictest confidence."

"I will."

"What have you learned?"

"I've done the background and credit checks," I said. "There's nothing unusual. Destiny Greaves, age thirty-seven. Born in Denver. Liberal arts degree from the University of Denver. Started a Master's program at Regis University in nonprofit management but hasn't finished. In fact, she hasn't taken a class in five years. She has no criminal record and nothing civil. She hasn't sued anyone or been sued. Her credit report is spotless. There's no evidence of outstanding debt. She owns a historic home in Capitol Hill, a three-story, four-thousand-square-foot house, built at the turn of the century. She lives on the top floor and rents out the others. The deed is in her name only."

Before we met, Destiny, with help from her parents, had bought and refurbished the house on Gaylord Street. Four months earlier, her father had paid off the balance on the mortgage, as "birthday and Christmas presents for life." Destiny and I had talked about transferring the deed into both of our names but hadn't.

"There's no mortgage on the house?"

"None registered in public records," I said mechanically. "No liens against the property."

"That's extraordinary. What is the house worth?"

"According to the most recent tax appraisal, nearly six hundred thousand, but most of that's come from appreciation and renovation. Destiny bought it twelve years ago for a hundred and fifty thousand."

"Her car?"

"She drives a late-model Maxima. The title must be free and clear. Again, no debt shows up."

"Fascinating," Carolyn said softly.

"You can stop worrying about blackmail. She seems to have enough money."

"What about her personal habits? I assume you've had a chance to follow her."

I gave a terse recital from memory. "She's at work by eight and rarely leaves for lunch. She stays late, until seven at least. Most evenings, she stops at a gym on Fourth and Broadway and spends about forty-five minutes. Afterward, she picks up dinner, usually at Whole Foods or a Mexican restaurant. At the Lesbian Community Center, she seems to be in the middle of a big project, something to do with outreach to teenagers, but you probably know that."

After a long pause, Carolyn said in a low voice, "Does she have someone special in her life?"

I had done so well, kicked into autopilot, as if discussing a stranger. Now, I had to pause and debate. I knew the safe answer, the words Fran had coached into my subconscious, but I longed to scream the truth, oblivious to shock or consequences.

Instead, I erased myself.

"I'm not aware of anyone."

"Good," Carolyn said flatly. "I have a tip for you."

I swallowed hard. "Okay."

"I believe Destiny will be at an event at the Botanic Gardens on

Thursday night. I suggest you attend as well. I'll leave a ticket in your name at the front gate. The setting should give you the perfect opportunity to watch her. Should you, perchance, see me as well, don't approach."

"What's the event?"

"A fund-raiser for Urban Teens, a program for homeless youth."

"How does that involve you?"

Borrowing the tone of a kindergarten teacher, Carolyn said, "Most homeless teenagers have dropped out of school. Through Urban Teens, we can contact them and encourage them to attend one of our alternative high schools."

"How does the Lesbian Community Center tie in to Urban Teens?"

"It doesn't, but studies have shown that a high percentage of runaways identify as gay or lesbian. I'll introduce Destiny Greaves to influential community leaders. If she can leverage these connections, they'll lead to further alliances, which should satisfy her agenda. And mine."

"Her agenda?"

"You should have uncovered this by now. The young woman is on a mission to save every gay and lesbian teen from the trauma of coming out. A quaint, but naïve, pursuit, wouldn't you agree?"

"Mm," I said indifferently.

"I suppose, though, her ardor is part of what excites me," Carolyn said slowly, choosing each word as if she had to pay for it. "Her boundless zest and enthusiasm, her commitment. She is committed, isn't she?"

"I wouldn't know."

"Then you must not be astute. Everyone I've spoken to remarks on her dedication. I must say, that's a turn-on, too."

"About Thursday—" I said abruptly.

I never finished the sentence, because Carolyn O'Keefe had disconnected. She'd assumed, without confirmation, that I'd follow her marching orders.

If she hadn't cut me off mid-sentence, she would have heard me say, "I can't make it Thursday."

• • •

I'd made plans with Destiny for Thursday night.

Our date, sketched out weeks in advance, included a movie at the Mayan and dinner, not schmoozing and wine and cheese at the Botanic Gardens.

I glanced at the phone, prepared to erase Carolyn O'Keefe's number from caller ID and Fran's notice, but once again, it had registered as "Restricted."

Trembling, I pounded Destiny's number into the keypad.

Before I could bring up the subject of our date, she apologized in the most gentle, provocative voice. "Kris, I hate to do this, but I have to skip the movie Thursday. I might be able to make a late dinner, but I need to attend a fund-raiser earlier in the evening."

"Can't you get out of it?"

"No. It's a benefit for Urban Teens, at the Botanic Gardens. Dr. O'Keefe invited me, and people I need to meet will be there. I can't miss this chance."

"All right," I said quietly.

Destiny missed the despair in my voice. "Thanks, honey. I knew you'd understand."

• • •

I didn't understand, but I couldn't spare the time to vent. I was already fifteen minutes late for an appointment with Nell Schwartz, the daughter of Hazel Middleton, the owner of the Fielder mansion. Nell had canceled on me twice the week before, and I didn't dare call and give her the opportunity to postpone again. I raced out the door, hoping for the best, but I needn't have worried.

When I arrived at the sprawling ranch house in Bonnie Brae, one of central Denver's most expensive neighborhoods, I saw a barefoot woman kneeling in the garden. Behind her was an array of geometric figures, sculpted out of bushes, shrubs and privet hedges. The neatly trimmed squares, circles and rectangles helped break up the expanse of yellowish-green lawn on the oversized lot, and wooden planters, filled with geraniums in several shades of pink, formed a colorful border around the concrete front porch of the blond brick house.

Before I could hop out of my car, the woman, who wore light blue capri pants, black kneepads, a long-sleeved white cotton shirt and a straw hat, stood and removed her gloves. As I approached, she walked toward me and introduced herself.

Nell Schwartz had a round face, full lips, red cheeks and long, wavy black-and-gray hair pulled back into a ponytail. She'd lost her chin to the folds of her neck, but a vibrancy in her eyes and an easy grin gave her a youthful look.

"Do you need some help?" I offered.

"I'd never turn down an extra set of hands," Nell said, dropping to the ground. "Go around back, through the gate on the side. In the toolshed, you'll find gloves, a digger and a cushion."

"Okay," I said, heading around the corner.

"Kristin—"

"Yes?" I stopped and turned.

"On your way, could you take that sack and set it by the trash can in the back?"

"Sure," I said, resentfully eyeing the overflowing Hefty.

The mere thought of touching an empty black bag made me hot, and Nell had filled this one past capacity. I could barely lift it with both hands, and when I started to drag it, balancing most of the weight on my right foot, the side tore. Cussing under my breath, I bent and hoisted it to stomach level, ensuring stains on my pale yellow shirt and white shorts.

I staggered into the backyard, and after I deposited the bag next to a plastic trash can, I entered a toolshed the size of a starter home. A quick search produced gloves and a digger but no cushion.

"Hey, does my grandma know you're taking those?"

"She said I could use them," I said defensively to a prepubescent boy who was enjoying the shade of the covered patio.

Lying on his back on a lounge chair positioned at a slight incline, he wore baggy shorts, flip-flops and a tank top that exposed flabby arms and a big belly. Unruly brown bangs hid all of his forehead and the tops of his eyes. "You better not be lying," he said in a bored tone.

"Why would I come here to steal gloves and a tool?"

He sniffed. "Because you don't own any."

"Do I look like a thief?"

He considered me with vague curiosity. "You have big muscles for a girl."

"Thanks," I said, smiling expansively, not caring whether he'd meant it as a compliment or an insult. "Think about it, though. Would I haul that trash bag back here during the commission of my crime?"

He giggled, a high-pitched sound. "Grandma filled it too full, didn't she?"

"What do you think?"

He grinned, exposing silver braces, which were a wise investment. "She always does that, and it makes my dad mad."

I put on the gloves and leaned against the patio table. "What're you reading?"

He held up the cover. "Nothing special."

"A Harlequin?" I said, trying to delete surprise from my voice.

"Adult romance. My mom gives them to me."

"You like them?"

"They're okay."

"Where's your mom? Inside?"

He fidgeted in his chair and adjusted his shirt. "In North Carolina. I live there with her and my sister and my mom's phony husband, Tate."

"What's a phony husband?"

"Someone who lies about everything. My dad's the only real husband."

"Your parents are divorced?"

"Supposedly," he said, pushing his bangs to the side.

"You're just visiting?"

He nodded. "For the summer. My dad lives here, but he's at work. We used to all live in Denver. I wish we'd move back."

"You like it better in Colorado?"

"Of course," he said, taking a swig from a Coke can. "It isn't as hot, and my sister's not here."

"She didn't want to come?"

He shrugged his shoulders in an easy fashion. "She has a job this summer and two boyfriends."

"Why aren't you helping your grandma?"

"I get a rash. I'm going to pull weeds later, after the sun goes down. Grandma said she'd give me ten cents for every root I dig up."

I surveyed the half-acre of dandelions. "You could make a hundred bucks, easy."

He scratched his cheek with the spine of the book. "Sweet! I'm getting rich this summer. My dad gives me ten dollars a week allowance, Grandma pays me extra for chores, and Great-Grandma Hazel gives me step-and-fetch money."

"Step-and-fetch?"

"A few dollars every time I get something for her."

"You won't help for free?"

His eyes narrowed behind the greasy hair. "Would you, if you were a kid and someone offered to pay?"

"Probably not," I admitted, straightening up. "I'd better get going. Maybe I'll see you later."

"Maybe," he said, his nose buried in the sheets of the romance.

CHAPTER 7

I came around the corner of the house and clapped my gloved hands. "What can I do to help?"

Nell Schwartz pointed to the hordes of dandelions that blanketed the lawn. "How about removing anything yellow?"

"I can do that," I said, squatting. I wrestled the first one out of the ground with the dull tip of the digger and said, "I take it you don't like Roundup?"

She shot me a chastising look. "Not when there's a healthier solution."

"It seems like a lot of work." I sighed, tossing a second weed toward the new trash bag she'd opened.

"Not like that," Nell corrected, when she caught me yanking a stalk without proof of an accompanying root. She demonstrated proper technique and watched me pull three more before she relaxed and concentrated on her own patch.

We chatted amiably for a few minutes before I came to the point. "So," I said lightly, "you're ready to sell the Fielder mansion?"

She gave a slight nod and tightened the drawstring on her hat. "I'll miss it, but it's time, past time. For years, I've tried to convince Mother to leave."

"Did you grow up in the mansion?"

"Some of the time. My parents bought the house when I was fifteen."

"When did your father die?"

"In nineteen seventy, when I was twenty-five."

"That's a long time for your mom to be alone."

Nell let out a snort. "She would tell you, not as long as their marriage."

"Your parents weren't happy?"

"No," she said briefly.

"You must have taken a chance on marriage. I met your grandson out back."

"Yes, that's Lyndon. I mean, Flax."

"Flax?"

Nell threw up her hands and rose to retrieve the garden hose. She took a drink from the nozzle before squirting her feet and hands. "He renamed himself this summer, but he has to remind me to use his new name. And yes, I did take a chance on marriage."

"Any husband now?"

She handed me the hose. "After the first two, I've settled for boyfriends. They provide the same benefits, without the legal mess. My last one, John, passed away in the fall."

"I'm sorry," I said, interrupting my long drink to meet her gaze.

"Don't be. He enjoyed a full life, as full as they come. He was a great help with the mansion, which is part of why I'm selling. My son, Dick, lives with me, but he has no interest in the property."

I shut off the stream of water. "Your mom's okay with the sale?"

"It's taken years to convince her, but she accepts the change, more or less."

"Where will she go?"

"Didn't Roberta tell you? Mother will live in the carriage house until she dies or needs to move for health reasons."

"Roberta didn't mention that."

"That's why we accepted Roberta's offer. Philip Bazi, the developer, would have given us almost a hundred thousand more, but he made it clear that he intended to tear down everything on the block. The woman from Save Our Denver, Elvira Robinson, promised to find a buyer who would allow Mother to stay in the carriage house, but she never bothered to meet her. Roberta is the only one I trust to work around Mother's needs. She refuses to leave her home. She says everything she cares about is close by."

"Your mother wouldn't prefer to live in the main house?"

"No, and she couldn't. Parts of it are uninhabitable. Squirrels have nested and ruined the woodwork and floorboards. It's not safe and hasn't been for some time. We shut off gas, electric and water to the main building, which has helped financially. Some winters, the utility bills ran in the thousands."

I let out a low whistle. "You haven't had tenants to help offset the costs?"

"Not in years. Our last renter was one of Mother's close friends, Constance Ferro. I'm sure she didn't pay much, but Mother enjoyed the companionship."

"When did Constance leave?"

"At least twenty years ago. One day she was there, and the next, gone. Mother said she moved to California to be with her niece, but she left behind everything she owned. Some of it's still there. Mother refuses to let me clear out the room. Oh, well," Nell said gaily, "Roberta will have to deal with her. I'm not sure she knows what she's getting into."

"Your mom?"

"Roberta."

I nodded sympathetically. "Why not wait until your mother passes away?"

"I wish I could, but I've been paying personal-care providers to come in and help Mother for the past year. My own funds are depleted. My son offered to lend me money or cosign a mortgage, but that seems foolish when the mansion sits empty."

"I agree."

Nell let out a long sigh. "Also, Mother seems lonely, although she'd never admit it. She rarely leaves the carriage house, only for doctor appointments and her trip to Blackhawk every Monday."

"She gambles that often?" I said, shocked at the prospect that slot machines in a former mining town represented Hazel Middleton's favorite pastime.

"And drives herself."

I cringed, recalling the narrow, winding highway with a rock wall on one side and a river on the other.

"This is the perfect solution," Nell said, whacking at a weed with relish. "If Mother won't leave her carriage house, I'll bring activity and stimulation to her."

I flashed her a questioning look. "Construction workers?"

"And Roberta."

I raised an eyebrow. "Will your mom see much of Roberta?"

"Roberta has promised to stop by the job site every day."

"Do they get along?"

"Famously. This is for the best," Nell said with forced enthusiasm. "After I sign the papers, I'll come home, drink a glass of champagne and toast new beginnings. For Mother and me."

I nodded. "I'm sure it'll be a relief."

Nell threw back her head. "You have no idea! When the sewer pipe broke last fall, the week after John died, I watched a backhoe tear up most of the yard and half of the driveway. After I wrote a check for fifteen thousand dollars, that's when I responded to Roberta's letter."

"Roberta had written to you?"

"Roberta Franklin has written every so often, for years. This time, I answered, but not until I sought the advice of a real estate agent. The agent made inquires, and before I knew it, I had four offers. I chose Roberta's, and here we are," Nell said, dusting off her hands.

I paused. "Um, Roberta's heard rumors, and this may sound crazy . . ."

"Yes?" Nell rose with effort and glanced at me sharply.

"Is there any chance the house is haunted?"

When Nell Schwartz shook with laughter, I could feel my face redden.

In the time it took for her to respond, I felt like an idiot for having asked the question.

When she spoke, her reply upset me even more. "That's what I'll miss the most—the ghosts!"

CHAPTER 8

The ghosts.

Apparently, they were more prevalent than I knew.

I spent the next few days in the Western history section of the Denver Public Library, where I discovered that many of Capitol Hill's grand homes were purported to be haunted.

Between trips to the library, I saw little of Fran, which was just as well, but on Wednesday, she caught me off guard when we crossed paths at the office.

"Bert gave me a jingle. Said she hadn't heard from you. Wants you to call her today with an update."

"Today?" I said, my voice squeaking.

"That a problem?"

"Not exactly, but I haven't made much progress."

"Must have. Haven't seen you in forever," Fran said amiably before slapping her forehead. "Hold up! You ain't switch-hitting on me, are you?"

"Please!" I said, avoiding a direct answer.

"You wouldn't double-cross me and try to work the Destiny case?"

I adopted a pained expression. "I've had trouble getting in touch with Elvira Robinson, the lady at the historic society. Philip Bazi, the developer, stood me up. And the Western history section of the library's only open limited hours."

Fran looked at me steadily. "Enough said. Spinning your wheels. Happens sometimes. Carry on. Just keep Bert in the loop."

I wondered what Fran was up to, but she didn't volunteer a progress report on Carolyn O'Keefe, and I didn't ask. I'd noticed that she was out and about a fair amount, but that didn't necessarily mean anything. Fran Green had more hobbies, interests and volunteer commitments than ten people combined. She carried two calendars to track it all and never confused a detail or date.

I barely could handle a limited number of engagements per week, with no desire for more, and when I woke up Thursday morning, I didn't need a single Daytimer to remind me of my most pressing appointment.

I couldn't have forgotten the fund-raiser at the Botanic Gardens if I'd tried.

It would be the first time I'd see Destiny with Carolyn O'Keefe, and the thought made my stomach ache. Who knew what indigestion lay ahead?

The day broke with gray skies, seventy degrees and high humidity. When I called the weather line, the forecast called for a forty percent chance of rain. Not the best weather for an outdoor event. Having grown up in Denver, however, I knew all too well the pattern of over-prediction and felt depressingly certain the Urban Teens fund-raiser would go on as scheduled at six o'clock.

Just my luck.

I passed the time in the morning as best I could by tackling the writing portion of Roberta Franklin's assignment. From a sheaf of notes, I compiled a first draft for the marketing materials and sales presentations, detailing the history and lore of the Fielder mansion.

Between sentences, most of which I borrowed from newspaper articles written at the turn of the twentieth century, my mind drifted, repeatedly rebounding to thoughts of Destiny. I pondered our recent lovemaking, unable to fathom Destiny's hands touching another woman. Maybe I'd exaggerated the danger Carolyn O'Keefe presented to my relationship and life. Maybe I'd blown it all out of proportion. How could Destiny, who displayed such passion for me, be falling for someone else at the same time? She knew every part of my body, exactly what I liked. Every time we made love, we shared something familiar and comfortable, yet different and remarkable.

How could Destiny fake that?

Again and again?

Before I could answer, the door opened with a bang, signaling the arrival of Fran Green in one of her more distinct outfits. Her neon pink shirt announced, "It's A Girl Thing," but she'd countered the femme look with work boots, a trucker's cap with an oversized bill and aviator sunglasses.

She threw the glasses and hat on the couch, moved her fanny pack around to below her gut and plopped into her chair with a thump. "Boy, dating ain't for pussies."

Accustomed to her drama, I barely glanced up from the computer screen. "Rough night?"

Fran let out a derisive moan and ran her hands through her hair. "You said it."

I pushed back from the keyboard. "Instant dating is tough?"

"Speed-dating, Kris," she said as she pulled a toothpick from the wooden beaver on her desk and began to gnaw on it. "Exhausting, but quite the fascinating experience at Java Jo's. Little coffeehouse on Pearl Street, had a room to ourselves. Mingled for a few minutes as everyone arrived, then at the stroke of eight, got down to business. Picked numbers out of a hat and took assigned seats. Spent ten minutes with each gal, boom, on to the next prospect."

"Did you meet anyone you liked?"

She raised a hand to stop me and pulled out a small notebook from the side pocket of her cargo shorts. "Have to fill you in from the beginning."

I rolled my eyes. "You took notes?"

"Jotted highlights. Recorded the event, too. I'll transcribe the tape for you later. Consider this a summary, full disclosure to follow."

I frowned. "Were you supposed to tape-record it?"

"Who knows? Made up my own protocol. You interested or not?"

I shifted in my seat and said good-naturedly, "No, but tell me about your dates."

Fran moved the notebook to within an inch of her nose, then out to the full reach of her arm. Back and forth, slowly and quickly, in fractional increments and gross movements, all the while squinting. "Forgot my specs."

"Do you want me to read it?"

"Impossible to decipher my codes. Have to manage myself. Here goes. Tall woman a possibility. Interesting story. Grew six inches one year in high school and gained forty pounds. Endured brutal physical therapy sessions to help accelerate muscle development. Nothing kept pace with those bones. Still has problems with tendons in her knees."

I stared at Fran, astonished. "You learned all of this in ten minutes?"

"In two. Episode defined her life. Gal wouldn't be a bad catch. Just a snag, or two, come to think of it. Height differences might be too extreme. Make an odd-looking pair, me eighteen inches shorter."

"That's a shallow reason for eliminating someone."

Fran retrieved a stuffed animal from her desktop menagerie, a purple penguin, and squeezed it distractedly. "Have to consider the practical aspect, Kris. Sex could be a problem. Bodies wouldn't fit together nicely. Too much of a workout, at my age, scooting up and down all the time."

"I'm sure you could get in shape. Weightlifting, cardio training," I said without a hint of sarcasm as I picked at a loose thread in my polo shirt and silently debated whether to make a run to Einstein's or Bruegger's for lunch. Caesar salad with a garlic bagel twist or sesame bagel with salsa cream cheese and tomatoes and cucumbers. One restaurant shared space with Starbucks, which meant an iced mocha. The other was around the corner from Jamba Juice, home of the orange cream smoothie.

Fran's reply intruded into my culinary reverie. "Don't know about the blue tint, though."

My head jerked up. "In her hair?"

"Skin. Round the time of Y-Two-K, drank a potion to protect her from disease. Made her own concoction by electrically charging silver wires in a glass of water. Now she's permanently discolored."

I suppressed a laugh. "Dark blue?"

"Baby blue," Fran said matter-of-factly. "Nice personality, though. Better than the alpaca farmer. Had to hear all about twenty-two colors of fleece. Dullsville! Lives on ten acres near Evergreen, building a herd. Not too compatible with my downtown lifestyle. Good-looking gal, though. Earthy. More chemistry there than with the one who sues people, that's for sure."

"You met a lawyer?" I said, impressed.

Fran discarded the toothpick and sucked her teeth. "Professional plaintiff. First car accident bought her a new house and trip to Italy. Second, lost sensation in her left foot but won a three-year sabbatical from teaching. Imagine that lifestyle, making yourself as disabled as possible."

"You're a tough critic."

"You ain't heard the half of it. Immediately crossed off the woman who wanted to paint turkey bones and sell 'em as Santa sleighs. Prayed for the timer to go off. Scampered out of my seat so fast, I knocked over a cup of coffee and a chair. Soakin' wet and got a shiner on my shin. Started me at a disadvantage with the bombshell who works for Denver Department of Health and Hospitals."

I did neck rolls, clockwise circles.

My inattention caught Fran's attention. "You listening?"

I grimaced when I felt a jolt of pain in my neck. As I kneaded the area, I said impatiently, "You met a bombshell."

"Sure did. Checks out houses and apartments for unsafe or unsanitary conditions. Better not let her near your place, Kris."

"Funny," I said, not amused by the somewhat accurate implication.

"She's got a nose that can smell the difference between rats and mice. Loves her work. More trash, the better. Gets to see progress after she issues a citation."

Fran retrieved a quarter from a ceramic butterfly dish and used it to buy a gumball from her desktop machine. She offered me a coin, but I declined. I'd chewed through three gumballs earlier in the day, and my jaw was sore.

"True advocate for the poor, the disenfranchised, the mentally ill. Heads into the worst nooks and crannies of Denver and never feels fear. Might care about her work a tad too much."

"Did you put her on your list?"

She smiled brightly. "First name. Reminded me of myself a little."

I cast a disapproving glance. "Your favorite out of the five women you met is the one who's the most like you?"

"You got it," Fran said, unabashed, as she cracked her gum. "Last minute, added the tall, blue lady to the docket. But I have to see if that blue skin glows in the dark. Better check it out in a movie theater. Might ruin the mood between the sheets."

"That would be a deal-killer?"

Fran blew a giant bubble and sucked it in successfully, leaving no residue on her lips or cheeks. "Got that right!"

"When will you find out if you have a match?"

"End of business today. The organizer'll send an e-mail. For now, I'm headed back to the homestead. Need to get started on the transcription."

"Good luck."

"Thanks, kiddo." Fran gathered her belongings and was halfway out the door before she added, "Weird feeling, waiting to see if my life's going to change."

"Tell me about it. Call me when you know something."

"Will do. Meanwhile, I plan to have that transcription available for your perusal in the morning."

Perfect.

Knowing Fran Green's two-finger typing, I calculated the transcription would take all afternoon and evening, forcing her to skip a round of following Carolyn O'Keefe.

Which meant she wouldn't see me!

• • •

At six o'clock, I was at the Botanic Gardens, trying to see without being seen.

I'd come in disguise, but nothing elaborate enough to hold up under close scrutiny.

Behind a vine-covered trellis, crouched against a marble bench, I watched the main stage of activity at the Urban Teens fund-raiser. Most patrons, dressed in summer casual, had gathered in a large square of grass sunken below the surrounding stone pathways. In the center of the lawn, servers dispensed beer, wine and soda from a drinks cart.

On the level where I stood, three tents sheltered overflowing banquet tables. One area was dedicated to salads: almond cherry chicken salad, lemon crab salad, smoked duck and mango salad and cucumber shrimp salad. I didn't hesitate to eat the richest food in the world, in support of some of the poorest citizens of Denver.

After sampling the salads, I made my way to the appetizer station and consumed proscuitto-wrapped asparagus tips, roast beef with caramelized onion glaze, ham with red onion marmalade and goat cheese and chive tea sandwiches. I topped off those by lavishing crackers with artichoke, black olive and sun-dried tomato spreads. I avoided the crab legs and chilled prawns, but not much else escaped my grasp.

At the third table, I set up a long-term stakeout. Devoted to all manner of desserts, I figured, accurately, that it wouldn't attract a crowd until later. Also, Destiny had sworn off sweets, and I wanted to avoid her and the certain confrontation that would have erupted if we bumped into each other.

While all of the desserts on the table tempted, I saved my desire for two chocolate fountains, dark and light streams of joy. From stainless steel apparatuses, warm chocolate cascaded down six levels of heaven. Unable to choose between happiness and too much happiness, I waded in both. I dipped pound cake, sponge cake and yellow cake, particularly enjoying wedges of cheese blintz. I sampled cherries, strawberries and raspberries and added frozen bananas, cubes of vanilla ice cream and chilled meringue balls. Ignoring glares from the caterers, I threw in cashews and homemade potato chips from an adjoining table.

I spent more than an hour alternating between snacking and watching ladies in stilettos drop into the grassy area, often missing the arms of their well-intentioned escorts.

Finally, when my stomach felt bloated beyond relief, Carolyn O'Keefe appeared with an entourage.

For some time, I watched her work the crowd with skill and ease. In every cluster of people, she seemed to know someone well enough to hug. That person generally introduced her to others, and she shook each stranger's hand with a double-handed clasp, making direct eye contact before release. She listened intently, eyebrows arched upward with interest, mouth turned downward in rest, until her thin lips broke into one of her frequent, charming smiles. If a monologue dragged, the smile froze and her eyelids opened and closed rapidly. In a few instances, she glanced at her watch, but most of her exits were seamless works of art.

She often gestured with her hands, waving them in counterclockwise motions, fingers stretched out.

And that's what I drew a bead on, her slender fingers.

I started to see them touching Destiny, inside her, driving her to ecstasy.

My thoughts became more wretched.

I no longer could see Carolyn O'Keefe standing in her green blazer and pants and white silk shirt with wide lapels. I envisioned her horizontal, wearing only the thick gold chain around her neck; her head thrown back, mid-orgasm, long neck fully extended, taut to the point of fracture; her light makeup glistening with perspiration; her strong cheekbones flushed from the rush of blood; her shoulder-length brown, gold and blond hair splayed across a pillow, the side part lost in tumbling; her dark, sunken eyes seized up in climax; her red lipstick tattooed across Destiny's body.

• • •

The sight of Destiny Greaves, at the Botanic Gardens, not in bed with Carolyn O'Keefe, highjacked my thoughts back to the present.

Frighteningly, I hadn't seen my lover arrive and could only hope she hadn't spotted me.

It alarmed me that I had no idea where she'd come from or when. She simply appeared one moment at Carolyn O'Keefe's side, and my pulse quickened with their every movement.

Destiny had approached Carolyn, the first person all evening to make that move. Nothing untoward about Destiny's handshake or Carolyn's usual grasp, but Carolyn broke pattern when she immediately dismissed the three women in her huddle.

She and Destiny were alone.

Facing each other, they appeared relaxed, but I noted Carolyn's animation had ratcheted up a notch. Her gestures stretched to the full reach of her limbs, her smile broadened, and her laughs grew louder.

When Destiny spoke, Carolyn tilted her head to the side and gazed at her thoughtfully. She often nodded vigorously and grabbed Destiny's arm tightly.

Her bare arm.

Despite the cool weather, Destiny had worn her mauve sleeveless shirt, and the blazer that matched her black pants was nowhere in sight. I felt like running and throwing a blanket over her.

When someone interrupted, which happened several times, Carolyn pulled Destiny to her side and claimed her with an arm draped loosely around her shoulder.

Her bare shoulder.

Each time, Destiny detached gently, without drawing attention to the withdrawal, and she focused on the newcomers until Carolyn discreetly dismissed them.

I could see what made Destiny good at what she did. She possessed the same people skills as Carolyn O'Keefe but applied them with less calculation.

Watching her, I couldn't help but think about her activism and the role it played in our relationship. Every day, as Destiny put her life on the line by walking through the front door of the Lesbian Community Center, I remained in the shadows. She claimed the separation was good, healthy even, that my leading a "normal" life outside the strife of conflict and politics helped ground her. But I knew it hurt, the short range of my risk tolerance and limits of my participation.

Destiny couldn't stop, and I couldn't start.

I couldn't stretch my activism past the ordinary rebellion that most lesbians expressed. Every day, I committed an act of defiance by loving a woman and, frankly, that was all I could muster. Unlike Destiny, I had no desire to defend all gay people. She supported them in their acts of heroism and stupidity, courage and cowardice, revolution and revolting behavior. She had more faith and determination than anyone I'd ever met, and she performed her job without question or fear, as if shielded by a protective dome of strength or denial.

The protests, the parades, the campaigns, the causes—I couldn't push myself to participate, other than as a sympathetic listener.

But Carolyn O'Keefe could.

Obviously.

I couldn't stand any more.

I knew I'd throw up if I kept watching my lover and my enemy. Twice, food had begun a lurching ascent, and I'd willed it down, but I wasn't sure I could continue to win the intestinal war.

I left my post and traipsed down a winding path until I reached the west end of the gardens. There, I sat on a slab of rock in the Japanese gardens and contemplated unBuddhist-like thoughts.

I hadn't gotten far in the possibilities for revenge when I felt a tap on my shoulder.

I turned and gasped.

CHAPTER 9

Destiny mistook my shock and guilt for surprise and pleasure and gave me a big hug.

I detached, afraid Carolyn O'Keefe might appear from behind a bush or tree.

She kissed my cheek. "No one can see us. If someone does, who cares? They'll never recognize you in this big floppy hat and sunglasses," she said, playfully removing both. Before I could invent a plausible reason for my appearance, she said excitedly, "How lovely! You came to support me."

I nodded and smiled meekly.

"I tried to get your attention earlier, when you were by the buffet table, but you must not have seen me."

"No," I said truthfully.

"Then I found Dr. O'Keefe, and I couldn't get away. I was afraid you'd left."

"I never saw you," I said untruthfully.

"I wish you had. A little of her goes a long way."

"She's the woman you showed me on TV?"

"Exactly. She wanted to introduce me to her colleagues."

"Who have you met so far?"

"No one with any influence. It's almost as if she wants me all to herself. She's too intimate."

"How so?"

Destiny must have heard the bristle in my voice, because she instantly backtracked. "Maybe I'm imagining it, but she touches my arm too often."

"I'm sure she doesn't mean anything," I said, calculating that a lie would elicit more than an accusation.

"Or maybe she does." Destiny sighed. "She seems to collect people. I only met her a few weeks ago, but she calls all the time, sends e-mails every day and asks personal questions, off topic. Twice, she's referred to me as 'her discovery.' Remember when you asked about women being attracted to me?"

"Of course," I said softly, my heart racing.

Destiny took a deep breath, her brow furrowed. "This might be one of those situations."

"What do you want to do?"

"What can I do, other than deal with her professionally and hope she'll do the same."

"Do you think she will?"

"She'd better," Destiny said firmly. "Especially at the conference."

I needed a defibrillation. "What conference?"

"Didn't I tell you?"

"No," I said evenly.

"At the end of August, the Colorado Association of Educators is meeting in Steamboat Springs. Dr. O'Keefe's promised to introduce me to the superintendents of other school districts in Colorado. Once we've successfully launched pilot programs for GLBT teens in Metro Denver Public Schools, she'll serve as a reference. If I want to roll out programs statewide or nationwide, her support is invaluable."

"She has that much power?"

"From what I hear, if she supports something, it gets accomplished."

"And if she doesn't?"

Destiny laughed nervously. "You don't want to get on her bad side."

"You're not worried about her personal feelings?"

"I can handle those," Destiny said cockily. "I have a great idea. Let me introduce you. If Dr. O'Keefe has a crush, it'll disappear when she sees how hot you are and how much we're in love."

"I am hot," I agreed, wiping clammy sweat from below my ears and replacing the hat and oversized sunglasses.

Destiny grabbed my hand. "Let's go find her and get it over with so we can go home. Give me a chance, and I'll show you how much these one-sided attractions make me want you more."

I grinned but wouldn't budge. "You go back to work. Press her for the connections she promised, and if she won't share, screw her. Make your own."

"Good idea. Screw Dr. Carolyn O'Keefe," Destiny said merrily.

"I'll meet her some other time."

"She's not going anywhere. If these programs take off, we'll be inseparable."

"Super," I said, smiling weakly.

Destiny had barely made it out of eyesight when I leapt to the nearest trash can.

The echoing taste of chocolate made me swear off fountains.

• • •

The following morning, for the first time since I met Carolyn O'Keefe, I awoke without dread. Destiny's reassurances had helped loosen the tightening in my chest, and I felt like a new person, euphoric almost.

Not even the dour Elvira Robinson, of Save Our Denver, could darken my mood.

"I don't believe Mrs. Middleton and her daughter appreciate the significance of the sale of the Fielder mansion."

"I believe they do," I said with a forced smile.

We'd begun our meeting at noon in the SOD office, which occupied a room on the first floor of a Victorian mansion on Franklin Street, and the building stood as a testament to SOD's preservation efforts. Painted to highlight intricate architectural features, the house looked as if it had been cared for every minute of its 120 years. Inside, SOD had decorated to imitate life in the late 1800s. Heavy drapes blocked most of the sunlight, and mahogany wood paneling added to the darkness. Antique furniture filled every corner, with each piece staged as a history lesson. On top of the twelve-drawer sideboard, ancient bathroom accessories such as razors, toothbrushes, combs and makeup jars rested on a lace table runner. A china cabinet with glass doors and shelves displayed kitchen utensils and dishes, and a marble coffee table showcased books and magazines from the era. Crystal lamps were placed throughout the room, but few were in operation.

I sat on a settee that felt as if it had come over on the Mayflower, tried to ignore the distraction of a cuckoo clock that sounded every five minutes and hoped the smell of cinnamon potpourri wouldn't infiltrate my clothes.

From my shadowy perspective, I had to strain to see Elvira Robinson. She had a narrow face, with pale skin, painted-on eyebrows and bright red lips. She'd tucked her gray hair into a bun, but the majority of it had fallen out. She wore a matching ensemble, a pink dress, shoes, hose and hat, which all hung loosely, as if she'd lost weight since their purchase at Sears decades earlier. I swear her pillbox hat was on backward, but I couldn't think of a polite way to broach the subject.

Her hearing aids must not have been adjusted properly, because she leaned into my every word and spoke loudly. "There are only a handful of homes in Denver on the scale of the Fielder mansion. It's a treasure."

"In the shape it's in?" I said, no longer distracted by the sharp whistle that accompanied many of Elvira Robinson's words.

"Oh, dear, yes. You couldn't duplicate the quality today, with its intricately crafted façade. That sort of decorative stone and brick work cannot be procured in this construction climate. For instance, you'd need a stone lintel and a stone sill for a window. These are made from Castle Rock rhylostone with a carved face. They can be imitated in concrete, but it's cost-prohibitive and produces a vastly inferior result." She sighed heavily. "I wish Mrs. Middleton could be persuaded to reconsider our offers."

"You submitted more than one contract?"

"Two. One buyer was prepared to perform architectural research, using original photographs of the house from the eighteen nineties, in an effort to duplicate the period. I understand both offers were higher than Roberta Franklin's. Do you have some knowledge as to why Mrs. Middleton rejected them?"

"I believe Nell and Hazel felt more comfortable working with Roberta. She's going to allow Hazel to continue living in the carriage house."

"Does Mrs. Middleton remain in good health?"

"According to Nell, she's still driving."

Elvira let out a judgmental cluck. "I don't know how she manages. Pulling a car out of the driveway and steering it down the alley can be a challenge." She shook her head sadly. "You're certain there's no hope for one of our buyers?"

"Roberta seems committed," I said vaguely.

Elvira's face bunched up, and her upper lip disappeared. "That's a shame. Sometime before I retire from the board of SOD, I would like to see one great house rise again to the glory of the late eighteen hundreds."

"It must have been a time of richness," I said with empathy.

"You cannot imagine! More millionaires lived in Capitol Hill than anywhere on earth. They made their fortunes in gold, silver, soil and industry, and they didn't hesitate to compete to build the most ostentatious living quarters. They spared no expense in bringing the best craftsmen and materials from Europe, and the homes took years to construct. Many owners died before completion."

"Without enjoying the luxury?"

"Yes, but most, I would venture to guess, enjoyed the process as much as the finished product."

"Can you tell me about the history of the Fielder mansion?" I said, eager to add to my library research.

"It would be my pleasure." Elvira rose to retrieve papers from a rolltop desk next to the fireplace. "I have a fact sheet I prepared for one of our grant applications."

Elvira Robinson handed me a sheet of paper with a checklist of information and two photographs of the Fielder mansion, one vintage, one recent.

"If you wouldn't mind reading aloud," she said, moving stiffly, returning to the loveseat across from me. "I'm having trouble with my eyes."

"Sure."

She sat in absolute repose, and I cast a furtive glance to make sure she hadn't fallen asleep before I recited the first bulleted point. "Built in eighteen ninety-three for the Fielder family, who made their fortune in silver. Peach sandstone was used in the stairs of the porte cochere, Pikes Peak granite in the entrance door threshold and Yule marble in the fifteen fireplaces."

Elvira swayed in her seat but resisted toppling. "The finest white marble in the country, from a quarry near Aspen."

"The house has an exceptionally high attic," I continued.

"Yes, yes," she said, her head bowed.

"Numerous spires and turrets. A hipped roof and wooden corbels. Rounded and angled towers and a mixture of window styles, including a two-story bay window. Combination of classic Queen Anne and Richardsonian Romanesque."

"Combined brilliantly," she said excitedly. "Asymmetry, textured surface, classical ornaments, art glass, high brick chimney and wraparound porches and balconies from the Queen Anne period. Add to that massive, rough-faced stone masonry, eyebrow dormers, squat towers and round arches of the Richardsonian Romanesque architecture, and you have a masterpiece of its time, for all of time."

I stifled a yawn. "The Fielders never moved in?" I surmised from the next entry.

"No. The Sherman Silver Act was repealed in eighteen ninety-three, and silver lost its value. Many families lost fortunes overnight, including the Fielders."

I cleared my throat. "The Fielders sold the house to Dr. and Mrs. Benedict the next year. The Benedicts made changes to the front porch and enclosed the back porch. They owned the home until nineteen thirty-two but didn't live in it continuously. They traveled around Colorado for extensive periods of time and often rented the home to other well-to-do families who were having mansions built in the area. It was sold upon Dr. Benedict's death for ten thousand dollars to the Alsops. Only ten thousand?"

"Far less than the cost to build the house, but common for transactions during the Great Depression."

"The Alsops turned the private residence into a boarding house, supervised by their housekeeper, Mary Flesch."

"Yes, many of the homes that survived the economic downturn suffered the same fate as the Fielder. They were converted into multiunit buildings, broken into an assortment of living arrangements, various configurations of shared baths, hot plates and iceboxes."

"It looks like the Alsop family held on to it for a while. They sold it in nineteen fifty-nine to the LaTourettes, a couple who attempted to remodel the structure into office space."

"Unsuccessfully, thank goodness."

"The following year, Herman and Hazel Middleton purchased it. They've had the longest period of ownership," I observed. "More than forty years."

"Yes, and until recently, I would have deemed them suitable custodians." Elvira smiled fleetingly. "At least the building won't be destroyed. I tell my committee members we didn't win, but we didn't lose. If Philip Bazi had wrestled away the mansion, we'd all have had a good cry."

"The developer? You're not a fan of his?"

Her nose wrinkled. "He's demolished seven significant buildings."

"Historic landmarks?"

"No, although we were in the process of applying for protective designation on three. All seven structures, however, were unique. The buildings were razed to make room for parking lots, an apartment building, a loft project and a chain video store. It's disgraceful!"

"I'm sure Roberta will do a fine job with the Fielder," I said reassuringly. "You'll be pleased."

Elvira raised both eyebrows and threw up her hands. "I'll cross my fingers. Many in the neighborhood would mourn the defacement of the Fielder's character. Particularly Halloween tour guides."

I sniggered. "You believe it's haunted?"

She tugged at the ends of her hair, unraveling what was left of the bun "Yes, I do."

I looked at Elvira Robinson for signs of humor but could detect none.

She continued, unfettered, "Growing up playing in these streets, I'd heard rumors about the Fielder mansion, but they were all in fun. Noises, sensations, movement of objects, shadow forms, strange smells. Most I dismissed as amusing distractions."

"Nothing to be concerned about?"

"Nothing to believe until I had the opportunity to meet with the owner who sold the house to the Middletons. Her tale gave me pause."

I consulted the sheet. "Mrs. LaTourette?"

"Yes, Madeline LaTourette. She and her husband purchased the building from one of the Alsop children. The LaTourettes intended to gut the building, and they began construction on the north wing. They didn't advance far," Elvira said dramatically.

"Demolition problems?"

"Yes, but not the sort you might imagine. For security purposes, they erected a chain-link fence around the property and hired watchmen to patrol at night. When each guard quit in quick succession, they turned to a pair of Doberman Pinchers. That plan, regrettably, lasted but one night."

I had an uneasy feeling. "Don't tell me someone hurt the dogs."

"Someone or something. The LaTourettes discovered a grisly sight in the morning."

I grimaced and said hurriedly, "What?"

"Both dogs lay sprawled on the sidewalk, dead. It seems they had leapt from a second-floor window in the turret."

My jaw dropped. "Over the security fence?"

Elvira nodded. "A sizable distance."

"Why had someone left the window open?"

"They hadn't," she said loudly. "The construction worker who was the last to leave swore the window had been secured."

Goose pimples formed on my arms.

"To gain access to the room, the LaTourettes had to pry open the door, even though it had no locking mechanism. There were claw marks on the inside of the oak door, and the dogs had scratched through it."

I involuntarily shuddered. "No!"

"Before they jumped, those poor animals had slashed until their pads where shredded. They had to escape whatever torture was inside that room," Elvira said, her voice fading. "There's no other explanation."

"Unless," I said, employing a theatrical whisper, "they were flung."

CHAPTER 10

The ghoulish tale of the Dobermans bonded me and Elvira Robinson.

I spent hours listening to more of her stories of boom and bust, and when I returned to the office at the end of the afternoon, Fran greeted me gruffly.

"Nice of you to show up."

Every feature in her face telegraphed defeat. "No luck with the speed daters?" I said mildly.

"Plenty of luck, all bad. Only one hit. The tall, blue lady e-mailed me yesterday, couple of minutes after the organizer sent out matches."

"I know she wasn't your first choice, but it's a start."

"Could have been but wasn't. I didn't want to bother writing back and forth. Breeds a false sense of intimacy. Figured I'd ring her up but didn't want to seem antsy. Planned on calling this afternoon to invite her for a walk in the park or a cup of coffee. Shouldn't have stalled."

"What happened?"

"Blue e-mailed me this morning, shared that she'd hooked up with the alpaca farmer last night."

"Hooked up as in—?"

Fran slumped in her seat until she was more horizontal than vertical. "You think I wanted gory details. I have a stitch of pride left. Hooked up as in doesn't want me. Can you believe it? I failed at speed dating. Not fast enough."

"You don't know that," I said soothingly. "Maybe the sleigh-maker, or the professional plaintiff, or the alpaca farmer selected you."

"Big whoop! What's the thrill in being wanted by someone you don't want?"

"Good point. What's your next plan?"

"Plan?"

"You always have a plan."

Fran smiled shyly and sat up straight. "You been reading my mind. Next step is to answer this ad in *Westword*." She dug in her tattered backpack and retrieved a page from the weekly newspaper. "Saw it this morning."

"A personal?"

"Missed connection ad," she said, her eyes alive with promise. "Check this out. *'You: gray hair, broad shoulders, natty dresser. Me: flowing brown hair, blue eyes, red dress, black pumps. Last Tuesday, at the King Soopers on Ninth Avenue, you let me cut in line. I loved watching you watch me. Can't get that look out of my mind. Let's meet again at the Imperial Ball next week.'*"

"You think this is you?"

"Has to be. I shop every Tuesday at that store."

"Natty dresser?" I said, fixing on Fran's rumpled T-shirt that proclaimed, "Speed Kills!"

Fran glanced at her paint-stained sweats and bedraggled sneakers. "This ain't the only look I sport. I have more sophisticated outfits."

"Meaning you iron one of your T-shirts with a less provocative saying and change to jeans?"

Fran nodded and cracked a mischievous smile.

I peered at her closely. "You remember this, er, woman from King Soopers?"

"Not specifically, but it could have happened. Me, with the full buggy, I always let women with a few items cut in. Common courtesy must have paid off. Good thing I spotted this ad. Gives me a second chance at fate."

"And you know about the Imperial Ball?"

"Never heard of it."

I couldn't contain my laughter any longer. I burst into an explosion of peals that caused tears to run down my cheeks and aches to form in my sides.

Fran looked more confused than amused.

As soon as I could catch my breath, I enlightened her. "The Imperial Ball is the drag queens' annual coronation."

A look of dismay crossed her face. "It's not me?" she said weakly.

"I hope not," I said haltingly, the words eked out between spasms of laughter.

After a long pause and a hard stare, Fran rummaged in her backpack again for a typed sheet of paper, which she thrust at me. "Forget that then. Gimme your opinion of this."

I read the personal.

Lesbian, 67 going on 47. Wholesome, financially independent broad loves golf, snowboarding and Fantasy Football, looking for same. Forget about candlelight dinners and moonlight walks, let's share more substantive adventures.

Fran gave me a hard look. "Think it'll draw response?"

I shrugged. "The financially independent part should do it."

"I don't want that to be the slant. How about you punch it up for me? Add a few lines that'll lure the girls."

"You want me to rewrite this?"

Fran dismissed my put-upon pout with a wave of her hand. "Or start from scratch. Your call. With my attributes and your wizardry, gals'll be lining up for a crack at the Green."

The green, indeed.

• • •

I couldn't stop smiling as I constructed Fran's personal ad. I'd asked her to leave the office, because it was impossible to exaggerate her attributes when I could look across my desk and see the truth. In her absence, I'd cracked myself up with dozens of versions of an ad, none suitable for publication. Around five o'clock, I realized I had to set aside frivolity and concentrate. The ring of the phone, however, interrupted my best intentions.

I answered pleasantly, still in a relaxed mood from Fran's foibles, but at the sound of Carolyn O'Keefe's voice, I tensed.

"I believe I directed you to attend the Urban Teens fund-raiser at the Botanic Gardens." Before I could reply, she added in the same clipped tone, "Where were you?"

"Most of the time, next to the chocolate fountains."

"Oh."

A long pause ensued, one which I refused to fill.

"Did you have a chance to observe Destiny Greaves?"

"Yes," I said, feeling dizzy.

"And?"

"And what?"

"Can you understand why I've fallen in love with her?"

I choked out, "Yes."

"Did you sense the feelings were mutual?"

"I have no idea, Carolyn," I said, a quiet rage building inside me. "You're paying me to look into her background and trace her movements. I can't get inside her head."

"Did you watch us together?"

"Briefly."

"Could you feel the electricity?"

I rubbed my arm so hard I could feel a bruise forming. "Not from a distance."

"You will," she said and disconnected.

• • •

My foul mood didn't improve one bit when Destiny popped in unexpectedly an hour later. She wanted to take me to dinner, to our favorite Italian restaurant, to celebrate.

"Kris, you'd be so proud of me," she said, bouncing with enthusiasm. "I've gained Carolyn O'Keefe's confidence. We brainstormed this morning and came up with a program to introduce to the schools, in phases, depending on the support of administrators. I know I'm not supposed to talk about work, but can I tell you about this?"

Destiny pulled me out of my chair and swallowed me in a hug, an intimacy that made me recoil when I smelled perfume in her hair. The scent that had coated my office and stuck in my throat, the whiff of Carolyn O'Keefe, now clung to Destiny's body.

"Go ahead," I said, almost shaking.

"We'll bring posters into high schools, advertising suicide-prevention hotlines, safe sex options and access to community support. That should be relatively easy, right?"

I plastered on a smile. "If you say so."

"Carolyn's heard about funding for studies that tie in the prevalence of gay slurs to the number of dropouts. A national agency's tackling this, but she thinks we can piggyback with their efforts and obtain numbers for Colorado."

"What will numbers do?"

"It's part of the process," Destiny said patiently. "On a more practical front, we'll encourage student councils to accept same-sex couples at dances and other functions."

"How?"

"We haven't figured that out yet, but Carolyn has fantastic ideas. She's sure we can include topics on homosexuality in sex-ed courses for elementary and middle schools. There's been talk of it for years. That would give kids exposure and support before they hit adolescence. How exciting is this?"

"Won't conservative parents object?"

"Care says she can handle them. She wants to press for training for all high school counselors on sexual orientation awareness and coming out. Wouldn't that be helpful?"

"But—"

"And mandatory awareness training on gay issues for all coaches in the high schools. She's working on that immediately. In Arizona, she used a curriculum that encouraged coaches to monitor their language, not only for its effect on gay and lesbian athletes, but for the message it sent straight kids. She says training could help coaches support kids in transition, as they come out and have to deal with locker-room harassment. She knows it can work, Kris. She believes in me and my ideas."

"It sounds like most of the ideas were hers."

Destiny looked hurt. "Not necessarily. I proposed grants for schools to form gay-straight student alliances. I also suggested we print brochures to educate parents of gay children. I told her we could contact Parents and Friends of Lesbians and Gays about printing an initial run of five thousand. I offered practical ways in which schools could make use of gay speakers' bureaus. Care had no idea we have volunteers ready to come into the schools to talk about sexual orientation and gender-identity issues. I asked if we could force a mandatory session, as part of a civics class. She agreed to talk to the heads of her social studies departments, to get their feedback."

"Would these be your programs or hers?"

"We're not fighting over credit at this point," Destiny said, still defensive.

"I hope Care isn't stringing you along," I said, wanting Destiny to notice the way I'd spit out the nickname.

She became utterly still. "Why would you say that? Are you jealous?"

"No."

"I've found a mentor, someone to guide me. What's wrong with that?"

I stared at my desk pad. "Nothing."

Destiny moved closer to me. "Why are you so negative?"

I raised my head. "How can these things be possible? If they were, why hasn't someone done them?"

"They have," she said bitingly. "Every one of them. In different schools around the country. But no one has done all of them, in a comprehensive approach. Probably because no one has ever formed the partnership that Carolyn and I have. She's an expert on school politics, and I'm an expert on gay and lesbian issues. Together, we create something incredible, very potent."

I felt as if someone had kicked me in the stomach. With no emotion, I said, "What's your next step?"

"We'll set priorities. We'll make phone calls and send e-mails to put the plan into action. I might have to work extra hours for the next few months. You don't mind, do you?"

I looked at her steadily. "How many?"

"As many as it takes," Destiny said, clearly resentful that I hadn't immediately acquiesced.

I could feel a power struggle coming on, along with a dull headache.

CHAPTER 11

"Roberta Franklin will fail. Consider that a guarantee, not a prediction."

Ridiculous words, and they weren't the worst that had come out of Philip Bazi's mouth. Without contradiction, I had let pass bold statements, boastful declarations and flat-out lies as I sat in his nightclub, Xstatic.

My head ached from a hangover of anger, but I was determined to control my temper.

Needless to say, the night before, Destiny and I hadn't gone to any Italian restaurant to celebrate. She'd gone home, presumably, and I'd spent the night at the office.

On a pull-out sofa in the back, I'd tossed and turned, changing positions at least a hundred times. My clothes had strangled me, but no more so than my thoughts.

I'd wanted to cancel my Saturday morning appointment with Philip

Bazi, but I knew if I did, I'd spend the day sulking. After which, I'd have to call ten times to earn another time slot with the developer who coveted the Fielder mansion. Better to get it over with.

On the way to Xstatic, I'd stopped off to brush my teeth, wash my face, comb my hair and exchange wrinkled clothes for ironed ones. Fortunately, Destiny hadn't been home at the time.

Now, I was wishing she had been, so we could have fought for a few more hours, a more rewarding activity than spending time with this jackass.

In person, Philip Bazi looked twenty years older than his published age of thirty-four. He had large, dark eyes that darted back and forth and eyebrows that extended to the sides of his face. He had dark hair, but only a bit of it, which he'd slicked down around his ears, leaving a massive surface of shiny dome. His dark shadow of whiskers made it seem as if it were ten o'clock in the evening instead of in the morning, and the stubble only exaggerated the extreme length of his face and pitch of his massive, beak-like nose. Hair sprouted from the backs of his fingers, almost enveloping a gold ring on his right hand, barely allowing the inlaid onyx to emerge. He wore a silk shirt, thankfully buttoned high, or I'm sure I would have seen a mass of black chest hairs.

His body language disgusted me, to the point I'd started to imitate it in a childish game. We both laced our fingers, stretched them above our heads and rested our intertwined hands on our necks. Twice, I'd mirrored the almost imperceptible thrust of his pelvis, a creepy move that had to be conscious on his part.

We were meeting in the bottle-service-only VIP room of Xstatic, a club he operated out of 12,000 square feet in one of the buildings he'd developed in the Golden Triangle neighborhood. Bounded by Speer Boulevard, West Colfax Avenue and Lincoln Street, the Golden Triangle was home to an eclectic mix of residences, businesses and organizations, including the Denver Art Museum, the main branch of the Denver Public Library and Denver Health Medical Center. Bail bondsmen still held their own, but nightclubs had pushed out meth clinics, mid-rise luxury condo buildings had replaced falling-down Victorians, and cafés and galleries had sprouted on vacant lots.

Philip Bazi had served as catalyst for most of these changes, according to him. All for the better, again his opinion.

I sensed that my lack of fawning over his achievements and obvious zoning out when he repeated himself pestered him, but he had a long way to go to reach my level of aggravation.

My agitation had begun as soon as I met him or, more precisely, smelled him. An overdose of cologne sparked my irritation, which accelerated with his limp handshake, undoubtedly reserved for women only, and nearly exploded as he scanned my body.

The intrusive exam lasted until he stalled at my breasts for the second time, at which point I said stoutly, "Not sold separately."

He pretended not to understand, and I didn't foist an explanation. Extra words only would have prolonged a visit I longed to cut short.

I felt as if I were in another world, living someone else's life.

The VIP room was separated from an onyx dance floor and two aluminum bars by folding garage-door walls. While Bazi had spent more than a million dollars on the luxe nightlife destination, nothing in the designer showcase of custom furniture, lighting, sound and visuals emitted warmth or comfort. The look probably appealed to the "hip, upscale" patrons he wanted to attract, but it did nothing for me. The décor, dominated by red velvet couches, iridescent ceiling-to-floor orange drapes and glass walls with black metal blinds, made my head spin.

Chinese symbols floated above a mirrored lounge area, and in the darkness, after a few drinks, they probably fit in. In the harsh light of day, however, without the crutch of alcohol, they looked ridiculous. As did the track lights hanging from all variety of wires strung from wall to wall and dangling from exposed pipes in the ceiling. The tables appeared as if the designer had stolen an infant's set of learning blocks and copied them on a larger scale of primary colors and shapes.

My mod white chair, a companion piece to the chic plastic bar stools, represented the ultimate in discomfort. I shifted on it, slouched, sat erect, tucked a foot under me and used my hand for lumbar support, but nothing helped.

I took my time with a sip of orange juice before I said, "How can you possibly know what Roberta Franklin can or can't do?"

"No novice, no matter how well-intentioned, will succeed with a project this size."

"You think she'd fail with twelve units?"

"I know she would."

"While you would succeed with two hundred and twenty?"

"I would," he said, infinitely tickled. "Who wouldn't want to live in a secure, high-rise condominium building with a rooftop pool and swim-up bar, two nightclubs, a gourmet grocer, a spa, a sushi bar and a French restaurant? Underground parking and state-of-the-art fitness center—who would turn that down?"

"You're sure of yourself, despite nothing close to this scale existing in Denver?"

"After clients see the quality throughout, the copper-trimmed domes, the imported stone, the gold medallions, they'll compete to buy. Pro athletes, empty nesters, dual-income couples—they'll fight for access to this exclusive, elegant address."

"According to Elvira Robinson, the director of Save Our Denver, the neighbors will never allow this type of building."

"Neither she nor any neighbor has the right to block this project. Zoning took that away years ago by allowing the height and density of the building I'm proposing."

"What about blocking the views of nearby buildings?"

"I wouldn't have gone to this much trouble," Philip said indulgently, "if I couldn't promise my buyers a panoramic view of the mountains, with a guarantee that nothing will be built to the west. It appears that other high-rise developers didn't have the same foresight."

"You don't have much respect for other developers, do you?"

"None."

"Every other developer within a five-mile radius with a multiuse, multiunit project has tabled it because of the soft market, but not you. You're still putting pressure on an elderly woman."

"They're afraid to change the skyline. I'm not. I'll continue to bring reasonable offers to people of all ages, until the day they die. At their funerals, I'll woo their relatives."

"Two hundred and twenty more units can't be absorbed in the near future, according to local economists."

"Who cares about the near future?" Philip Bazi said over my words. "Other developers are afraid to pull the trigger on a deal this big. You know why? Because they have to obtain a certain percentage of pre-sales before they break ground. I don't."

"You don't care that two buildings in the immediate vicinity of Hazel Middleton's house sit half-empty, waiting for buyers who may never materialize?"

His wan smile turned into a scowl. "None is like this. Not even the two luxury towers I completed and sold in the Golden Triangle in the last three years. By the time other developers with less vision revive their plans, they'll have missed the window of opportunity. My philosophy is simple. Can I find two hundred and twenty people who will enjoy the privilege of living in the finest building in the western United States? Yes. Will the majority of those sales take place well after the building is under construction. Yes."

"It'll take years for this real estate market to turn around."

He smiled benignly. "Metrowide vacancy rates can pass ninety percent, interest can skyrocket into double digits, and I won't feel concern. My product has never sat on the market. Nothing can stop me."

"Except for Hazel Middleton."

He licked his lips. "She can delay me, but I'm a patient man."

"Or Roberta Franklin."

"She'll never follow through with this purchase."

"Have you met Roberta?"

"No."

"How can you know she's not capable?"

"If she had real estate development experience, I would have met her by now."

"She has experience."

"Has she made dreams rise from dirt?" he said with an unpleasant undertone.

"If you're talking about building from scratch, no. But she's successfully undertaken numerous remodels."

"It's not the same. Not all developers can turn a property into a financial success. It takes fiscal responsibility, market possibilities and guts."

"Which do you presume Roberta lacks?"

"That's obvious—the guts. She's a senior citizen, for Christ's sake. If she had the balls, she would have done something before now. You can't show up for your first hand of blackjack and expect to play at the high-roller table. That's not going to happen in this city."

"Does that mean you believe the numbers are sound, that the market would support a twelve-unit concept?" I said without inflection.

He shot me a shrewd look and answered after a slight hesitation, "Yes."

"Then why wouldn't you do a project like that?"

"Because I've had to swallow too many cups of Hazel Middleton's weasel-piss coffee to settle for entry-level scraps. I did fix-and-flips ten years ago, when my father cosigned my first loan. I'm not going back to that. How could I maintain the respect of investors and contractors?"

"You have no desire to preserve the building and make a million? You have to tear it down to make ten?"

"Try twenty, and we understand each other," he said crossly. "Tell Roberta if she can get the old bag to sell to her, I'll buy her out for half again the price she pays Hazel Middleton. Same day, cash transaction. She can wrap up one closing, attend another and make a quarter-million or more. No risk, no hassle. Guaranteed success."

I shook my head. "She won't go for that."

"I'll make it worth your while to persuade her. Say ten thousand, off the books, for one conversation we never had?"

I stiffened. "No, thanks."

"Easiest money you'll ever earn. What's stopping you?"

I shot him a withering look. "Integrity."

He laughed, an intimidating sound. "If you won't take that message to Roberta Franklin, maybe you'd rather take this one. If she insists on buying or developing the Fielder mansion, she'll encounter dire consequences."

"Guaranteed?" I said sarcastically, mimicking his earlier predictions.

He cocked his head to one side, raised both eyebrows and cracked a half-smile. "I wish her the best of luck," he said insincerely. "A lot can go wrong in development."

I matched his frozen stare with an icy smile. "Such as?"

"Shady financing."

"She has all her funds in place."

"Uncontrollable construction costs."

I could feel my face redden. "She's hired an engineer and architect to assess the costs. Three general contractors have given her bids within ten percent of each other."

"A downturn in the economy."

"She needs to sell a dozen condos, not several hundred," I said pointedly. "She breaks even at six."

Philip Bazi unclenched his left hand, and I saw a twitch in his forearm. "A crowded field."

"You said yourself, for one-of-a-kind products, there is no competition."

The last caution, which he leaned forward to deliver, close enough that I could smell his foul breath, made me exit without a word in farewell.

He didn't deserve consideration, not after tossing off, "Workplace accidents."

CHAPTER 12

My cell phone rang later that afternoon, with Destiny caving in first. "Are you ever coming home?"

"Yes."

"Why haven't you called?" she said, her voice breaking with emotion.

"I was out on an appointment."

"Are you still mad?"

"No," I mumbled. "Are you?"

"A little. Can we talk some more?"

"Not right now."

"Fran's there?"

"What do you think?" I said woodenly.

"She sees more of you than I do." Destiny paused before adding, "Will you please come home tonight?"

"Probably."

"When?"

"Soon."

"I love you."

"Thanks," I muttered. "I'll see you before seven."

• • •

My attempt at cordial brevity hadn't fooled my officemate in the slightest.

Fran Green overheard every word, filled in the blanks and shot me a dirty look before I could return the phone to my pocket.

"Are you two fighting?" she said loudly, pointing to her T-shirt, "Love Is The Answer."

I cleared my throat. "Maybe."

"About what?"

I avoided eye contact. "Nothing."

"You letting this Carolyn O'Keefe situation eat away at you?"

I didn't respond.

"You want to be single? You got the idea that's the way to go?"

"It'd be easier than this," I said petulantly.

Fran pounded her fist on the desk. "Cut the crap. Destiny would never cheat on you."

"How can you be sure? You don't know this Carolyn O'Keefe, what she's capable of."

"I know Destiny, don't I?"

"So do I."

"Not well enough, evidently. That girl adores you. Always has. Always will, unless you keep screwing things up. Let it go, you hear me?"

I nodded, a slight movement.

"You haven't had any contact from O'Keefe?"

I shook my head.

Fran scowled. "Doesn't feel right. Too quiet. No sign of O'Keefe at all?"

"None," I said, leaving out my trip to the Botanic Gardens and her nasty follow-up call.

Two little lies.

Fran studied my impassive features. "You haven't heard from O'Keefe since you gave her the report on Destiny?"

I willed innocence into my tone. "No. Do you think I should call her?"

"You got the number?"

"No, but I could track her down at the school district office."

"Nah. Sit tight. Wait for her next move." Fran scratched her chin. "Surprised it hasn't come yet, but you stay out of it."

I let out a long sigh.

"I mean it. Let me take care of this, and it'll blow over."

"What's going on anyway?" I said testily. "What have you been doing on the case?"

"Plenty," she said firmly. "But this ain't the time for an update."

"Why?"

"First off, you're too hotheaded. You wouldn't be able to view it rationally. Second, I'm still compiling my report."

I glared at Fran. "When will you care to share?"

"Before you know it. Meantime, you can believe Fran Green's got everything under control."

She stared at me hard, until I said in a monotone, "Okay."

"Gonna let it go?"

I shook my head but said, "I suppose."

"You better." She approached me, and I tried to brush off her hug, but she squeezed me tightly.

Let it go.

Easy for Fran Green to say.

She didn't have to spend a day in my mind, which, granted, was prone to paranoia.

But not this time.

I was certain Carolyn O'Keefe posed a distinct threat, even if no one believed me.

• • •

That evening, Destiny and I made it through dinner without arguing, an accomplishment, given our recent history.

She waited to broach any tender subjects until we were in bed.

"I feel like I'm losing you," she said, cupping my cheek in her hand. "You're so far away."

"I'm right here," I replied feebly.

"Is it that case you're working on?"

"A little."

She propped herself on one elbow and studied me with concern. "Can you talk about it?"

"No."

"Don't let it get to you, Kris. I know you care about your cases, but no one's worth this."

"You're wrong," I said, looking directly into her eyes.

She kissed me tenderly. "Let me make love to you."

"Not tonight," I said, detaching, unable to bear her hands touching me.

"Fooling around always makes you feel better."

"Not now, please."

She pulled back. "Are you sure?"

"We'll make love soon," I promised, stroking her hair.

"Tomorrow?" she said eagerly.

I smiled faintly. "Not that soon."

"A week from now? A month?"

"Not that long."

She grinned at me playfully. "You promise I'll have sex in the next thirty days?"

"Yes, Destiny," I said quietly, my heart aching.

"While I'm waiting patiently," she said, pulling me close, "I'll hold you until you're ready."

I lay in her arms, stiff, for a long time.

When she finally fell asleep, I moved to the far side of the bed, where I lay on my back, wide awake.

I longed to close my eyes, but every time I did, scenes of Destiny and Carolyn played out on the backs of my eyelids.

Exhaustion eventually won out over horror, and I fell asleep shortly before the sun rose.

• • •

"We've got a problem."

A ridiculous way to open a Monday, but I should have expected it, knowing Fran Green seldom bothered with tact.

My face went slack. "Is this your way of telling me you finally have an update on Destiny and Carolyn?"

Fran nodded. "Spare a minute?"

"Can I sit down first?" I said irritably, my blood pressure rising.

"Take your time," Fran said sociably. "Can I get you anything? Water, soda?"

I shook my head glumly.

"What do you want first, facts or opinions?"

"Facts."

She opened her notebook. "Plenty of those. Fact number one, Destiny and suspect have met on three occasions."

"Could we call her Carolyn?"

"Fair enough."

"For dates?"

"Wouldn't label 'em that. Hardly romantic settings. Sweet Tomatoes, Chili's, Applebee's. Middle of the day, middle of the 'burbs. I performed surveillance from the car, using high-powered binoculars purchased from a reconnaissance Web site. I'll submit the receipt later."

"I could care less about the receipt. What I need is—"

"You're a stickler for financial details," Fran interrupted. "Wanted to put you at ease concerning my bookkeeping."

"What about my lover?" I practically screamed. "Put me at ease about her."

"Can't do that," Fran said solemnly. "But making progress. Chalk up these liaisons to business meetings."

"Could you get to the point?"

Fran's tone and speed never changed. "Two of 'em arrive separately. Destiny's always a few minutes early. No signs of guilt or subterfuge. Shakes O.K.'s hand when they leave the restaurant. Never walks her to the car, never lingers, never looks at her with lust. Nothing out of the ordinary."

"O.K. is what?"

"Shorthand for O'Keefe."

"Could we *please* call her Carolyn?"

"Limiting, but you're the boss. Fact number two, three days ago, Destiny received a two-hundred-dollar bouquet of flowers."

"From Carolyn?" I said frantically.

"No, that's the perplexing angle. From Shirley Bassett."

"The one you believe is Carolyn's lover?"

"Yep."

"Have you confirmed they're lovers?"

"Not yet. Got some feelers out, the old Fran Green search engine. Takes longer than Google but produces better matches. Should hear back soon."

"How do you know how much the flowers cost?"

"Noted the quality and quantity, queried the floral experts next door."

My chest heaved. "Why would Shirley Bassett send Destiny flowers?"

"Didn't. Fact number three, S.B. brought them to the Lesbian Community Center herself, along with a hundred-K donation."

"Cut it out, Fran," I said testily. "I can barely absorb all this, much less translate your shorthand."

"Shirley Bassett. One hundred thousand dollars," Fran said easily.

I gasped. "Shirley Bassett wrote a check to the Lesbian Community Center for that amount? Are you sure?"

"Saw it myself."

"Destiny showed you?"

"Nope. The cutie-pie in charge of fund-raising gave my eyes the treat. Her and me, we've always been tight."

"Lola?"

"Thought she preferred Layla, but you're probably right on the pronunciation."

"She's worked there for a year."

"Never corrected me. How am I supposed to know? Anyway, trusts me enough to share the secrets. More than Destiny's doing with you." My reaction—a mixture of hurt and anger—must have shown, because Fran hastened to add, "Destiny's more mature than Lola. Stinker gossips every time I drop by the Center. I'll have to talk with Destiny about her when this blows over."

"In the meanwhile, you'll use her for information," I said snidely.

"Heck, yeah. Make that blabbing work to my advantage. Already dug up some nuggets. You won't believe what cause the money has to support. Take a guess!"

"Tell me."

"Anything but youth programs. That's Bassett's only stipulation."

My eyes widened. "That her contribution not support the cause her lover and Destiny most support?"

"*Précisément.* That's French for precisely. Oh, and also, the money has to be matched with funds from the community."

"That's common."

"Everyday occurrence, according to Lay . . . ola. You should see it, kiddo. The Center's a beehive of activity. They're setting up a phone bank, calling in markers from community leaders, partnering with every social organization in the city. Lola's determined to match and earn every cent. She has thirty days to do it."

"Thirty days?"

"Mysterious coincidence or planned manipulation?" Fran said, cocking her head and dramatically lifting an eyebrow.

"Did the tight deadline surprise Lola?"

"More like invigorated her. She claims a deadline's good. Creates buzz and a sense of urgency. Draw it out and folks lose interest."

"Does she expect to match it all?"

"Destiny told her to shoot for half. They've got an order out to a sign company to whip up a poster they can display in the lobby. Bar graph type thing to mark the progress every morning. They hired a graphic artist to typeset ads they can place in—"

I cut her off. "A graphic artist? Why? I could have done those ads."

In Fran's exaggerated shrug, her shoulders almost touched her ears. "Destiny's trying to honor boundaries, maybe."

"I would have done the ads for free!"

"Destiny knows you're dedicating yourself to the detective work full-time. Maybe she wants to respect that."

"Is this you talking or her?"

"Me talking for her," Fran said with a grin. "But if you asked, which you can't, I'll bet she'd say the same."

"I wonder why she hasn't mentioned the donation," I said unhappily.

"All in a day's work, and you gals agreed to cut back on shoptalk, correct-a-meundo?"

"Yes, but—"

"Leave it to me, Kris."

"Don't you find it a little odd that Carolyn O'Keefe wants to have an affair with Destiny at the same time as her lover is giving Destiny's organization the largest donation in its history?"

"Put it that way, more than odd. Too much courting going on, that's for damn sure."

"Could Shirley be having an affair with Destiny?"

Fran shot me a blistering look.

"Trying to have an affair," I amended.

"Possibly. But if so, she ain't doing nothing to hide it. Lola says she's stopped by a half-dozen times, has meetings with Destiny with the door wide open, chats up the rest of the staff."

I could feel the frown between my eyes deepen. "What the hell's going on?"

"Beats me. Let's table speculation for the time being. Get back to the facts. Fact five—"

"Four," I said automatically.

Fran consulted her notebook and said affably, "Got me. While our girl Destiny's behavior has been above reproach, I can't say the same for Carolyn O'Keefe. Fact number four, Carolyn has followed Destiny."

"How do you know?" I said, filled with alarm.

"Because I've been following Carolyn. One day, I latched on to her at work and tailed her to the LCC. I watched her sit in her car for a good hour. She cranked the engine when Destiny came out, and she took off after her, me in pursuit behind the two of 'em. The chase ended after four blocks."

"Why?"

"Suspect—excuse me, Carolyn hasn't got the surveillance skills you and I possess. She's terrible at tailing, won't run the yellows. Pretty obvious about it, too. It's a miracle Destiny didn't spot her."

"Maybe she did."

"Doubtful. You know how Destiny drives that Maxima, floors it with the stereo blaring."

"It's good she lost her, right?" I said, jittery. "Carolyn doesn't know where we live."

"Not so fast, chickee. Fact number five, On Wednesday at six-oh-nine p.m., I spotted Carolyn O'Keefe parked across the street from your abode."

"Doing what?"

"Watching."

I felt a chill run up my spine, and my voice sounded strange when I spoke in a torrent. "How did she find us? For Destiny's protection, our address is unlisted."

"You didn't give it to her?"

"Of course not! I told her Destiny owned a home in Capitol Hill, but I never gave her the address."

"Dang!"

"Destiny must have told her, or she followed Destiny home. Did Carolyn see me on Wednesday?"

"No, siree. You were camped out at the office. Remember, I called to give you the bid on central air installation? Sorry about the fib. I had to make up some reason for tracking you down."

"Whatever," I said distractedly. "What am I going to do?"

"Play it safe. Park in the neighbor's garage, the one I used the winter I bunked with you. Use the back gate, back stairs. Inside, lower the blinds before you turn on any lights."

"Like I've done something wrong!" I cried. "I have to hide in my own home and pretend Destiny's not my lover?"

"Any better ideas for staying a step ahead of crazy lady?"

"No," I said, suddenly hit by a wall of depression. "I can't take much more. How many facts are left?"

"Only one, but it's a whopper."

"I'm glad you're enjoying this," I said roughly. "While my life unravels, you're patting yourself on the back for your sleuthing abilities."

"Sorry about that," Fran said sheepishly. "Got caught up in the excitement of the hunt. I'm talkin' like we do on all our cases and lost sight of the sensitivity. Can you accept my apology?"

I gave her a blank look and gestured sluggishly with my hand. I felt unbelievably tired.

"Found out this at the second business meeting. Might give you better insight into the depth of my concern."

"Just give it to me," I said dejectedly.

And then get the hell out of here.

"Fact number six, Carolyn's managed to shoot Destiny hundreds of times."

My heart stopped. "Shoot her?"

Fran nodded grimly. "All kinds of poses, none posed. She must have used a telephoto lens. She captured her, that's for sure."

I stared ahead and shook my head, in movements that became smaller and smaller.

CHAPTER 13

I felt like going home and sleeping for a year.

Unfortunately, I had to stop by Hazel Middleton's house, to see if the owner of the Fielder mansion genuinely wanted to sell to Roberta Franklin. On the drive, I considered the facts Fran had dumped on me.

Destiny and Carolyn had met three times. That alone wasn't striking. Destiny had been known to schedule multiple meetings in pursuit of money or alliances.

Destiny had received a large bouquet of flowers from Shirley Bassett, who presumably was Carolyn's lover. This bothered me more than the six-figure donation. Why was Shirley Bassett going after Destiny? What was Carolyn and Shirley's true relationship? Lovers? Roommates? Friends?

That was the least of my worries.

Back to the facts.

Carolyn had followed Destiny at least once, maybe more. My only consolation was that Destiny loved to drive dangerously, which should put an end to that.

Carolyn had watched the house, which meant she knew where Destiny lived and possibly that I lived with her.

Finally, I couldn't shake the image of the photos. Fran had seen them spread across the passenger seat of Carolyn's car the second time Destiny met with Carolyn. Leaving the restaurant, Destiny could have spotted them if she'd parked near Carolyn or walked by her car. Yet, Carolyn didn't seem to care, almost as if she wanted Destiny to discover her obsession.

That fact—that one frightened me more than all the others!

• • •

Fast forward an hour, and I was in the midst of another frightening topic.

"Nell always did exhibit a fascination with death," Hazel Middleton said absently. "I thought she'd outgrow it, but it sprouted faster than she did."

"Nell's certain the house is haunted," I said persistently.

I'd had plenty of time to form my own opinion of the Fielder mansion after knocking on the front door of the carriage house for ten minutes, with no reply.

The foreboding three-story turret on the main house reminded me of a medieval tower of torture. The porte cochere, designed to shelter carriages as they pulled up to the front entrance, had a decided tilt to it. The massive wraparound porch had missing railings and resembled a sinister, toothless smile. The porch floor, crafted from fine hardwood, was buckling and rotting. Many of the bay windows, projecting out from the front and sides of the house, sported plywood, and the ones with glass had panes missing, behind which tattered sheers blew in the wind. Shingles had peeled away from the steeply pitched roof, and gutters dangled at odd angles. The friezes, cornices and pediments had lost their charm at the hands of a mad painter, and the distinct red-orange Manitou Sandstone was marred by shadows of discoloration.

What Roberta Franklin saw, beyond decay and negligence, I had no idea.

All I saw was trouble.

I'd almost given up on my appointment when Hazel Middleton had pulled into the mosaic driveway in a late-model, maroon Lincoln Continental.

Through lightly tinted windows, I could see an angel hanging from the rearview mirror and the outline of a head, barely poking above the steering wheel. Large, round sunglasses masked most of the driver's face.

Once Hazel exited the car, she shut the door with the assistance of a hip thrust, and I had a better look at her. Her frame was thin, as if made from strong, flexible wire, and she walked without a cane or walker, in conscious high steps. The dramatic movements gave her the gait of a puddle-jumper, almost that of a hopscotcher when she took big steps. She had perfect balance, without a hint of a wobble, and no deep wrinkles or bowed posture. Most vividly, her eyes were as bright as a newborn's, wide open and alert.

She'd served me iced tea and kept me engaged with all sorts of topics, the most recent of which was ghosts.

"The house is not haunted," she said emphatically. "That sort of thinking merely allows Nell to be part of something mysterious."

"What about the opinion of historians that the building was designed architecturally in such a way that attracts evil spirits?"

"Phooey! I see a house patterned after chateaus in the Loire Valley, an elegant mansion for its simplicity. I take comfort in the sturdiness of its walls. I appreciate that we provided lodging for many families over the years. I'm still in awe of the expanse of the reception hall with its grand oak pillars and marble."

"Has Nell told you everything that happened to her in the house?" I asked, relieved Hazel had decided we'd be more comfortable meeting in her side yard than in the "stuffy confines" of the carriage house.

We sat on park benches, opposite each other, near two concrete lions, and I used one of the animals as a makeshift footstool. Before I'd seen the property, I'd felt sorry for Hazel Middleton, having imagined her step down from the splendor of the main house to the dredges of the garage, but the pity had dissolved with my first view of the carriage house, which resembled a charming two-story English cottage.

Hazel smiled patronizingly. "Nell has told and retold her stories to any audience she can find, embellishing them with each retelling. She has elements of a fragile personality, my daughter."

"Nell couldn't have imagined everything," I said mildly. "She claims tenants moved out in the middle of the night, forfeiting deposits."

"My husband viewed those as cash windfalls."

"Did you?"

She hesitated momentarily. "I felt their occurrences were the unfortunate downside of property management."

I consulted my notes. "Do you recall the toilet on the first floor flushing incessantly one night in December, when Nell was a senior in high school?"

"Oh, my, yes! I attributed that to my husband Herman's limited handyman skills."

"How about the cigar smoke in the library?"

"Smell isn't one of my keenest senses, thank goodness."

"What about the chair that started rocking itself, on the north wing porch?"

"Wind currents."

"The sounds of a woman wailing?"

"The heating system, with its old pipes and radiators."

"The Dobermans?"

Hazel shook her head reluctantly. "That happened before we moved in."

"The dogs belonged to the owners before you, who held on to the property for less than a year, before they sold the mansion at a loss."

"For a mere fifty thousand dollars," she said, delighted.

"Didn't they discount the price because they thought the house was haunted?"

She giggled and clasped her hands. "They did."

"The LaTourettes left the dogs overnight to guard the house and found them sprawled on the sidewalk, dead, the next morning," I said rigidly. "They had jumped from the second-story window in the turret. How do you explain that?"

"I never tried," Hazel said sweetly. "I viewed it as serendipity."

"What about the couple whose baby wouldn't stop screaming?"

She frowned, trying to reconnect with the past. "Our tenants, the Jenkins? With the two-year-old?"

"Yes."

"Mr. Jenkins had been offered a job out-of-state and wanted to be released from the lease."

"Nell says the wife called you and Herman in the middle of the night, and you witnessed the episode."

"Balderdash! We saw nothing except a fireplace grate near the baby's crib. We had no proof as to how it came to be there. We were witnesses to a room in disarray and a child crying, nothing more."

"As if he were possessed?"

"At the top of his lungs," she admitted. "But they could have upset him intentionally."

"You didn't believe the Jenkins' story that they were in the other room when the grate was ripped from the wall and flung at their son?"

"No," Hazel said stolidly. "There is nothing unnatural or otherworldly about wanting out of a lease agreement."

"Another baby the same age died in the house sixty years earlier of 'unexplained causes.' You didn't find that coincidental?"

Instead of squirming at the memory, Hazel burst into laughter. "Nell's a card, isn't she? She must have shown you the articles about that pioneer doctor. What was his name? I can't recollect."

"Dr. Benedict."

"Oh, yes. The physician who covered a large territory in the early nineteen hundreds."

"Two thousand miles," I said, without glancing at my notes.

"My, yes. I'd forgotten how extensive. It was his child who died, if I'm not mistaken?"

I nodded. "His eighteen-month-old son, in nineteen oh-five."

"His poor wife killed herself soon after. Some type of poisoning."

I scrunched up my face. "Cyanide."

She smiled faintly. "I haven't thought about these circumstances in years. Nell used to recount them every Halloween, expanding facts into fiction, but she stopped some time ago. The dear child probably doesn't want to frighten me, now that I'm up in years."

I leaned forward. "She didn't make up the séance in 'sixty-eight, did she?"

Hazel snorted. "A séance did take place. Nell and her friends brought in a medium. The whole affair was quite a production."

"Didn't it lead to the discovery of the secret room in the basement?"

"Dr. Benedict's lab? Yes, and in some ways, I wish we'd never known about the hideaway. We had to remove unusual apparatuses and thousands of bottles and instruments. Afterward, I bolted the door and hid the key."

"Nell says her personality changed every time she went into the room."

"That's why I hid the key," Hazel said matter-of-factly.

"Have you been in the lab room since the 'sixties?"

"I don't believe I have. No, I take that back." She paused, concentrating. "At some juncture, fifteen years ago or thereabouts, I opened it for a furnace repairman who needed access. His personality didn't change, to my recollection."

I smiled. "Could I go in there?"

"At your own peril," she teased, a twinkle in her eye. "I'll see if I can lay my hands on the key."

"This may be off the subject, but what about your friend, Constance Ferro? Nell swears she disappeared in the middle of the night."

Hazel's face lost some of its color, but her voice carried with full strength. "Oh, honestly! This nonsense has gone too far. Constance did nothing of the sort. She'd been in ill health for some time, a weak heart. She moved to California to be near her niece. I know she left in broad daylight, because I accompanied her to the airport."

"Why didn't she clean out her stuff? Is she still alive?"

"She most certainly is not. She passed away suddenly, peacefully. Her niece, who was her only relative, had no interest in her belongings. I haven't had the heart to dispose of them."

"When did Constance die?"

"On March sixteenth, nineteen eighty. At eight fifty p.m."

I looked at her closely. "Shortly after she moved to California?"

Hazel closed her eyes for a moment, and when she spoke, she struggled to compose herself. "I'm sorry, what did you say?"

"Did Constance die in California?"

Hazel rose abruptly and began to pick at flowers in the full-size, old-fashioned wagon that had been converted into a garden. "She most certainly did."

"You must have cared for her deeply," I said softly, "to recollect the precise time of her death."

Hazel started, her back to me. "She was the love of my life."

"Hmm."

Hazel turned and added hastily, "A dear, dear friend. We were inseparable. I miss her, but we've remained close. She's with me always." I must have looked confused, because she continued, with an anxious smile. "In spirit, not in ghost form. We'll never be separated."

"Were you lovers?"

"Oh, no, dear. Not in the sense of what you see today. We didn't dare. We were two widows who wished we hadn't married the men we did. If circumstances had been different . . ." Her voice trailed off.

"Or the times were different?"

She shrugged, a slight movement. "Back then, we wouldn't have known how to go about it. One simply couldn't adopt a new lifestyle. Constance moved into one of the units shortly after Herman died. She'd retired from her job at the library but wanted to remain within walking distance of the downtown branch. She arrived at the perfect time in my life."

"It sounds like it."

Hazel had a faraway look as she spoke. "Constance understood my loss, not so much for a man I never loved, but for the erosion of self-esteem. She accepted me for the shell I was and used to say she enjoyed watching me fill out."

"You seem quite full now," I said, smiling warmly.

Hazel laughed shyly. "Thank you. I've tried to make the most of my remaining years. I had no idea I'd be given this many, or I might not have lived the last decades with such urgency."

"Urgency's good."

"I suppose it is."

"After Constance left for California, you stopped renting units in the main house?"

Hazel nodded. "I no longer felt comfortable living among strangers. Also, I'd grown weary of placing advertisements, showing the apartments, receiving calls at all hours of the day and night, struggling to hold on to a competent handyman, filling out paperwork and tax forms. It became too much."

"But you never considered selling the house?"

"There was no need, and I couldn't bear to look across the driveway and see a new owner."

"Now you can?"

"My daughter tells me I have no choice. I've accepted that I have to part with the main house."

We chatted for a few more minutes before I closed my notebook and rose.

After promising to search for the key to the locked cellar room, Hazel walked me to my car, and from the street, we stood side by side and eyed the Fielder mansion.

I looked at her intently. "You don't find the house foreboding?"

"Not in the least."

"After you die, you won't come back and haunt it, will you?" I kidded her.

She cracked a smile. "You have my word on that. When I'm finished, I'll be done and gone. But I refuse to be hurried on my journey. Roberta Franklin had best be clear on that, no matter what type of deal she and my daughter have cooked up. She will not touch the carriage house, not one inch of it, or enter it without my permission, until I've died."

"That's the agreement," I said as I shook her hand. "Thanks for your time, and for the good news about the house not being haunted."

"You're welcome. I enjoyed our visit. Give my best to Roberta."

"I will. You'll be seeing a lot of her, now that the deal can go through."

Hazel looked perplexed. "Was there any question about its completion?"

I winked and said, "Roberta won't buy the house if it's haunted."

She looked at me sideways. "You're putting me on."

"I'm serious," I said, shaking my head in amazement.

Hazel sidled closer and whispered conspiratorially, "Roberta Franklin will refuse to buy my house if it's haunted?"

I shrugged nonchalantly. "As I understand it."

"I'll be darned," Hazel said neutrally, but as she pulled away, I could see a contemplative look in her eye.

CHAPTER 14

I spent the rest of the afternoon counting the minutes until I could approach Destiny about the $100,000 donation from Shirley Bassett, the one she'd conveniently failed to mention. I confronted her immediately after she walked into the house at eight.

"Have you received a large donation recently?"

Destiny set a pizza box from Antonio's on the kitchen island and looked at me suspiciously. "Maybe."

"Six figures?" I said casually as I lounged on the living room sofa.

"How did you know?"

"Lucky guess."

"What's going on, Kris?" She crossed the room, shifted my legs and sat next to me.

I didn't move a muscle in my face. "You tell me."

Her eyes flickered. "A large gift came to the Center. The donor wants to remain anonymous."

"Was it an individual or foundation?"

"A personal contribution," she said at last.

I sat up and pulled my knees to my chest. "From a woman?"

"Kris, don't do this."

"It was a woman," I said triumphantly.

"Yes, but I can't break a professional confidence."

"Even for me?"

"She didn't give me permission to gossip with my lover."

"Nice," I said, my tone harsh. "Did she give you permission to tell me about the four dozen red roses she brought?"

Destiny blanched, but her voice remained calm. "Where are you getting this from?"

"I can't say."

"Are you spying on me?" she said gravely.

"I came across the information in a case I'm working on."

"What case?"

I shrugged.

She moved back a few inches. "Who hired you, and to do what?"

I smiled thinly. "You know I can't reveal a professional confidence."

Destiny's face became a mask of anger. "Come off it, Kris! What's going on?"

"Honestly, Destiny, I can't say."

"Is Fran helping you?"

"No," I said, not necessarily a lie, because Fran's actions hardly felt beneficial. "Don't go running to her for information."

"You really won't tell me?"

"You tell me who gave you the money, and I'll tell you who hired me," I said heatedly.

She looked stricken. "I can't. My situation is different."

"Your work and integrity are more important?"

"I didn't say that, but my donation doesn't involve you," she said deliberately.

"How do you know?"

Her look of surprise seemed genuine. "Why would it?"

"Think about it, about ulterior motives."

Her bewilderment increased. "Kris, I have no idea what you're talking about. Why do I have to defend a contribution to the Center? We receive thousands every year, and I don't run home and tell you about them. It's none of your business."

I took a deep breath, and my shoulders tensed. "What you're doing at work is none of my business?"

"Correct."

Our eyes locked. "Then why do I have to listen to you talk about it every night?"

The look of devastation on Destiny's face penalized me more than her prolonged silence. When she spoke, a cold furor had replaced hurt. "You really resent me, don't you?"

"I resent that your work always comes first."

Her breathing became shallow. "You knew that when you met me."

"I thought it would change."

"Well, it hasn't," she said furiously. "And it won't. When I'm eighty years old, I'll be setting up a hotline or sending out a press release. It's what I do."

"It's who you are."

"So what?" she yelled, throwing up her hands. "Why do you say that like it's an accusation? It *is* who I am, and I'm proud of it. I can't help it that I love my work when you're struggling with yours."

"I am not," I said mechanically, my voice barely above a whisper.

"What do you call it, Kris? Since you quit your real job, you barely work. Your sister tries to give you freelance projects, but you refuse."

"I can't go back to that," I said, lowering my head. "Even if that was real and what I'm trying to do now is unreal."

"I didn't call it unreal," she said, exasperated.

"You implied it."

"What if I did? How realistic is it that you can make a living as an investigator? What are you moving toward? You barely have enough work for yourself, and now Fran's a partner. You shouldn't pay her to be your companion."

"How dare you!" I said, my voice rising.

"Can you deny it? Most days, the two of you do nothing but play solitaire and argue about what's on talk radio."

"How would you know?" I said, steely-eyed.

Her insincere smile came and went. "Because you tell me."

"And now, you're using it against me."

"No, Kris, I'm simply pointing out how miserable you've been. Not working affects you. Would you at least agree with that?"

I avoided her gaze. "Maybe."

"The type of work you do is hard on you," she said without rancor. "You never talk about it, but do you think I don't notice when you pull away when I try to kiss you or when you disappear from the bedroom in the middle of the night?"

"Only sometimes," I said in a small voice.

"More lately."

"You don't respect me anymore."

"Of course I do," Destiny said plaintively, reaching for my hand, which I yanked back. "I can't relate to people as well as you do."

I couldn't say anything. Tears began to trickle down my cheeks.

"Not on the deep level you touch them. My work is about connecting with people, but I do it superficially. I come up with ideas and agendas. I keep everything running, and I fight for the big picture of how to improve lesbians' lives. But I don't hold their hands or watch them cry or listen to their darkest secrets. That's why I hire program directors and counselors," she said with a wry smile. "I can help all of the women in Colorado, but I don't have any interest in one."

"You're sure?" I said pointedly, staring at her until she caught the double meaning.

Her sigh was almost inaudible. "The donor doesn't interest me, only the donation. You should know that by now."

I looked at Destiny steadily, but my voice quivered when I said, "What are we going to do?"

She squeezed my hand, which this time I let her control. "We're going to do what we've done for three years. Trust each other. I'll trust that you're working on something that involves me, at least peripherally, but you can't talk about it."

I nodded.

"Yet?" she said hopefully.

"Or maybe ever."

Only her raised eyebrows signaled a protest. "You'll trust that women can make huge donations, in the millions if they want. I'll allow them to buy services, but never me. Okay?"

"I guess," I said, unable to stop trembling.

Destiny lifted my chin and kissed me on the forehead. "Do we have a deal?"

"Yes," I said quietly.

Her eyes glistened. "Do you trust me?"

"I can't not," I said, my voice husky.

• • •

The next day passed awkwardly.

Destiny and I tiptoed around each other, craving the closeness we'd destroyed, yet reluctant to expose ourselves again, frayed from the opposing emotions.

As my relationship unraveled, Fran moved ahead, in full pursuit of one, and on Wednesday morning, she greeted me enthusiastically, before I could make my way through the door. "I need a minute of your time."

"I just got here," I said grumpily.

"Need a second opinion."

I plopped down in my chair and rubbed my eyes. "About what?"

"The love of my life. I have the responses to my *Westword* ad. She's in here somewhere," Fran said, gesturing with a swoop to a stack of letters on her desk.

I yawned. "Aren't you being a little unrealistic?"

"Nope," Fran said firmly, patting the correspondence. "I can feel it. Loved the part you added about 'attractive, sometimes beautiful.' Must have been an attention-grabber. Don't know where you came up with the other tripe, but it worked." She flipped open the weekly newspaper and read aloud. "*Mature lesbian, attractive and sometimes beautiful, wholesome and financially independent, seeks same. Looking for a profound love, one in which I can give all that I am and realize what more I can become. Enjoy a full life, including golf and snowboarding, but am missing the essential: a partner/lover/friend/soul mate. If you feel the same, let's begin each day as if it were our first and could be our last. Please write, as much as you feel comfortable sharing.*"

"Not bad," I said, admiring my work.

"They charge by the word at *Westword*, you know. But I ain't complaining. Wait till you see the haul." She fanned out the letters before depositing them on my desk. "Thirty."

I sat up straight. "You received thirty responses?"

"And counting. Check out the gluttony of options."

I rifled through the stack. "What are the dots?"

"Color codes. I borrowed some stickers from the cabinet in back. Hope you don't mind, office supplies for personal use. Red for hot. Yellow for warm. Blue for cold."

I stared at her, astounded. "What did you use for criteria?"

"Ranked the dames in six categories. Gave 'em scores of one to ten in each, high score ten. Perfect score, sixty."

"You gave equal weight to each category?"

"Think I should have calculated weighted averages?" Fran said, her brow furrowed.

"No, no." I hastily glanced at the matrix she'd drawn. "Are these the categories? Handwriting?"

"Yep. Good penmanship's a real turn-on!"

"Communication style?"

"She's gotta get to the point, hold my attention."

"Humor?"

"I ain't expecting a belly laugh in every sentence, but there better be a few giggles."

"Assertiveness?"

"I want a gal who knows what she wants, goes for it."

"Description of self?"

"Has to be reasonably good-looking. If the adjectives make me pant, scores galore."

"What's this sixth category, miscellaneous?"

"Gut feel."

"Did you grade on a curve?"

"Hilarious, Kris. Didn't have to. Most in the top echelon. Sad to say, a few didn't crack the teens, and a couple of nutcases scored zero."

"Zero," I commented mildly. "That's cold."

"How about an opening line of, 'I was and am highly desirable to homosexual men.'"

I gasped. "Yikes."

"Then there's 'I'm married with children, yet still I seek the feelings of another woman.'"

I scowled. "You're too old for those games."

"Got that right. Get a load of 'People have said I'm devastatingly beautiful. I'd like for you to meet me.' "

My eyes widened. "Scary."

"Didn't appreciate 'I'm the best friend I've ever had.' "

I smiled. "I kind of like that one."

"You wouldn't if you saw her name. Bambi. How could any woman command a gnat's worth of respect with that moniker? And what's she got against using capital letters at the beginning of sentences?"

I studied Fran. "Have you memorized these letters?"

"Practically. It's addicting, all the attention. You'll see after thirty."

I groaned loudly. "You want me to read all of them?"

"I'd welcome the feedback," Fran said, flashing her most pleading smile before she moved to the couch.

I sighed. "I don't have to use the dots and scoring, do I?"

"Nah. Feel free to make up your own system."

I took a letter out of its envelope, unfolded it, smoothed it down with both hands and prepared to read. Before I could absorb the first paragraph, I had to stop. "I can't do this while you're staring at me."

"Why?" Fran said innocently.

"You're breathing too loud. I can't concentrate."

"Well, excuse me!"

"Couldn't you do something else while I read?"

"Be happy to," she said, reaching for a *Curve* magazine I'd left on the couch.

"Not here," I said emphatically. "Do me a favor. Go next door and pick out some flowers I can give Destiny. Tell Beth to put them on my tab."

"You in the doghouse?"

"Don't ask," I said, returning to the task at hand. "Make it a big bouquet."

• • •

Five minutes later, Fran returned with a bounce in her step and pulled up in front of my desk. After she lowered the floral arrangement, she frowned when she saw the stack of responses, already rubber-banded.

I handed her the one letter I'd separated from the rest. "Here she is."

"You can't be done," Fran said, doubt mixed with reprimand. "Took me two hours."

"I'm finished," I said firmly.

"You read all of the letters?"

"Parts of them."

"How'd you choose this one?" she said, turning the yellow paper, bending it and slapping it against her palm.

"I tried to picture you with each one. This one, from Robyn, stretched my imagination the least."

"Picture? As in bed, in kinky sex positions?" Fran said playfully.

"As in a restaurant, in a conversation."

She aimed a disdainful flick at the paper. "Pages ripped out of a spiral. Smacks of careless, lazy."

"How about spontaneous, unpretentious? A nice contrast to her work as an insurance contracts analyst."

"Boring!" Fran exclaimed. "Worse, only two months have passed since her breakup. I don't have time for reminiscences of lost loves."

"How about Peggy, the four-page letter written in green ink?"

Fran shook her head in disgust. "Too much, too soon."

"What about Dolly, the postcard, the one who wants you to call after midnight because she works the swing shift?"

"Too little, too late."

"Obviously, we have different tastes," I said, exasperated.

"Why couldn't you choose Tess, the one with the partial photo?" she said, referring to the letter that had included a torn photo, taped facedown.

"I didn't like 'Turn this over to see the back of me and call if you'd like to see the front.'"

"I found it intriguing."

"She'd cut someone from the photo!"

"What's the harm? I've got albums full of irregular photos myself.

Some missing sides, others tops, one a middle. Ruth was everywhere, now nowhere, but it's hard to part with the good snaps."

I threw up my hands. "Out of all the responses, Tess was your favorite?"

"Should have guessed by the three red dots," Fran said curtly.

I replied carefully, "She wrote to you on Snoopy stationery."

"Whimsical touch, eh?"

"I knew a girl in high school who collected Snoopy stuff. She had a weird attachment to that dog. You'd better watch out."

"You and me, we'll have to agree to disagree," Fran said brusquely, gathering her belongings. "I've gotta run."

"Now?"

"I have to follow up. Better do it at home. The atmosphere ain't right here. Thirty'll take time. I plan to call the five high-scorers, drop the rest a line."

"You intend to answer all the letters? What will you say to the ones you turn down?"

"Something like 'I appreciate you taking the time to write, but I haven't selected you. Nothing personal.' That should do it."

"Rejection is always personal."

Fran allowed a half-smile. "Course it is, but no sense stirring up a psycho."

CHAPTER 15

I saw little of Fran Green over the following two days and less of Destiny. My lover and I spoke by phone several times a day but rarely crossed paths in person.

On Friday night, however, I paid a surprise visit to the Lesbian Community Center, where Destiny was alone, hard at work, sending e-mails to patrons and asking them to match Shirley Bassett's donation. She had dark circles under her eyes and seemed groggy but maintained she felt fine. We shared Thai food I'd picked up from Tommy's on Colfax Avenue, and at nine o'clock, I kissed her and left.

I waited outside, in front of the building, but no one came to visit, and Destiny never left.

At eleven, the lights went out, and I raced home, narrowly making it up the stairs and into bed before Destiny arrived. I pretended to be asleep, and she pretended to believe me.

Destiny worked through the weekend, and I passed the time painting the fence in the backyard, something I'd meant to do all summer. I'd hoped manual labor would take my mind off Carolyn O'Keefe's machinations, but it had the opposite effect. With each stroke, I replayed images of her and Destiny at the Botanic Gardens, unable to dismiss the notion that they shared something special.

I recalled Carolyn pulling Destiny to her side, claiming her. Both of them greeting people with ease and grace. Two of the most powerful women in Denver, together.

I felt like aborting the handyman project after three feet but couldn't stand to leave distressed counterparts next to gleaming sections. Twice, I ran out of paint and had to run to Home Depot, and by the end, the 200-foot job had consumed all of the weekend's daylight hours and rendered me sore and cranky.

Monday morning, at the office, Fran Green forced me to endure an equally unbearable exercise.

"There has to be another way," I whined. "Why do I have to go?"

"Need your insight. Want you to see Shirley Bassett in action, at the podium," she said, referring to the president of the Denver Women's Chamber of Commerce and her role at their upcoming luncheon on Wednesday.

"I'd rather clean the bathroom with my tongue."

"No need for histrionics," she said mildly.

"What if we run into Carolyn O'Keefe?"

"Won't. She's heading a school board committee meeting at the noon hour."

"How do you know?"

"Scoped it out on the Web. Stalker's pipeline of info, that Internet."

"Why do I need training? How hard can it be to sit at a table, make meaningless conversation and listen to dreary speakers?"

"More to it than that. Have to get you ready for the stampede. Let's practice. Stand up."

I rolled my eyes and let out a resentful grunt, but complied.

Fran stood across from me and squared my shoulders. "Starts with the business card. Put those babies in your right blazer pocket."

"I'm not wearing a blazer," I said reasonably. Fran had begun this pointless demonstration as soon as I'd returned from a three-mile jog on Seventh Avenue Parkway, and I was still dressed in a tank top and running shorts, no pockets on either.

"Pretend. The card comes out every time your hand moves to greet and shake. Left pocket, that's for the ones you land. Give it a try."

"Do I have to do this?" I whimpered. I felt lightheaded, possibly from the physical exertion of the past hour and weekend, more likely from the emotional exhaustion of the past weeks.

"Not as easy as it looks, is it?" Fran commented, when I accidentally put an invisible card she handed me into the wrong imaginary pocket. "Let's move on. Gotta perfect the elevator speech."

"What the hell's that?" For the ninth time in ten minutes, I regretted having agreed to attend the chamber meeting.

"Follows what you'd say to someone in an elevator. Also known as the thirty-second promo. All the pros got one. You say your name, name of the business, product or service you sell, benefits. Wham, bam, no more, ma'am."

"What am I supposed to say? I can't go as a private investigator."

"Got a point there. Tell you what, we'll whip up a set of cards on the laser printer. Make you a multilevel marketer. Perfect cover. Gives you a reason to talk to folks, and no one will linger or call later. No one clears a room faster than an MLMer. What do you want to hawk?"

"Nothing," I said stoutly. "I didn't successfully build and sell a business only to come back as a Mary Kay lady."

"Loads of other possibilities. Scrapbooks, prepaid legal, kitchen items, household products, sexy underwear, you name it."

I sulked.

"How about candles?"

I closed my eyes tightly. Unfortunately, when I opened them, Fran still stood before me, smiling expectantly. "Fine," I muttered.

"Key to these luncheons, keep moving. Meet as many folks as you can. You won't offend someone if you cut her short. Everyone does it. Don't take offense if someone's talking to you, looking at you with one eye, meantime scanning the room with the other. Unseemly, but common."

My shoulders slumped. "This is disgusting."

"Pay attention, Kris. Next tip, divide prospects into categories: gold, silver, bronze. Gold, you'll exchange cards, engage, nail down a date for a follow-up meeting. Silver, same thing, except push for a meeting but don't schedule it. Bronze, skip the meeting. Give some excuse about your schedule being booked."

I glared at her. "You do realize that I'm not really trying to get business?"

"Just telling you how it works. You may not use the technique, but watch out or someone will lay it on you."

"How do you stand to go to these meetings?"

Fran smiled in response to my dark look. "Got nothing at stake."

I shook my head, suspicious. "What's the real reason you go?"

"Better than a bar. Lots of gals in one room, most of 'em sober."

I laughed loudly. "You go to chamber meetings to pick up women!"

"You never know," Fran said with a wink.

• • •

After I'd satisfied Fran that I remembered which business card went where, she dismissed me, and I drove over to Hazel Middleton's.

My intention was to pick up the key to the lab room in the basement of the Fielder mansion. In applying down-to-earth logic to the illogical spirit world, I'd decided to spend time in the room that had changed Nell Schwartz's personality. Why chase ghosts across four floors of a mansion if I could narrow my search to one small area?

The plan might have worked, except Hazel greeted me at the front door of the carriage house with the news that the key was nowhere to be found. She invited me in, and I followed her to the kitchen, where she hit a button on the blender and shouted over the whir. "The secret to my longevity."

I cast a skeptical eye at the unattractive mix.

"My own juice concoction. Carrots, celery and apples."

She offered me a taste, but I declined, certain a mere sip would curdle in my stomach.

"Do you have any other secrets?"

Hazel nodded. "I read as often as I can, and I write in a journal every day, to keep my mind active."

We moved to the living room, where we sat in matching wingback chairs.

"What do you write about?"

"This and that. Would you like to see?"

"I'd love to."

From the circular table between us, Hazel Middleton handed me a perfect-bound book with a pink floral pattern on the cover. I opened it to the bookmark in the middle and read two recent entries.

July 22: Charlotte came over. Brought some yummy cookies. Said Dee won't be able to make it for pinochle on Monday. Been feeling puny. Will send her a card. Washed blouses, nightgown, bras and panties. Also put new bulb in nightlight in bathroom. Watered the cactus.

July 27: Nell and Lyndon/Flax came by, and we had a picnic in the park. Ham sandwiches and deviled eggs. Afterward, we went to the grocery store. They told me to load up as there were two people to help me. They carried all the stuff to the kitchen, and I took my time putting it away.

"That's nice," I said. "Every time I've tried to keep a journal, all I did was complain."

Hazel smiled faintly, a move that drew attention to her light green juice mustache. "I like to emphasize the good. The more you focus on the good, the better life becomes. The better life becomes, the easier it is to focus on the good."

No wonder my brief journal-writing stints had brought on depression. I'd taken a different approach than Hazel Middleton, highlighting fights with lovers and slights from family members, spotlighting frustrations and failures, and I'd never felt the therapeutic effects of purging others claimed to enjoy.

Maybe I'd try again, this time documenting the superficial, pleasing aspects of life.

I started to close the book, prepared to set it on the table, when a familiar name caught my eye.

July 29: Philip stopped again, with chocolates, wrapped truffles from Godiva. I like them, but they don't like me. Too rich. He's a kind man. Wants me to reconsider his offer. I'll leave that up to Nell.

• • •

After I read the entry, which undoubtedly referred to Philip Bazi, the menacing developer, I excused myself from Hazel Middleton, and drove back to the office, at unsafe speeds.

When I burst through the door, out of breath, I startled Fran, who nearly tipped over in her chair. Her legs fell off the desk, awkwardly hitting the floor, and the letters in her lap, more replies to her *Westword* ad, flew in all directions.

While she gathered them, I sat at my desk, fanning myself with a client file, recounting my visit to Hazel Middleton's.

"Roberta Franklin has to make a decision," I said frantically. "Philip Bazi is worming his way into Hazel's life."

"Cool it," Fran said, straightening up. She handed me a tissue, which I used to wipe the sweat from my forehead. "Bert can't move forward till she has conclusive evidence. What's the verdict, ghosts living there or not?"

I threw up my hands. "Who knows?"

"That won't satisfy her, Kris. You need to make a recommendation."

"How can I?" I said defensively. "Hazel, who should know best, laughs at the suggestion. She claims the spirits exist only in her daughter's imagination."

Fran handed me a battery-operated, hand-held fan from her bottom desk drawer. "The daughter claims the place is haunted?"

I nodded. "Nell spent almost two hours telling me about incidents. In ninety-degree heat, I had to weed her entire front lawn and act sympathetic."

Fran smiled broadly. "Hot sun, chilling tales."

"Funny," I countered tersely. "If you'd taken this case, you might not be joking about it."

"Easy there, girl."

"Sorry," I said half-heartedly. "I've never felt so confused."

"Give me the five-minute recap of Nell's two-hour spiel. Helps to have two noggins tackle it."

"Nell Schwartz is sure that at least four or five ghosts live in the main house," I said with a heavy sigh. "She believes they were there when the family moved in. She and her parents lived in the north wing, on all three floors, which were originally the library, a suite of bedrooms and a children's play area. Almost from the first night, she heard clicks in the dark."

"Clicks?"

"Rhythmic, soft ones. Only after dark, and only in her bedroom, which had been the playroom. She attributes these to a benevolent presence. Maybe the toddler who died in the house in nineteen oh-five, the son of Dr. and Mrs. Benedict."

Fran shrugged. "Sounds harmless."

"Maybe, but it's hard to discount the mirror incident. One night, a heavy mirror moved from hanging on the wall to resting against a couch."

Fran guffawed, as she moved her hands in circles. "Fat chance."

"Several friends of Nell witnessed it, too," I said steadfastly. "They were upstairs when they heard a noise on the main floor. They thought someone was breaking into the house, but when they came down, the only thing out of place was the mirror."

Fran's lips turned downward. "Could have fallen."

"It cleared two love seats and a coffee table and ended up leaning against the outer edge of the couch."

"Intact?"

"Not a hairline crack."

"Someone playing high-jinks on the family," Fran said, more a statement than a question.

I moved the fan to the back of my neck. "Nell also heard footsteps off and on. One night, they approached her bed, evenly paced as they crossed the room. At the bed, they stopped, and seconds later, she heard a ferocious bang." To emphasize my point, I brought my fist crashing to the desk, which made Fran jump.

She said harshly, "Could do without the sound effects."

I grinned. "Nell felt a thump in the middle of her mattress, under the box spring. It shook the bed and terrified her. She remembers running into the hall with her eyes closed, screaming."

"Were the parents clued in on these mysteries?"

"Yes, but neither believed her. Nell did have an advocate in high school, a teacher who told her to pray for the beings to move on."

"Someone told her prayer would solve this mess?"

"Nell swears from the time she started talking to the spirits, they shifted their energy. When the clicks would start, she'd plead that she had a test next day and had to get to sleep. They'd stop immediately."

Fran sucked her teeth. "You been in the mansion?"

"Not in the main house. Only in Hazel's carriage house and side yard. I don't want to go in there. I'd probably break my ankle in the rubble. And," I added half-seriously, "I'm scared about what happened to the Dobermans in nineteen fifty-nine, when the LaTourettes tried to convert the mansion into office suites."

"Nell spin a tall tale about pooches?"

"Not Nell. Elvira Robinson, from the historical group. Two dogs were hurled out of a second-floor, locked room, through a window, over a security fence, to the sidewalk." I clapped my hands together. "*Splat*! Instant death."

Fran raised her eyebrows, first the left, followed by the right, back to the left. "Another episode like that could ruin Roberta."

I nodded. "It would if she were partway through construction and had to sell."

Fran cupped her chin with both hands. "Way I see it, we have but one choice."

"Tell Roberta to walk away?" I said hopefully.

"Not so fast, skipper. Can't break Bert's heart without proof. Nope. We need to hire ourselves a paranormal investigator."

I cocked my head. "And where will we find one of those?"

"As it happens, I know an expert. Didn't want to interfere as you plodded along, but—"

"Plodded along—"

"Know you've been doing your best, but time to speed it up. Witchy Woman. I'll call her tonight."

I groaned. "Witchy Woman?"

"Real name's Cassandra Ambrosia Antonopolus. Course that's a made-up handle, too. Born Joanne Berger. Changed her name in her teens."

"Where did you meet her, in a graveyard on Halloween?"

"No need for sarcasm. Hooked up with her at Gay Bingo."

"Why didn't you say something sooner?" I huffed.

"Didn't want to mash any toes. What's more, couldn't see you embracing someone whose business card reads, 'Paranormal investigations and space clearings.' "

"You're right," I said, irritated at Fran's accuracy and at having to resort to this.

"She has a top-notch list of clients," Fran said cheerfully.

"Who would hire her?"

Before Fran could answer, I added with a resigned exhale, "Besides us? And why?"

"All kinds of folks, mostly on account of strange odors. Foul smells, those are Cass's bread and butter. Other things, too. Temperature change in a section of the house. Sensation of dread, someone watching them. Areas pets avoid."

"She specializes in haunted houses?"

"Any type of confined space. Apartments, offices, cubicles, stores, garages. Clears 'em out, good as new."

I gave Fran a penetrating look. "You believe in this?"

"It ain't hocus-pocus. Cass takes technical readings and measurements, makes calculations."

"What's she use, a Ouija board?"

"Get with the times, Kris. Cass has twenty grand invested in equipment. Thermometers, motion sensors, Geiger counters, microphones, electromagnetic field detectors, infrared video cameras, nightscopes, digital cameras. Engineer's dream, that stash in the trunk of her nineteen-seventy Cadillac. Has a few old-fashioned tricks up her sleeve, too: rice, flour, dowsing sticks, compass."

I shook my head in disbelief.

"This gal ain't no night flight. She's dedicated, organized and experienced. Grew up taking trips with her daddy to historic asylums across the East Coast. How many kids you know can claim that pedigree?"

"None, I hope."

"She's worked at it and developed herself into a true professional. Got training and everything."

"Where? Spirit University?"

"Joke all you want," Fran said, but by her tone I could tell she'd run out of tolerance. "You won't be laughing when Cass chases an icy blue form off your fanny. She works hard at her trade, no different than you or me. Last week, told me about an assessment form she created."

"For what?" I said, only slightly interested.

"Uses the form to clarify the client's goals. Showed it to me. It's an impressive, succinct document. Let's say you got a problem in your sunroom. Before Cass steps foot in your pad, she wants to know the details of the hauntings: times of day, correlation to cycles of the moon, duration of shenanigans, what person or event links to the sensation or smell, past and present uses of the space."

As Fran spoke, she became more agitated, which gave me an inkling, sans fancy equipment. "I didn't know you had a problem in your sunroom."

"Cigarette smoke," she blurted out.

I smiled broadly when I saw her blustery embarrassment as she rose and paced the room. "You hired Cass for a clearing!"

"Worked, too," Fran said between militant strides. "Got rid of every plume. Couldn't stand the reminder of Ruth."

"Ruth's not dead, and she's never been in your house," I said blandly.

"Probably sent her decidedly departed mother to haunt me. We showed her. Cass vamoosed her out in thirty minutes."

I didn't bother to conceal a smile. "How much did this cost?"

"Two hundred and fifty for the initial consult, another hundred for the shove. Worth every penny. We do the same for Bert, she'll thank us in the end."

"Hmm," I said doubtfully.

Compared to Roberta Franklin's skepticism, I imagined mine would rank as trivial, but I authorized Fran to contact Witchy Woman.

How low had I sunk?

CHAPTER 16

No lower than Fran Green.

The next morning, she straggled into the office with a tangled nest of hair, bloodshot eyes and cheeks dotted with rash-like splotches. "Hope you're not expecting much work out of me today," she said by way of greeting.

"Another date?" I replied, less than amused.

"Two. On a Monday night, no less." She lowered herself to the couch, inch by inch. "First went so poorly, needed a corrective experience. Followed your advice and called the insurance analyst, Robyn. What a dud. Rushed her home by eight."

"You and Robyn didn't click?"

Fran stretched out, covered her eyes and moaned. "That's putting it mildly. Took her to dinner, and the tedium began with a thirty-minute reading of the menu. She wanted the chicken if it wasn't stringy, the beef if it wasn't gristly or the fish if it wasn't fishy. The waitress suggested the special, grilled vegetables and cactus fajitas."

"Cactus is edible?"

"Not for this cat. Hold the prickles, I said, and my dinner companion called my humor juvenile and inappropriate."

"Well . . ." I said with a shadow of a smile.

"Try snappy and erudite," Fran replied, her voice raspy.

I rolled my eyes.

"After dinner, the broad chewed on me again for unbuttoning the top notch of my pants. Told me the come-on was crass. Was she smoking something? Furthest thing from sexual. I ate too much, filled up the trousers, was dying for relief."

"Date number two must have been more successful, if you're this debilitated."

"You got it," she said with a lustful smile. "Tired from tussling with Tess."

"The one with the Snoopy stationery and perfect score?"

She nodded, the slightest movement. "Tess Thompson, thirty-something taxidermist."

I shot Fran a look. "Thirty-something?"

She sat up slowly. "Thirty on the nose, but spare me the grief. Age difference is meaningless, according to her."

"Taxidermist?"

"Extraordinaire. She has a deer hanging on the wall, so lifelike it looks like the fella's drinking from a stream."

I winced. "She makes a living at this?"

"Don't scoff. Two hundred for a small bird, couple thou for the big mounts. It's a booming business."

"Her life's work is to help people hang corpses on their walls?"

"It's an elaborate art form," Fran said, animated. "These ain't no rags jammed inside a skin. Anatomically correct eyes, teeth, antlers. Wouldn't believe what she can do with a bullet-riddled carcass. Brings the dead to life. Gives you chills."

Fran rotated her neck, dropping her head to her left shoulder, back to center and to her right shoulder. I'd seen more range of motion in ceramic dolls, and with each micro-movement, she stifled a cry.

"Did looking at all those dead heads give you a sore neck?"

"Tess slept on my shoulder all night, and I couldn't move that side of my body this morning. Had to grab my hair to pick up my head, and there ain't much to clutch. Took a hot shower and been massaging the muscle on the top of my shoulder."

"Maybe you should see a chiropractor."

"I don't need a cracking. Get plenty of those in snowboarding season. This pinch'll work itself out."

"Dating's painful," I said with mock sympathy.

"Ain't that true! Young Tess pressed another nerve when she made a crack about love at the break of dawn. Too early, I told her, and I didn't mean in the day. She said true love has no timetable. I'm her first, case you can't tell."

"Relationship with a woman?"

"Relationship, period, but she's done her share of reading. Must have memorized *Lesbian Sex*. Quick learner, too. Caught on to the Green tricks, the ones never mentioned in the books."

I shook my head in wonderment. "You have your own methods?"

"Gems. Ought to publish 'em. Nah, take the fun out of it. Tough, really."

"Writing about sex?"

"Being someone's first. It's not that appealing. Last, now that makes you a winner."

"You want to be the last?" I said with a note of concern. "You feel this strongly about Tess?"

"Might. Tell you what, I sure am attracted to the attraction."

"Aren't you worried about moving too fast? About getting her hopes up, or yours?"

"No cares whatsoever," Fran said smugly. "What could go wrong?"

• • •

That evening, at the opposite end of the spectrum from Fran Green, I found myself involved in the less sensual aspects of love.

Over the course of our relationship, Destiny and I had talked about drawing up wills, adding my name to the deed on the house and merging our finances, but we hadn't done any of these.

We kept promising that we'd get around to the details tomorrow.

Tomorrow, the day after today that never came.

I'd decided earlier in the day that there would be no more tomorrows, that I had to talk to Destiny today.

"We need wills," I said as she walked into the bedroom.

She crossed the room to kiss me. "It's a depressing thought, but you're right. Every time I offer the free legal seminar for lesbians, I feel guilty that we haven't done any of the things recommended."

"Sandy and Jan just did everything," I said encouragingly.

"They hated it. They fought for weeks." Destiny sat on the edge of the bed. "We'll have to decide rights of survivorship. What if we die separately? What if we die together? What if the people we designate as heirs die before we do? Do we have to think about all that right now? You know my parents would give you everything, if anything happened to me."

"I'd feel better if we did it legally," I said, grabbing her hands. "Wouldn't you?"

"Yes," she said softly.

"I want my name on the house, too."

She smiled widely. "Done."

"And we need to merge our finances. Completely."

"Finally!" she practically shouted. "I've been begging you to share."

"One checking account."

"Yippee. You'll do the finances? Pay the bills, balance the checkbook, tell me how much money I can take out of the ATM?"

"Yes," I drawled, shooting her a chastising look, because she knew I'd been doing those tasks for her for more than two years.

"Good," she said resolutely. "I'll call Kate, the lawyer we use at the Center."

"Thanks."

Destiny kissed my cheek and stood. "Isn't it a little late to be talking about this?"

"In our third year?"

She glanced at the bedside clock. "At midnight."

"When else can we do it," I said, keeping my tone light, "if this is when you get home?"

Destiny sighed. "These hours won't last forever."

"They can't, or you'll collapse."

"I wish everything hadn't come in all at once. The big donation is driving me crazy." She took off her flats, pink scoop-neck shirt and black linen pants and tossed them onto the overstuffed chair next to the bed, where they joined other outfits she'd worn recently.

"Why are you putting in so many hours? Isn't Lola in charge of fundraising?"

Destiny turned back the covers and slid into bed next to me. "She's doing all she can, but it's overwhelming. We have a short window to match the funds. Whatever we can't match, we lose. I hate stipulations. I understand the philosophy behind them, but in practical terms, they put pressure on donors and staff. I feel like a used-car salesman, twisting people's arms to meet a deadline that benefits us, not them."

I stroked her hair. "Are you sure you can't postpone some of the work with Carolyn O'Keefe, at least until the grant period expires."

"I tried. But she's insisting on meeting almost daily, in person or by phone. She wants to prepare as much as possible before the educators' conference in Steamboat Springs. Which makes sense," she said, her voice disappearing, "but this schedule is killing me."

"It'll be over soon."

"I hope so." She snuggled against me and murmured, "Thanks for understanding, Kris."

"Sure," I said, unconvincingly to my ear, but she didn't notice.

Within minutes, she'd fallen asleep, and for a long time, I left the light on and watched her.

• • •

Wednesday at noon came all too soon, but as long as I kept breathing through my mouth, I knew I could last ten more minutes.

While I sat fully clothed on the toilet in the ladies room at the Westin, three hundred yards from the source of my avoidance, I put a hex on Fran Green. She'd brought me to the Denver Women's Chamber of Commerce meeting thirty minutes earlier, only to abandon me.

"We'll get more done if we split up," she reasoned, then she headed straight toward the most attractive woman among a crowd mingling near the registration table.

In her absence, I'd tried several times to hold a conversation that lasted longer than ten seconds, but nothing clicked.

Failing at networking, I staked out a seat at a back table and killed a few minutes acting as if I were intensely interested in my newcomer's grab bag. I took out each item, studied it and pretended I wasn't in a windowless, arctic-cold room, surrounded by people who were ignoring me.

By the time I'd emptied the bag, I could only conclude that the women's movement had been a figment of my imagination. Forget the free consult for Botox, 20-percent off coupon for treatments at a day spa and booklet on dressing for success. The stack of recipe cards, swatches from an interior designer and child-rearing tips really raised my ire. Only the miniature highlighter and key-chain flashlight had a chance of escaping the nearest trash can.

I played with both for a while, but when three coworkers at a utilities company sat across the round table for eight and dismissed me after brief introductions, I'd had enough.

I figured the bathroom would be a safe refuge for the remaining minutes, but I hadn't factored in the stench. The floral deodorizer was only managing to coat, rather than eliminate, the ripe smell. Nonetheless, I waited until the last possible second to exit the bathroom, barely allowing enough time to scurry to my seat before Shirley Bassett took the stage.

From two tables away, Fran tendered a slight wave, but I didn't reciprocate. Instead, I focused on Carolyn O'Keefe's lover, who cleared her throat, tapped on the microphone repeatedly and instructed everyone to take a seat. She intensified her pleas until we all had shuffled into place.

Wearing an apple blossom print jacket dress with matching flyaway jacket, Shirley Bassett used the podium to sound the battle cry for continued growth of chamber programs, participation in more national events and outreach to members outside the Denver metro area.

None of which interested me, so I turned my attention, out of the corner of my eye, to the woman on my right.

Middle-aged, she had black hair cut short to disguise balding on top, and she'd attached a few bobby pins, but their effectiveness seemed minimal. Large rectangular black glasses gave her small, narrow eyes a cartoon look, and a weak jaw and drooping mouth made her face seem on the verge of collapse. When she pushed a smile, her dour look transformed into a smirk, with gums overshadowing teeth. She wore a peach sundress, sandals with no panty hose, and three-inch long beaded earrings that lengthened her already oversized ears. Black cat hairs, spread across her chest and lap, were a sharp, almost comforting, contrast to the excess of cosmetics, perfume, accessories, hairstyling, pantsuits, short skirts and leather briefcases that filled the room.

My scrutiny must have caught her attention, because she leaned close and whispered, "Have you met our president, Shirley Bassett?"

The wall of alcohol hit me before her words, and it took me a second to reply. "No, you?"

"We knew each other quite well when I lived in Phoenix."

Jackpot.

I smiled inside and said conversationally, "Really?"

"We mixed in the same crowd. We called ourselves committed feminists."

"Lesbians?"

"Women-loving women," she said, chuckling.

I extended my hand. "I'm Kristin Ashe."

She grasped it firmly with both of hers and wouldn't let go. "Patty Ossorio."

"Nice to meet you."

"My pleasure," she said, slurring her words.

Shirley's recitation of chamber news prevented my reply.

In the vacuum of excitement that accompanied the announcements, I stole a glance at Fran. Her stage whispers to tablemates had begun to turn heads, and for the first time, I felt grateful for our separation.

Patty startled me by sliding a note next to my salad plate.

I opened it and read, "Are you as bored as I am?"

"Probably," I wrote back.

During the clapping for the speaker Shirley introduced, Patty said out of the side of her mouth, "You hate these functions, don't you?"

I replied under my breath, "Is it that obvious?"

"Why did you come?"

"My business partner forced me. You?"

"Memory loss," she said with a friendly smile. "I forget how stressful they are, and I return."

"Seriously?"

She nodded as we directed our attention to the front of the room, where a spokeswoman from the mayor's office had begun a spiel about how we, as women, could get involved in the political process.

I fidgeted in my seat and yawned through the civics lesson on the interdependency of local governments. I ate most of my salad and very little chicken, or maybe it was pork, through the protocol for contacting government offices. I gave silent thanks for women's perpetual dieting as I downed several large slices of cake that our table had been given to share. I needed the chocolate to perk me up through the power of donations.

The chart of government offices was enough to put anyone to sleep, but I soldiered on, resting my chin in my hand, when another note appeared. "The speakers aren't always this awful."

I returned the correspondence. "Do you come often?"

"Third Wednesday of every month."

"Why?" I wrote back, accenting my question with exclamation points.

"It's the best marketing I do."

The tepid applause that followed the speaker's departure gave me a chance to whisper, "I can help you implement marketing you won't hate."

"You'd do that?" Patty said, almost delirious.

I pushed back my chair to stretch my legs. "Absolutely."

"What kind of work do you do?"

"Marketing for small businesses," I lied, falling back on my former career. At least the fib felt better than posing as a multilevel marketer, Fran's suggestion.

"I need a Web site. The company I rep for has one, but I want my own. Could you write it?"

"Maybe. What do you want?"

"Nothing fancy. A bio of me, response-oriented copy, benefits of customer appreciation gifts, importance of brand identity, something along those lines."

"What kind of business do you own?"

"I distribute customized promotional products. The flashlight in your bag came compliments of me."

"Thanks," I said sincerely. "What else do you sell?"

"Anything that will hold a logo. Calculators, pens, shirts. Some items sell for as little as a nickel."

"What could I get for five cents?"

"A personalized mint."

"Mm."

"I consume a fair amount of those, as you might have guessed."

"Are you drunk?" I said, matching Patty's wild smile.

"A little. Do you mind?"

Before I could respond, Shirley Bassett interrupted our conversation with closing remarks, but few women in the room heard them; most had fled or begun to pack.

Shirley's return caused Patty Ossorio to comment dryly, "For being so wealthy, you'd never know it. She works the room as if she has to earn last month's rent."

"How rich is she?" I said casually.

"Rich. With her trust funds, she ought to be able to buy a better girlfriend."

The hair on the back of my neck stood at the mention of the woman who had hired me to follow Destiny. "What's wrong with the one she has?"

"Some would say," Patty Ossorio replied, rather loudly, "that Carolyn O'Keefe has an unnatural attraction to women."

CHAPTER 17

An unnatural attraction to women.

Coming from a lesbian, what the hell did that remark mean?

I never found out.

Patty Ossorio became sidetracked by a woman who interrupted to complain about binders she'd ordered but never received. As soon as I politely could, I broke in to schedule an appointment with Patty to work on her Web site, and we shared a loose hug before she turned to the irate customer.

I left in search of Fran and found her at a drinking fountain in the hall.

She straightened up and wiped her lips. "You try those breadsticks? Tough as rebar."

I gave her a scathing look.

She cleaned her teeth with her tongue. "Any interesting scuttlebutt at your table?"

"None."

"Nothing on Shirley B. or Carolyn O.?"

"Nothing."

"Didn't see you doing much schmoozing."

"Your point?" I said, barely controlling pent-up rage, raring for her to call me to task.

"Never mind. We'll work it from another angle," Fran said easily. "By the way, need to take the day off tomorrow."

"For?"

"Personal reasons. That a problem?"

"No," I said, my tone clipped.

"How many days we get?"

"I have no idea."

"Better set a policy. Meantime, I'll take this one without pay. How's that sound?" Fran smiled, an engaging move I was meant to match.

Only the secret that I possessed a lead she didn't allowed me to smile genuinely for the first time in hours.

• • •

Fran must have meant to ask for a day and a half off, because she didn't saunter into the office until close to noon on Friday. No wonder Destiny thought we never worked.

She greeted me with a boisterous, "Guess what Tess and I did yesterday?"

My resentment bubbled to the surface. "Tess?"

"Went spelunking."

"In a cave," I said, my temper barely in check. I'd assumed Fran had spent her day off trying to save my relationship with Destiny.

"Where else? Tess showed me a beaut. Can't tell you where. The entrance is a closely guarded secret. Stalactites and stalagmites take a thousand years per square inch to form, and dummies run off with them in seconds."

"What are you talking about?"

"Cave formations that hang from ceilings or grow from floors. Probably heard them referred to as speleothems."

"I've never heard of them as anything. Are you speaking a foreign language?"

"Close. Guess what's the difference between a spelunker and a caver?"

When I glowered, she answered herself.

"Two extra light sources."

"Is that supposed to be funny?"

"Thought so at the time, but loses a little in the light of day. Another difference: Cavers rescue spelunkers."

I didn't crack a smile. "This is how you spend your day off, when we're in the middle of two major cases?"

"Gotta have my rest and relaxation," she said lightly. "Ain't you wondering if I had fun?"

I gritted my teeth. "No."

"Had a blast for the first ten minutes. Loved the gear. Insulated coveralls, knee and elbow pads, helmet with a headlight. Didn't look forward to packing out my own urine, but skipped my morning fiber, blessedly."

I almost smiled. "What happened in the eleventh minute?"

"Started sucking spiders. Not literally. Caver term for having your head close to the ground in a confined crawlway. Lots of tight squeezes in caving, practically nothing but. Can't tell you how many times I had to suck in my gut, especially in Widowmaker."

"Widowmaker?"

"Nasty section of the cave. Had to navigate the fissure by pressing my back against one wall, feet against the other. Had the pleasure of inching sideways, while I tried not to think about the chasm below." Fran dropped to the floor and demonstrated.

"What was it, a two-foot plummet?"

"Joke all you want, but add about fifty to that estimate and thank your lucky stars Fran Green made it back alive," she said, crawling into her chair. "Terrifying experience, but nothing compared to what happened an hour later. Tripped and broke a tiny icicle. No biggie, thousands more like it within arm's reach, but Tess panicked."

"Was she afraid other spelunkers would find out?"

"That's it. Went downhill from there. She gave me a big lecture, which echoed, so heard it twice. Shrill ranting about the cave being alive and me killing part of it. Then, she pulled a prank. Wanted to teach me a lesson about the power of nature. Took my headlamp and hers and turned 'em off, made us sit in the dark for a full minute. Freaked me out."

"You couldn't handle sixty seconds?"

"Doesn't sound like much sitting here in the sunlit office, but go down there with bats and drips and water, you'll know what darkness is. All black, nothing to focus on but sounds. The void. Still creeps me out if I dwell on it."

"I take it you won't be returning."

"Not anytime soon, but did agree to help Tess dig out her own cave. On the weekends," Fran added hastily.

"Where? In her basement?"

"Laugh all you want, but my new girlfriend could become famous."

I was still reeling from the use of the word *girlfriend* when Fran continued.

"Every caver's dream is to discover a new cave. Tess found an opening not marked on the maps, near Fulford Cave, outside Vail. She's hoping it's an entrance that filled with dirt. She's spent two years digging and has reached a small chamber. She can't stand in it but can sit. I told her I'd help burrow, long as I stay within reach of daylight."

I looked at Fran with increased skepticism, well aware of her penchant for invention. "Are you making this up?"

"Not a word. Ask her yourself," Fran said, gesturing to the door.

"Tess is coming here?" I said anxiously.

"Any minute. Wanted to bring me lunch. Told her to pick up enough grub for you, too. Arby's okay?"

I didn't have a chance to reply before Fran's cell phone rang.

• • •

Fran held a brief conversation, during which she said very little, but when she clamped the phone shut, she broke into a wide grin. "Everything's confirmed with Cass for Saturday night. Bring your sleeping bag."

"We're spending the night at the Fielder mansion?" I said, my voice cracking.

"You betcha."

"The whole night?"

"If we dare," she said with an evil cackle.

"That might not be such a good idea. I have to bring Flax, Nell's grandson. When I told Nell we were hiring a paranormal investigator, she wanted a representative from the family present."

"The more the merrier."

"Actually, I think she wants us to entertain him. According to her, all he does is go online and play Gameboy."

"No problem! I'll pack an extra set of gear. Kid'll ghost hunt in comfort. State-of-the-art hot/cold thermos, air mattress, down pillows, collapsible chair and footstool. Nothing like roughin' it!"

"Forget about Flax. I could use those luxuries."

"Fair enough. Give the kid your Army Surplus hand-me-downs. You and me'll luxuriate in the latest Eddie Bauer has to offer. I'll bake a batch of triple-chocolate brownies, for good measure. Gonna need the sugar boost if we gotta keep our eyelids propped open all night."

"Yummy. What time?"

"Five sharp. Cass wants plenty of time to set up the equipment before we lose daylight."

"What if we don't—"

Fran interrupted with a hearty, "To be continued, kiddo. There's my gal."

• • •

Undeniably, there she was, a gangly woman with stilts for legs, walking through the door.

In her arms, she carried two overflowing bags, and against her flat chest, she balanced three drinks, using her chin for support.

"The dumb asses didn't have any drink holders. Tell me how you run out of those at lunch."

Fran jumped to help Tess, but she brushed off her assistance and headed to the nearest counter. On it, she set the items, meticulously loosening each from the pyramid.

To her credit, she didn't spill a drop of soda on her white tank top or lose a fry in the massive pockets of her camouflage cargo shorts. Once unencumbered, she grabbed Fran, strangled her in an embrace, planted one on her lips and spun her around, tangling her T-shirt, "Wither Without You."

Only after completing the twirl did Tess acknowledge me. She dropped Fran and extended a stiff arm. "Tess Thompson," she said, using her free hand to brush back a clump of wayward hair.

Light brown strands, streaked blond from the sun, drooped from her scalp like strands of yarn. Judging from the web on her head, she must not have owned a comb, and she could have used one on quite a few parts of her body. Shrouds of light-colored hair covered her arms, legs, pits and upper lip, even her toes, which were on display through sandals whose ties reached to her knees and whose use she'd extended with duct tape.

My eyes widened at the sight of massive veins on her sinewy forearms and triceps, but I valiantly offered my hand, which she crushed against the beaded leather bracelet on her wrist.

Introductions aside, she took over the role of hostess, unpacking food and distributing straws, napkins and condiments, all in a flurry of motion.

"Is ham and cheese okay with you? Fran said you eat it all the time, but I'll trade out my roast beef, if you'd rather."

"No, thanks. I like ham."

"All the meat at Arby's is too processed for my taste, but that's because I grew up on game."

"Oh?" I said politely.

"I like wild duck especially. The meat tastes better when the animal has to run for its life, don't you think, Fran?"

"Couldn't say. Not enough experience to comment."

"We'll fix that," Tess said, reaching across Fran's desk to teasingly cuff the side of her head. "I love fresh lobster, too. Especially when I can choose one from the tank."

"You don't mind that while you're eating your salad, the lobster is boiling to death?" I said mildly.

"Not really," she answered childishly. "Do you, Fran?"

"Myself, I prefer a little distance between the murder and the meal."

I laughed, but Tess didn't.

Fran's girlfriend peered at me. "I've heard a lot about you."

"Likewise."

"Destiny, too. I'm in love with her."

"So am I," I said pointedly.

"I mean her politics. I admire everything she does. I donate to the LCC every time they send a fund-raising letter."

"Great."

"You have to support good causes. I also give to HRC, PFLAG, Sierra Club and PETA."

"PETA?" I said, surprised Tess would support an organization dedicated to the ethical treatment of animals, when she made her living stuffing them.

"It balances out my work."

"Wouldn't it be easier to choose another occupation?" I said reasonably.

"Not in a million years. I love what I do. I become the spirit of the work. Has Fran shown you the piece I gave her?"

"Not yet."

Tess looked around the office. "Frannie, you said you'd bring it in."

"Sure enough," Fran said, shooting me a nervous glance. "Must have forgotten."

"The piece is of two squirrels mating."

I tried unsuccessfully to halt a grimace.

"The detail's magnificent," Fran said. "Award-winning."

"Did Fran tell you we're going to start our own nonprofit?"

I cast a glance at Fran, but she studiously avoided eye contact. "She hasn't mentioned that."

"I told you I'd ponder it. Haven't committed yet."

"You will. We're going to buy land south of Castle Rock, where we can rescue and rehabilitate birds."

"I didn't know Fran had such an avian interest," I said, unable to conceal a smile.

Fran persisted in avoiding my gaze. "Just learning about the critters."

"We'll make it happen," Tess said confidently. "Did Fran tell you we're going on a big-game safari next summer?"

"No, she didn't," I said perkily, enjoying Fran's discomfort.

"Photographs only. No killing."

"That's what you think," Tess said, aiming at Fran, her fingers coiled in the shape of a gun.

And so it went for the next hour.

It turned out there was quite a lot Fran hadn't told me, and for good reason. I would have laughed at half and cried about the rest.

Fortunately, the happy couple had an appointment at a mountaineering shop, to outfit Fran with a climbing rigger, and they departed in a rush, leaving behind a faint trace of Tess's body odor.

I'd barely had a chance to clear my desk, or the air, when the door opened again.

• • •

"Hey, stranger," Roberta Franklin said, entering with a friendly wave. She was dressed in pointy-toed cowboy boots, a snap-button, shimmery white Western shirt, a black suede vest with fringe and tight blue jeans. Large gold hoop earrings dangled below a tan Stetson.

I cast a frantic glance out the window. "You just missed Fran."

"I was hoping to catch you alone. Is this a convenient time?"

"Sure," I said, gesturing for her to take a seat at Fran's desk. "I'm making progress on the case, but—"

"We'll get to that in a minute. I have something of a more personal nature I'd like to discuss." Roberta paused and crossed and uncrossed her legs.

I gulped. "Okay."

She said eventually, "If I don't broach the subject now, I'll lose what little courage I've mustered. If you don't mind . . ."

"Jump in," I said, disturbed that her left eye had begun to twitch in the deep recesses of her wrinkles.

She cleared her throat. "It's about Frances."

I tried to suppress a groan by converting it to a cough, but the leak didn't escape Roberta's notice.

"It's not my intention to put you on the spot, but would you happen to know if Frances is available for courting?"

I took a deep breath and doled out the exhale. "Define *available*."

"Has her relationship with Ruth concluded?"

"Months ago."

"Has she taken up residence with another woman?"

"No."

"Or pledged her love?"

I looked away for a split second. "Not that I'm aware of."

"Is she seeing someone?"

I started to bite my nails. "You really should be asking Fran these questions."

"I'll take that as a yes."

"I didn't say that."

"You didn't have to," Roberta said with obvious regret. "Fifty years of interviewing witnesses has taught me a thing or two about admission and omission. I appreciate your candor."

"Don't give up," I said hesitantly. "It's a dynamic situation."

She cast an appraising glance. "Are you implying that Frances would be receptive to an overture?"

I shrugged. "You never know unless you try."

She chuckled. "I can see I've met my match in wordplay. Has Frances said something about me?"

I answered with a sly smile. "Perhaps."

"Something complimentary?"

"Always."

Roberta straightened her bent back. "Does she find me attractive?"

"You'd have to ask her that."

"I've hesitated to take this step for fear of compromising our professional relationship."

"That shouldn't be a problem. Fran's busy with another case, and I'm in charge of yours."

"It's settled then."

I felt the block of ham sandwich and potato cakes harden in my belly. "I guess so."

"You wouldn't intentionally direct me down a path of certain peril and questionable reward, would you?"

"Define *peril* and *reward*," I kidded.

Roberta reached forward and squeezed my hand. "You're a stinker. Let's talk about a few ghosts, shall we?"

I'd worried needlessly about Roberta Franklin's reaction to hiring

Cassandra Antonopolus, the paranormal investigator. That hardly fazed her. In fact, she welcomed the feedback as a means to break the stalemate brought on by the disparate opinions of Nell Schwartz, Hazel Middleton and Elvira Robinson. Roberta promised she'd maintain an open mind in regard to any data that Fran, Flax, Cass and I could gather from our night at the Fielder mansion.

In all, she seemed heartened by the progress on the case, until I updated her on Philip Bazi.

When I recounted his antics—from his thinly veiled threat of workplace sabotage to his relentless pursuit of Hazel Middleton— Roberta Franklin went into a tizzy.

She sputtered, cursed and left in a huff, vowing to take care of "that rapacious developer."

CHAPTER 18

That evening, I came home to find Destiny lying on the couch, an ice pack on her head.

Before I could ask about her day, she looked at me with dead eyes and said, "Sometimes, Kris, I really hate my job."

I knelt on the floor beside her. "Cheer up! It's Friday, the beginning of the weekend."

"What difference does that make? I have to work all weekend."

"You're just tired. You're working all the time. You'll feel better after you've rested."

"When am I supposed rest?" she said, dejected. "When will the world stop assaulting, insulting and abusing lesbians so I can take a break?"

"Not this month," I said with a sympathetic smile. "What happened?"

"Nothing and everything." Destiny threw the ice pack to the floor and sat up. "I'm sick of Carolyn O'Keefe. She's all talk and no action. She feels no sense of urgency to implement anything, and we keep talking about the same issues and ideas, in circles."

I joined Destiny on the couch. "Could you table the youth programs, at least until your donation-matching period expires?"

"No!" Destiny said, scaring me with her vehemence. "You don't get it, do you?"

"Get what?"

"I want to help girls in high school, that's all I care about."

"What about your other causes? You were adamant about gay marriage last month."

"Screw gay marriage."

"Since when?"

"Since I realized that we're going about this all wrong. Instead of fighting for the privilege of having heterosexuals recognize our love, let's take away their rights. Let's refuse to acknowledge any bond exists. Let's allow them to live together for thirty years, buy houses, wash dishes, bear children, share money, bury parents, have sex, and let's pretend they aren't coupled."

"Destiny," I said gently.

"Let's not let them into our families. Let's introduce them as Jane and 'her friend Jim' after fifteen fucking years. Let's not honor their relationships. Let them break up, and we'll deny the devastation of their divorce, because we never accepted their marriage. Let's do that instead of pushing for some county clerk to issue a piece of paper a legislative body will later declare invalid."

"You know what this is really about, don't you?"

"What?" she muttered.

"The whole issue boils down to weekends in June."

She looked at me as if I were crazy.

"Straight brides don't want us competing with them for prime wedding dates," I said, poking her in the side.

Destiny didn't crack a smile. "This isn't funny, Kris."

"Okay." I sighed. "You want to take a break from the gay marriage issue for a while?"

"You could say that," she said snidely.

"What about your ideas for the next Coming Out Day, the 'We Exist' slogan?"

"I'm over that, too. So what if there are one or two gay people in every extended family, hundreds in a neighborhood, thousands in a city, tens of thousands in a state, millions across the U.S., tens of millions worldwide? I'm supposed to send out a press release declaring that we perverts pay taxes and obey laws and volunteer in our communities? That we start small businesses and perform heroic acts and vote and show up for work every day? That we mentor children and look in on seniors and give birth and save lives and follow spiritual paths? And, yes, that we dare to live with, make love with and devote our lives to women? You want me to do that?"

I shrugged, at a loss for what might decrease, or at least not increase, her wrath.

"Forget it," she snapped. "I don't want to educate the public, Kris. That no longer interests me. I want to help one girl, in one high school."

"All right."

Her voice broke. "You have no idea what high school was like for me, do you?"

"How could I? You never talk about it."

"I lost every friend I had."

"I didn't know," I said quietly.

"One day, I was popular and well-liked. The next day, I was invisible."

"How did they find out you were gay?"

"I told them. All of them, each time hoping for a positive reaction. I was foolish enough to believe my friends would be happy for me when they heard that I'd met someone and that we were dating and falling in love."

"You were?" I said, unable to hide my surprise at hearing this for the first time. I'd assumed Destiny's first love had been a woman she'd met her sophomore year in college, although she'd never said that exactly. "Who was she?"

"Raja Schuler. I met her in calculus. She was a foreign exchange student from Germany. After the rumors about us circulated, I could have withstood the isolation. I know I could have, but they crushed her."

"You were her first girlfriend?"

"And last. After she realized the consequences, she reacted by changing her sexuality, a luxury I never had. She started sleeping with every guy she met, including one who took her to the prom."

"I'm sorry," I said, reaching for Destiny. She let me clasp her hand but didn't return the squeeze.

"Last I heard, she was living in Berlin with two kids, a sheepdog and a husband who knows nothing about 'our adolescent fling,' as she labeled it."

"I'm sure you were more to her than that."

"What was between us will always be between them," Destiny said, resigned. "That's my only consolation."

"If the environment in your school had been different, do you think you might not have lost Raja?"

Destiny's eyes glistened. "I might not have lost myself."

"Didn't your parents offer support when you came out?"

"My mother was in a fog, and my father was worse. When I dropped out of everything—debate team, student council, soccer, tennis—he finally noticed something had changed and asked me what was wrong. I told him everything, including how Raja had cheated on me. He had two comments: 'Can you blame her?' and 'Don't tell anyone you're a homosexual.'"

My eyes bulged, and I took a deep breath. "Now, I get it."

"I need to put resources in the schools, Kris, right down the hall. When girls and boys feel alone, excluded, confused or ashamed, I want them to have somewhere to turn."

"That would be nice," I said, desperately wishing the solution didn't involve Carolyn O'Keefe. "On a lighter note, or maybe a more serious one, I'm glad you couldn't change your sexuality as easily as Raja could."

"Never," she said, and with the flicker in her eyes, I saw a measure of Destiny's resilience return.

• • •

When I left the house at ten the next morning, Destiny was still on the couch, fully clothed, with a pillow over her head. She'd skipped dinner and breakfast and was snoring lightly.

I left her a note and headed to the office, where Fran Green met me with glee.

"Guess who called last night?" she said, rising to dance a jig.

"Ruth."

"Never happen. Still got her call-blocked."

"She's managed to use cell phones and pay phones to get through."

"Not this time. Think hot broad," Fran said giddily.

"Tess."

"Can't deny it, she called, too. She rings me up every night, sometimes every hour," Fran said, her arms flapping. "But that ain't what's got my heart thumping."

"I give up," I said wearily, dropping my sunglasses and keys onto the desk.

"Bert. She called to invite me to a cozy dinner."

My eyebrows jumped as I conjured up surprise. "She asked you out?"

Fran blushed. "She made a query as to whether I would be available for a romantic evening."

"How sweet!"

"The lady has class. You wouldn't believe the life she's led. She's traveled all over the world. Won every award legal eagles can invent. I could have listened to her all night. That sexy voice ripping up my insides. As it was, didn't put down the receiver until after midnight."

"She called that late?"

"She rang me up at seven."

My jaw dropped. "You spent five hours on the phone with Roberta Franklin?"

She shrugged. "Seemed like four."

"What did you talk about?"

"What didn't we? Couldn't stop. Didn't want to."

I gave Fran a sharp look. "You didn't bitch about Ruth, did you?"

"Not a word about the smoking or hypochondria. Took your advice and kept my trap shut."

"Did Roberta complain about any ex-lovers?"

"Couldn't. She's never been in a long-term coupling."

"Are you sure she's a lesbian?"

"Ask my loins."

"Fran!"

"She's done her share of dating, met her quota of one-nighters. That dame's all about the women, no worries on that score."

"Aren't you concerned that she hasn't lived with anyone or made a commitment?"

"Bert's made a pledge to her career. Law's her vocation and avocation, she says. Didn't need more. Also, had a serious drinking problem most of her life. Been sober ten years and grateful she didn't drag anyone else through the gutter, is how she explains it."

"What if you fall in love? Won't you want a commitment?"

"Whoa, girl. You've got the cart so far ahead of the horse, the two are in different pastures. I agreed to a date. Rich food, good wine—" Fran reacted to my admonishing frown. "Scratch that. Rich food, tantalizing conversation, finger touches across the table, smooch at the door. My needs are simple."

I shook my head. "That peck might lead to trouble."

"Who said anything about a peck?" Fran said, wrapping up her dance with a flourish and dropping into her chair with a crooked smile.

• • •

Fran left at noon to bake brownies and pack for our ghost-hunting expedition, and I made a trip home, where I found Destiny in a lounge chair on the deck.

We ate lunch together, after which I left for an appointment with Patty Ossorio, my new best friend from the Denver Women's Chamber of Commerce. Unfortunately, my time with Patty extended past my initial estimate, which meant I not only missed out on a nap but also had to race back to the house to gather supplies and change clothes before heading to the Fielder mansion.

When I arrived for the ghost hunt, Fran was already there, leaning against her purple Ford Ranger, arms folded across her chest. I could barely make out "Butch It Up," on her T-shirt.

She stirred only enough to wave two fingers.

"I'm not late, am I?"

"Five o'clock. On the button."

"Where's Cass?"

Fran inclined her head toward the main house. "Checking out the lay of the land. Went in without equipment. Wants to get a feel for which rooms might be active. Soon as she chooses, you and me get to schlep equipment. We'll haul, she'll position."

"What time did she get here?"

"Thirty minutes ago, same as me."

"I'd better check in with Hazel."

"Done. Bumped into her when she came outside to give the flowers a drink."

"What did you tell her about why we're here?"

"The truth. Didn't figure the real deal would alarm her."

"Is she okay with it?"

"Thinks it's hilarious. Wants us to keep a close eye on Flax. Doesn't want him running down the street to Seven-Eleven to buy candy. Other than that, no concerns."

"You told her we'd be here all night?"

"Righto. She said not to worry if we see her light on into the wee hours. Likes to read, falls asleep mid-page. There's our expert," Fran said as Cassandra Antonopolus came out the front door.

Lost in thought, Cass wove toward us, her attention directed at the sky. As she walked, one slow step at a time, she muttered to herself.

"What's with the hair?" I whispered to Fran, referring not to the color, a candy apple red, but to the unusual styling. Parted in the middle, the waist-length hair on the left side was curly, but the hair on the right was straight.

"Has naturally frizzy locks. Goes to a salon every month to have one side straightened Japanese-style. Takes hours, sets her back two bills, but gives her a look no one else has. Brings attention to the business."

"Doesn't the car do that?"

Witchy Woman's black Cadillac, parked in the circular drive, had silver goth lettering on the doors, windows, hood and trunk. My favorite tagline: "There are no bad ghosts, only bad ghost behavior. Call today for corrective action."

"She drives the Caddy to gigs. Rest of the time, tools around in a Saturn and parks that baby near a major intersection. No better billboard. Brings in at least one call a day. Not all good ones, but enough. Come here, I'll introduce you."

With that, we crossed the stone driveway and caught up with Cass.

In her mid-twenties, she was short and slightly plump. Dressed in black, except for gold sequins on her thigh-high boots, she wore a low-cut, form-fitting knit top and cotton miniskirt. She had a large nose that flared at the nostrils, a broad forehead and intense black eyes. Her mouth was turned up in a half-smile, and when she widened her grin, deep dimples formed in her cheeks.

"Thanks for coming," I said, returning her smile and handshake.

"Thanks for the job."

"You're welcome. Fran's said great things about you."

"Enough of the lovefest," Fran broke in gruffly, wrapping her arms around our shoulders. "What's your gut tell you after the reconnaissance?"

"Do you really want to know?" Cass said, breaking away to survey both of us, pausing to stare at me for a moment too long.

I nodded bleakly, and Fran said tentatively, "Better spill it."

Cass's eyes blazed, and she smiled brightly. "We're in for a wild night!"

CHAPTER 19

Sixty minutes later, no one was smiling.

Fran and I had burned through the hour carting equipment into the house, virtually all the contents of the backseat and trunk of the Cadillac, plus loads from Fran's truck and my car, while Cass fiddled with the temperamental equipment.

Adhering to Cass's instructions, we'd unloaded the bulk of the technical gear into two areas: the bedroom suite Hazel's friend Constance had occupied in the turret on the northwest corner of the second floor and the children's playroom in the third-floor attic.

For the moment, Cass had directed us to leave the camping supplies on the main floor, because she hadn't decided where we'd sleep.

She had a specific plan, however, for the lead-up to slumber.

We'd set up and experiment with the equipment before splitting into two teams to gather data. After four hours of this, we'd spend two additional hours awake and relaxed (easy for her to say). After that, we'd try to sleep for six to eight hours.

On past expeditions, this combination of activity and inactivity had brought optimal results.

Some ghosts liked to show off for the equipment, some preferred to casually join the social circle, and some enjoyed startling mortals out of deep sleeps. With Cass's proposed itinerary, we'd have all the bases covered.

I couldn't believe I was doing this!

The more I tried to take ghost hunting seriously, the more absurd it seemed, but I didn't vocalize this thought.

Instead, I left to pick up Flax just as Fran lumbered into the house under the weight of three sleeping bags and Cass tossed a dead battery pack out an upstairs window.

• • •

On the drive to Nell Schwartz's house, I couldn't stop thinking about my "marketing" meeting with Patty Ossorio earlier in the afternoon.

I'd spent a good portion of the time praying she wouldn't need another drink.

Patty had chosen our meeting place, a Starbucks on Colfax Avenue, and after settling in, I'd made my first mistake by rising and asking, "Can I get you anything?"

From her comfortable nest in a deep sofa chair, Patty had given me a seven-part drink order. Latté, decaf, single shot, hint of vanilla, light foam, extra hot, *grande*. Something like that. I repeated it twice, incorrectly, before fleeing for the counter. From there, I caught the girl's attention and had Patty shout her preferences. The barista screwed it up three times before calling it back correctly.

When it was my turn to order, I could only say, "Ice water." When the girl asked if I had any special requests, I couldn't tell if she'd laced the question with facetiousness, but I answered politely, "Extra ice, please." I added two blueberry muffins to the order and threw in a generous tip.

Mistake number two occurred when I asked Patty what she'd brought. She'd carted in two tote bags the size of small suitcases. Across several tables, she dumped mouse pads, caps, golf balls, computer screen brushes, business card holders, pens, watches, umbrellas and travel mugs. Customer appreciation gifts, as she called them.

To view the trinkets as gifts was a stretch, but I did take a liking to the miniature "magic answer ball." In sixth grade, my friend Trish had owned a full-size version of this interactive, pseudopsychic device, and we'd spent hours posing questions.

As an adult, I once again felt its pull, and I shook the ball.

Is Destiny having an affair with Carolyn O'Keefe?

Chalk it up to fate or poor workmanship on the Chinese import, but no definitive answer surfaced, only "yes" and "no" floating in a clump.

My attention snapped back to Patty after she unpacked brochures, flyers, screen shots of competitors' Web pages, catalogs and fact sheets. Among the stacks, she'd included a photo of herself for the bio page.

When I came across it, I almost exclaimed. Either the photo was twenty years old, or she'd brought a snapshot of her daughter.

I delicately broached the subject. "This one would work, but do you have a more recent picture?"

Patty's cheeks reddened. "Do I need one?"

I fumbled. "You've changed the color of your hair and your glasses." From blonde to black, tiny silver frames to massive black ones.

"Should I have a new photo taken?"

"Either that or leave it off."

"Off."

"Okay," I agreed, noticing she was wearing the same dress as she had on in the photo. A purple sundress, similar to the one she'd worn to the chamber meeting. Evidently, she didn't possess much range in fashion, but who was I to talk?

I had on a variation of my networking outfit, too, this time green pants, not khaki, and a blue top, not burgundy. My loafers with no socks hadn't changed, and I'd carried a legal pad, pen and calculator into the Starbucks in my hands, no need for a purse or briefcase.

I shuffled through Patty's materials, and we began to work on her Web site.

After we covered content, navigation, page layout and links, she offered to give my name to other chamber members in need of Web site content. "I'll refer so much business, you won't have to attend any more chamber meetings."

"One was enough," I said emphatically.

"That government speaker was ridiculous! Shirley must have owed the mayor a favor."

Capitalizing on the nasty tone Patty had employed, I said, "You're not fond of Shirley Bassett?"

"I was at one time. She'd deny it, but we went on a date years ago, when we both lived in Phoenix."

"How did that go?" I said neutrally.

"Not well. She couldn't stop talking about her lover, Carolyn. They were in a trial separation, which didn't last long, a week or ten days, something like that. Unfortunately, they decided to give it another try."

"Which put an end to your relationship with Shirley?"

"Indeed, but whooee, it wasn't easy letting go," Patty said, an enchanted look in her eyes. "I was physically attracted to her, that's for sure, like an explosive chemical reaction. Usually, I prefer women on the higher end of the butch scale. I've dated an electrician, a plumber, a master carpenter and a landscape architect."

"Your house and yard must be in good shape."

She matched my smile. "You could say that."

"How long had Shirley and Carolyn been in a relationship when you went on your date?"

"At least ten years. God, time flies when you're getting old. That means they've been together twenty years by now. Shirley must be as demented as Carolyn."

"What do you mean?"

"Carolyn O'Keefe's infatuations are legendary in the women's community in Phoenix. Name a pretty lesbian, and the doctor has stalked her," Patty said, breaking off a fraction of her muffin. For more than two hours, she'd taken maddeningly small pieces of sugar and crumbs, most as tiny as pinheads, and placed them on her tongue. Presumably, they dissolved, because I never saw her chew.

I adopted a puzzled expression. "Stalked?"

"That might be too strong a word. Or maybe not." She added in a confidential whisper, "I shouldn't gossip, but it's so entertaining."

"Feel free. I don't know any of these people anyway."

That was all the permission Patty Ossorio needed.

With zeal, she recounted incident after incident, and the pattern was always the same. Carolyn O'Keefe would approach women in a professional capacity and offer to mentor them. They'd be flattered by the attention and drawn to her power, and before long, Carolyn would convince herself that the women were sexually attracted to her. None was, and when the targets became aware of Carolyn's obsession and tried to end the relationship, Carolyn's creativity kicked in.

Take Judith and Sue, for example, two in a long line of Carolyn's attempted conquests.

After Judith rejected Carolyn's advances, Carolyn arranged for her business line to be disconnected while she was on vacation in Europe, causing her to lose the most lucrative client in her educational consulting firm.

With Sue, Carolyn's revenge was even more clever. After the middle-school teacher threatened to report her for sexual harassment, Carolyn placed an ad in the local newspaper, offering free plants for the taking at Sue's home address. When Sue returned from an out-of-town school trip Carolyn had sent her on, she found her front yard stripped bare of the xeriscaping she'd spent years cultivating.

There were more women and more stories, but one topped them all.

At its conclusion, I had to excuse myself.

In the restroom, I struggled to regain my composure as I replayed "the airplane banner" tale, until it felt as if it had happened to me.

Five years earlier, during a high school graduation, Carolyn O'Keefe had paid a pilot to fly over a stadium in Phoenix with the following message trailing on a banner: *Dear Geri, don't cry. I forgive you. Je t'adore. Joan.*

Out of the crowd of 850 students and 5,000 friends, family and faculty, the dig was directed at the high school principal, Geri Cressman. Carolyn had tried to have an affair with Geri and became furious when Geri rejected her in favor of a first-year French teacher, Amy Mercer. Joan, the supposed author of the banner, was Geri's lover of twelve years who'd committed suicide three weeks before graduation, presumably after having found out about Geri's affair with Amy. Carolyn's timing was exquisite. The small airplane appeared on the horizon at the exact moment Geri rose to introduce the first student.

Jesus Christ!

The extent of Carolyn O'Keefe's manipulations made my eyebrows sweat and my legs weaken, and I fought to regain my breath.

When I stumbled back to the table, Patty caught me off-guard with a goofy smile. "Carolyn O'Keefe is coming after someone you know, isn't she?"

I hesitated, caught in the space between a truth and a lie. "Yes."

"I'm sorry," she said, almost flippantly.

"How did you figure it out?"

"You looked like you'd seen a ghost when you heard the message on the plane's banner."

"I'm not afraid of Carolyn O'Keefe," I said stoutly.

"Have you met her?"

"Yes. I'm a private investigator, and she hired me to follow my lover, Destiny."

"Destiny Greaves, the activist? You're her girlfriend?"

I sat down gingerly. "Yes."

"I didn't know she had a girlfriend."

"She does," I said tensely. "Do you know Destiny?"

"Only by reputation," Patty said, before she did a double take. "You're an investigator? What about my Web site?"

I sighed wearily. "I can write. I owned a marketing company for eighteen years."

"That's good to know," she said without a trace of shame. "Does Carolyn realize Destiny's your girlfriend?"

"No. She gave me ten thousand dollars in cash to find out everything I could about her. Carolyn said she had thirty days to decide whether to have an affair with Destiny."

Patty shook with laughter. "Only Carolyn O'Keefe would give herself a deadline."

"They're attending a conference together in Steamboat Springs, at the end of the month. I guess it's down to"—I paused to calculate—"six days."

Patty's face bunched up. "Destiny Greaves is way too smart and beautiful for Carolyn. You don't have anything to worry about. Why is your girlfriend talking to her at all?"

"Carolyn promised to help Destiny implement gay and lesbian programs in the schools."

"Is your girlfriend ambitious?"

"Extremely."

"To get what she wants, would she sleep with Carolyn?"

Spots started flashing in front of my eyes. I blinked rapidly. "She'd better not."

"Hmm," Patty mused. "I wonder if Shirley knows Carolyn's up to her old tricks again."

"She might," I said, pulling at my eyelids. "She's hovering, too. She gave the Lesbian Community Center an enormous donation, which has to be matched this month. She followed up with a bouquet of flowers, brought to Destiny personally."

"Your girlfriend told you this?"

"I found out through Fran Green, my business partner. She's doing surveillance on Destiny, Shirley and Carolyn."

Patty started, as if someone had woken her up abruptly. "You're having your girlfriend followed?"

"What else am I supposed to do?" I drew in a sharp breath. "At least I'm taking action."

Patty absentmindedly rubbed her cheek. "I wonder what's going through Shirley's mind right about now."

"Could you talk to her?" I said hopefully. "Tell her about the phone line, the plants, the banner."

Patty waved her hand dismissively. "Shirley knows about those already."

"You're sure?"

"The banner anyway. She was in the stadium when it happened, and they moved out of Phoenix a month later."

"She might not know about the other incidents. Couldn't you tell Shirley to confront Carolyn?"

Patty shook her head, sending hair in every direction. "I wouldn't be the right person for that job."

"You told me Carolyn O'Keefe takes revenge on women when they reject her. On whatever matters most to them, that's what you said. We can't let that happen," I pleaded. "Destiny built the Lesbian Community Center from scratch. It's all she knows, all she cares about."

"How wrong you are." Patty snickered. "Carolyn approached you."

The room started spinning. "What?"

"She knows your girlfriend better than you do. She won't attack the Center."

"She won't?" I said in a small voice.

I felt as if I were about to faint.

I put the glass of ice water to my head, oblivious to the fact that it had no ice or water left in it.

"No," Patty said affably. "Carolyn O'Keefe is coming after you."

CHAPTER 20

Carolyn O'Keefe is coming after me.

I was still digesting that thought when I heard a tap on the car window. "Hey, open the door!"

I flicked the electric switch. Somehow I'd arrived at Nell Schwartz's house, and I suppose I'd honked for Flax—because here he was on the street and there was Nell waving from the picture window—but I couldn't recall any of it.

Flax threw his backpack onto the backseat and hopped in front.

"How'd the online auction go?" I said half-heartedly.

"Okay."

When I'd phoned to arrange a pickup time, Nell had explained that her grandson might be occupied. With equal parts pride and astonishment, she'd relayed that one of her friends had hired him to select and purchase a laptop computer, printer and accessories. Flax charged by the hour for his expertise and used his father's credit card to process online transactions. He'd begun the sideline business in North Carolina and, for the summer, was operating out of the guest bedroom in Nell's home.

"Did you have the winning bid?"

"It hasn't closed."

"When will it close?"

"At midnight."

"Tonight?"

"Yeah. Too bad my sister's not here. Back home, I pay her ten dollars an hour to stay on eBay when I have to go to the orthodontist."

"How much do you charge the client?"

"Fifteen."

"Couldn't you make the same arrangement with your Grandma Nell?"

"She offered for free, but she sucks with computers. I try to teach her stuff, but she's too old."

I nodded sympathetically. "One time, I tried to teach my grandma chess. What a nightmare! And *Clue*, forget about it. Halfway through the game, she wanted to know when I was going to deal out more cards."

Flax laughed, a deep sound that seemed to come through his nose. "I tried to show Grandma Hazel my Game Boy, and she said it hurt her eyes."

"Back to the auction, couldn't you run over to your Grandma Hazel's and use her phone line to dial up?"

"She doesn't have DSL."

"Snob," I chided, before he added, "Or a computer."

We rode in companionable silence for several minutes.

"Grandma Nell thinks we'll see a ghost tonight," he said softly.

I shot Flax a quick look, but he didn't seem concerned. He'd lowered his seat to its most reclined position, and his eyes were slits. Only his right hand drumming on his baggy jeans betrayed any hint of disquiet.

"What do you think?" I said.

"I dunno. Who's gonna be there?"

"You, me, Fran Green—"

"Who's she?"

"My business partner."

"Is she cool?"

"Very. You'll like her. We've also hired a specialist, Cassandra Ambrosia Antonopolus, but she goes by Cass."

"Ambrosia, what kind of name is that?"

"It's a salad."

"With lettuce?"

"Mandarin oranges, marshmallows, coconut and something that holds it all together. And as far as names go, I wouldn't talk, if I were you, Mr. Flax."

He snorted. "What's she like?"

"We just met," I said, as I pulled up to the Fielder mansion. "You'll have to judge for yourself."

Flax's eyes widened at the sight of the vintage Cadillac and almost popped out of his head when Cass came leaping off the porch.

• • •

Fran exited the house a step behind Cass, patting herself down, shooing away imaginary bugs.

I made introductions all around, and the four of us took a tour of the house, with Cass in the lead.

Lucky for me, I didn't have allergies. A thick coat of dust lay on every surface, a fact which tickled Cass (because of the ghost-tracking possibilities) but made me sneeze. Fran handed me a tissue, which I used to wipe my nose and block the smell. If I'd had to develop a recipe for the strange odor, I would have mixed mildew, rancid cooking oil and urine.

In the dim light, we stepped around droppings, which I hoped had come from squirrels, rats or mice. Anything but bats.

All of us used flashlights to navigate, not only because the last rays of sun had faded from the day, but also because daylight wouldn't have made a difference. The few windows that weren't boarded up were opaque with streaks of dirt.

The deeper I went into the house, the more I believed that Roberta Franklin's estimate of a million dollars for renovations might be low.

In the bathrooms, which we glanced into but never entered, chunks of porcelain were missing from the tubs and toilets, and ceramic tiles were chipped and cracked. Classic claw-foot tubs sat askew next to light blue stools; many of the tubs had been ripped from the floor, presumably to correct plumbing problems, which must have been plentiful. Water stains marred the ceilings of most rooms, visible through thick shrouds of cobwebs.

I could see the home's rich history in the mahogany wood, high ceilings, rounded walls, wainscoting, antique fixtures and period wallpaper, some of it crafted from leather and fabric, but the present intruded in every glimpse.

The hardwood floors were stained black and warping, baseboard heating had been installed above gorgeous trim, storm windows were affixed to plastic strips nailed to original window casings, and wainscoting and wallpaper were peeling from the walls.

All attempts at modernization had only cheapened the original beauty. Patches of carpet had become teal and gold petri dishes for mold. Laminate cabinets in the kitchen and baths were falling apart at the seams. Pale green linoleum, which had been installed indiscriminately in four or five rooms, was pockmarked. A trash compactor in the pantry had frozen with rust. Metal miniblinds, crooked and bent with use, dangled helplessly. And in random pockets throughout the house, signs of long-ago plumbing and electrical repairs were still evident, because no one had bothered to patch holes in the walls or sweep plaster from the floors.

The trek through three floors left me restless and apprehensive, but it didn't have the same effect on my companions. Cass kept up a brisk, excited pace throughout, Flax shadowed her eagerly, and Fran made copious notes but no judgments.

The entryway was the only area of the house where I felt relaxed, and only because of its proximity to my car.

When we returned there, Cass sprang into action. "We'll split into teams. Kris, you take Flax and stake out the second-story bedroom in the turret. Fran and I will monitor the attic."

"What do you want us to do?"

"You'll be in charge of the EMF detector. Flax can run the thermal scanner. You'll record data on this sheet." Cass handed me a hand-held detector and a clipboard with a three-part carbonless form.

Flax received a gadget the size of a cordless phone. He turned the device over in his hands, mesmerized by the pistol-grip design and backlit display. "How's this work?"

"Point and shoot. A red dot appears on the object you're scanning, pinpointing a specific area. Don't aim it at Kris's eyes."

"No kidding," I said loudly.

"Stay in one place," Cass continued. "Try the rocking chair in the corner of the room first. Don't aim at windows, doors or the fireplace opening, or you'll receive false readings. Your temperatures may vary by up to five degrees. That's fairly normal, but when the scanner shows anything close to a ten-degree variation—hotter or colder—that could indicate a presence. Have Kris start snapping pictures."

"Which camera should I use?"

"All of them. The Polaroid's useful because it provides instant feedback, but it's the least perceptive. Use one of the thirty-five-millimeter cameras next. I've loaded them with highspeed film. One has color in it, the other black and white, Kodak Gold."

"Nothing but the best," Fran said, twirling a whistle on a rope.

"Click off a few shots and try not to twitch between shots. Then switch to the digital. You can shoot up to fifty-six shots on one memory card, and I've brought extra cards and a battery recharger, so go for it."

"Hundreds of shots?" I asked.

"If you like."

"How much time will I have?"

"Maybe seconds, maybe minutes. React as fast as you can, but stay calm and focused. The quality of the contact is more important than quantity. Note everything on the data form. Time, location, temperature and EMF readings, as well as your own sensory perceptions. The form's easy to follow."

"Thorough, too," Fran chimed in, glancing at her own clipboard.

"That's it?" I said.

"Pretty much. I have video cameras, tape recorders and motion sensors staged in other parts of the house, but if we can maintain active surveillance in these two rooms for the next three or four hours, that should take care of phase one."

"How does that EMF thing work?" Flax asked, pointing enviously at the device I cradled like fragile goods.

"It's an electromagnetic field detector. It operates on the principle that spirit entities are energy forms. If their energy disrupts the electromagnetic field, the meter will detect it."

"Sounds simple," Fran said, shaking hers like a bottle of dressing.

"You scan the area you're investigating by using a swaying motion."

I was afraid to move mine. "Side to side or up and down?"

"Either. Not so fast, Fran. Use a more gentle, even pattern."

"Can I try?" Flax said.

"Sure." Cass handed him her detector. "Easy, don't jerk it into position."

Flax moved his like a pro. "How come this one's different than theirs?"

"It's a more sophisticated model, the Trifield Meter."

Fran aimed hers at me. "Someone invented these to hunt ghosts?"

"No, they just happen to work for this application. The Trifield was designed to read activity of geomagnetic storms."

Fran, Flax and I resembled symphony conductors in slow motion.

Cass watched us protectively as she continued the training. "Anything registering in the two to seven milligauss range probably represents a spirit phenomenon."

"Can't wait," Fran said.

"I've set the alarm threshold at two so you won't have to continually stare at the meter. If it goes off, don't panic. Start snapping pictures and record the information. After that, mark the disturbed area with the bright-colored tape I gave you."

Flax double-checked his back pocket for yellow tape, and Fran patted the roll hanging from her toolbelt.

"Radio me on the two-way, and I'll come and recheck the area. If continued high readings occur, that's a bad sign. It means the anomaly is probably related to something electrical, not spiritual."

"How we gonna snag false positives if the juice to the house is shut off?" Fran asked.

"It's less likely, but I've seen it happen with outside power lines. Typically, though, a reading of two milligauss or more indicates a ghost."

"I want to do the EMF," Flax said. "The thermometer sounds boring."

"I'd prefer Kris use the EMF. It's tricky to operate."

Catching the crestfallen look on Flax's face, I hastily intervened. "He'd probably be better at it. People hire Flax to purchase and install computer systems."

"Please let me do it."

"It's up to you," Cass said, turning the decision over to me.

"We'll take turns," I replied diplomatically.

"Never knew you were such a gearhead," Fran ribbed Cass.

"You wouldn't know it, but I kept it simple tonight. I left the infrared film at home because it's easy to ruin. And I'm skipping the white noise generator, ion detector and Geiger counter."

"What do those do?" I asked.

"I know, I know," Flax said, jumping up and down. "An ion detector measures ions in the air, and I'll bet they show a disturbance when a source of energy is present. The Geiger counter's easy. Any fluctuation in radiation would also point to a disturbance, right? Does yours measure alpha, beta, gamma or x rays?"

Cass stared at him, openly impressed. "All of the above."

"I used one at a science fair in fifth grade," he said modestly, but his fidgeting indicated he'd enjoyed the compliment.

"Researchers have found that ambient radiation seems to increase or decrease in the presence of ghosts. Paranormal investigators have used Geiger counters since the nineteen seventies," Cass elaborated. "I'm glad someone on the team can appreciate the sophisticated techniques."

Flax beamed. "But I don't know what the white noise generator does."

"Stumped me, too," Fran readily agreed.

"The basic idea," Cass explained, "is that background noise, white noise, acts as a carrier for other sounds."

"Voices of the dead?" I said, my own squeaking.

"Precisely. The voices are generally too weak to detect, but in the presence of white noise, they become quite clear, sometimes loud."

"You've heard dead people speak?" Flax asked in an awed whisper.

"Many times," Cass said nonchalantly.

His disappointment was obvious. "Too bad we don't have that tonight."

"Yeah," Fran joined in lightly. "Why are you holding out on us?"

Cass flashed a disarming smile. "I didn't want to get too complicated."

"I wish I could be your partner," Flax said, scooting next to Cass.

Sensing my dismay, Fran hurried to deflect the insult. "You gotta keep an eye on Kris, techno-man. Me and her get on a team, first thing we'll do is run out that door."

Flax pouted. "You would not."

"Yes, we would," I assured him.

"Know what we'd do next?" Fran asked.

"No," Flax said, his lower lip protruding a full inch.

"Keep running down the block."

"And out of the neighborhood, and that wouldn't accomplish anything, would it?" I said reasonably.

"I guess not," he said grudgingly. "I better stay with you."

"That's a plan."

"The key to our success," Cass said, wrapping up the training, "lies with recordkeeping. We need scrupulous, accurate notes we can later match with photographs. In a typical overnight investigation, no single piece of evidence is conclusive, but when it's all compiled, you begin to see compelling patterns. If we can link positive EMF or temperature readings with photographic evidence—"

"Eureka!" Fran shouted. "Nothing flighty about that."

"We're aiming for practical research, under controlled conditions, without bias."

"Got it," Fran agreed.

"Understood," I said.

"Let's go!" Flax cried.

CHAPTER 21

Nothing like two hours of inactivity to dull any enthusiasm for activity.

When Flax and I had entered the bedroom on the second floor, my heart was racing at 200 beats per minute. Now, I could barely keep my eyes open.

We'd begun our vigil by taking elaborate notes of the contents and layout of the room in the turret.

A casual observer would have thought the bedroom was in active use, its occupant having stepped out for the evening. The rocker in front of the window was cocked at an angle to take advantage of views and sunshine, and a polyester light blue blazer was draped carefully over the back. The twin bed, dresser, vanity and nightstands were made of light maple and in showroom condition. The quilt, bed skirt and needlepoint throw pillows all had floral patterns, not matching but complementary.

Scattered throughout the room was further evidence of a life interrupted. An open jewelry box atop the dresser contained clip-on earrings, watches, broaches and necklaces neatly arranged by matching sets. A collection of Easter cards, addressed but never sent, remained on the dresser. In the drawers, underpants, nylons, bras, undershirts, pullovers and sweaters lay neatly folded, all smelling faintly of perfume. And on the nightstand were March 1980 issues of *Ladies' Home Journal* and *Redbook*, with mailing labels addressed to Constance Ferro.

The last tenant.

Nell Schwartz had claimed that Constance disappeared suddenly, in the middle of the night; Hazel Middleton had countered that she moved to California to be near her niece.

Canvassing the room, I was inclined to believe Nell.

Next to the magazines sat a framed headshot of Hazel. If Flax found it unusual that his great-grandmother's photo was in another woman's room, he didn't comment.

Shortly after our inventory and mapping, a frightening thought occurred to me. I pointed toward the window. "What direction is that?"

"North."

I gestured toward the doorway. "Do you notice anything unusual about the woodwork and trim?"

"It's different than the rest of the room."

"And the door itself?"

"It's not sturdy like the others. Why?"

"Excuse me," I said as I pressed the two-way radio to my chin.

"Green here," came the reply to my buzz.

"Why did Cass put us in the room the dogs jumped out of?" I whispered tersely.

"That you, Kris?"

"Who else would it be?"

"All kinds of weirdoes on these airwaves. Better repeat the question."

"The Dobermans," I said between clenched teeth. "We're in their room. Why did Cass choose it?"

The ghost supervisor herself answered. "Is something wrong?"

"Not yet."

"Do you want me to come down?"

My mouth felt dry. "If you don't mind."

"I'll be right there."

Unable to wait, I instructed Flax to stay put, and I left the room and started up the massive stairway, meeting Cass halfway through her descent. "We're in the room the Dobermans dove out of," I said, flustered.

She stood in absolute repose. "I'm aware of that."

"Did you pick it because of the possessions left behind or the tortured dogs?"

Cass tossed her straight hair over her shoulder. "Neither, really."

"Why then?"

She gave me a funny look. "Because it felt the most active."

"Felt how?"

"Instinct. Experience."

"Good active or bad active?"

"That's what we're here to measure tonight," she said evenly. "Would you prefer to switch rooms or partners? I could trade places with Flax."

"No," I said, momentarily disconcerted. "We'll be fine."

Cass smiled slightly and squeezed my arm for reassurance before I retraced my steps to the northwest corner bedroom, where I spent the next few minutes deflecting Flax's questions about why I'd left so abruptly. He accepted my evasive replies but seemed edgy.

To settle us down, I suggested we play twenty questions, using famous people, not objects. He agreed, and we played a number of rounds, only managing to stump each other once. He flummoxed me with Paul Allen, the cofounder of Microsoft, and I confused him with Aunt Jemima, the syrup queen.

Six questions into our last round, he snapped a photograph, catapulting me into alertness.

I scrambled to retrieve the clipboard. "Did you get a reading?"

"No, but Cass said we could take pictures anytime we felt something was near us or watching us."

"And you did?" I said excitedly.

"Not really. I was bored, but she'll never know the difference."

"Flax," I said, my chest heaving, "we have to document everything. I'm writing this down."

He pulled a face. "No, don't tell her."

"I can't lie. It'll throw off the data," I said flatly.

"Write down the camera went off by accident at nine-oh-seven p.m. Please!"

"Okay," I said, comfortable with that level of deceit. "Do the toilets still work on this floor?"

"Some of them, but there's no water. You have to go to Grandma Hazel's house."

"Fine. I'll be back."

On my way to the carriage house, I inadvertently set off one of the motion detectors, because I'd forgotten to call ahead on the two-way to tell Cass and Fran to disengage the system with the hand-held remote. In the ensuing chaos, I had to endure a piercing screech from the alarm and a good-natured harangue from Fran.

By the time I returned from my bathroom break, the lack of activity had caught up to me.

I could have cared less whether the house was haunted or whether I'd ever see a ghost.

Roberta Franklin's concerns meant nothing to me, and neither did this project.

Who had I been kidding?

Delegate the Destiny/Carolyn case to Fran and focus my attention on this one?

What the hell was the matter with me?

I'd never experienced a time in my life when my priorities were more out of whack.

I couldn't have cared less about the dead.

I had too much to worry about with the living.

• • •

I made a deal with Flax. He would show me a back exit, down the servants' stairs and out to the street, a route that wouldn't trip any of Cass's motion detectors. I'd be gone an hour or less, and he'd cover for me, if I'd bring back a Big Gulp and a bag of Skittles. I told him I had an errand to run, and he didn't press for details, funneling all of his interest to the sugar bribe.

I scurried out, hoping Fran and Cass wouldn't discover my dereliction but not concerned enough to change course. Five miles away, I brought my Honda Accord to a stop and pondered definitions.

Breaking and entering? Technically, no, not if I could find and use a key.

Criminal trespass? Maybe. But I wasn't really a criminal, and I didn't intend to do anything nefarious.

Simple trespass? I could live with that.

I was debating these potential legal perils as I sat outside Carolyn O'Keefe's house on Holly Street. After several minutes of conscience-gauging, I exited the car and walked up a concrete path, which cut across the lawn. On the porch, I nudged past a wooden table and chairs and veered toward a clay planter.

I was bending down to look under the planter when a loud whisper startled me more than a scream. "Howdy!"

I massaged the elbow I'd hit and slowly turned. "Hi," I said to a man thirty feet away, sitting on the porch of the house next door. He was partially hidden by a bamboo sun shade, which gave me hope that my silhouette was equally blurry. In case it came down to a police lineup, God forbid.

"Dr. O'Keefe told me you'd be coming."

"She did?" I said, somewhat vaguely.

"You're the new housekeeper, aren't you? Working late? You forgot your key, didn't you?"

I nodded.

"She moved the spare. It's under that bush," he said, helpfully designating a lilac next to the front stoop. "In a Tupperware."

How thoughtful of Carolyn, I thought as I retrieved the key.

I focused my attention more keenly on the old man's chatter when I caught the end of a phrase, " . . . good to see her spending more time in the house. It's an awful waste, only using the place for cocktail parties. It's about time she moved in. I told my wife it'll be good to have her around, someone to chat with on these warm summer evenings."

"Have you met Carolyn O'Keefe?" I wanted to shout, unable to fathom her granting this meddler five seconds, much less an evening. Instead, I disguised my voice by raising it a few octaves and adding a warble. "She's living here now?"

"Sure seems to be. She spent the last eight nights in a row, but you'll know better when you see inside. I couldn't say what you'll find, fixing as how the curtains are always drawn."

"I'd better get to it."

The neighbor dismissed me with a wave. "Good talking to you."

After fumbling for an agonizing few seconds with the key and tumbler, I scampered inside. I locked and chained the door behind me and flipped on the nearest light switch, which activated a bank of track lights. In the glare, I surveyed the living room, taking in the possessions Carolyn O'Keefe had chosen to reflect her lifestyle and taste.

A blackberry leather sofa and two matching chairs. A glass and ebony coffee table. Dried flower and grass arrangements, one reaching almost to the ceiling. A wide-screen plasma television resting in a built-in niche above the black marble fireplace. Contemporary papier-mâché lamps, molded into bird-like shapes. Matted and framed black-and-white photographs on every white wall, all desert scenes. Glass display cases, filled with snapshots of Carolyn preening with prominent Democrats—local, state and national elected officials.

My gaze wandered to the dining room, which had been transformed into a music room complete with a raised platform, theater-style floor lighting and a baby grand piano.

As I slid across gleaming hardwood floors, I passed a wet bar on the way to the kitchen, one well-stocked with hard liquor. In the kitchen, I paused on slate tile and located a switch that activated recessed lighting overhead. The calculator in my head couldn't add high enough to include all of the finishes, fixtures, appliances and gadgets. Extra-deep sinks, resting in rose marble countertops. Cherry cabinets with forged black knobs. Stainless steel oversized, sub-zero refrigerator. Built-in microwave, double-wide dishwasher and Viking six-burner gas range. Blown-glass light fixtures dangling over the island, almost touching the restaurant-grade espresso machine.

I backtracked to the hall that led to an empty guest room and a sparsely furnished master suite. Before I could thoroughly search the bedroom, however, I had to use the bathroom.

Again.

Nerves were taxing my bladder.

Secretly hoping to clog Carolyn's pipes, I pulled down sixty squares of toilet paper as I checked out the room. Concrete counters. A red sink resting above a copper cabinet. A steam shower. A stand-alone whirlpool tub. Taupe stone tiles.

I hastily finished my business and headed back to Carolyn's bedroom.

Here, I gaped at the wall of mirrors, the king-size forged iron bed and the silk kimono framed and hanging on a wall.

I sat at the foot of the bed and let out a spiteful laugh at the thought of Destiny and Carolyn together.

In this house. In this room. In this bed.

Twenty-four hours with Destiny, and the honeymoon would be over.

Messiness was my lover's worst trait, and she knew it but couldn't seem to correct it. In our first year of living together, we'd had countless "discussions"—read fights—before arranging a truce. She would try to confine her spillage to one room, her office, and I had permission to "transfer"—read throw, everything into that pit.

And I did.

Constantly.

Fran had mediated on more than one occasion, offering the use of her housekeeper as her best solution. But that wouldn't have worked. Before the poor woman arrived, we would have had to rearrange all the contents of the house.

In my mind's eye, I saw Destiny's discards as I sat in Carolyn O'Keefe's spotless oasis.

The magazines in every room—*Curve, Advocate, Time, People* and *Us*. The empty boxes in the entryway, the mugs in the bedroom, the discarded work outfits in the living room. The basement piled high with who knows what, the garage filled with mementos Destiny had forgotten but couldn't bear to discard. ATM receipts in the bathroom, annual reports in the kitchen, bike parts spread across the yard.

One time, a colleague of Destiny's, riding with her to a meeting, had asked if she'd had to stop suddenly. Kindly, the woman had expected that only braking could have explained the disarray. But, no, that was how

Destiny organized the files, clothes and trash in her Maxima. Randomly or not at all.

It had taken me a long time to admit she couldn't help herself, and neither could I.

At my urging, she straightened up every few weeks or months, but our house was never free of clutter. Surprisingly, she never lost anything and rarely wasted time searching. Somehow, her acute memory enabled her to pinpoint the location of all her treasures, which is why she had no incentive to change, according to Fran.

I scratched an itch on my chin and was thrust back to the present when I caught a whiff of Carolyn's perfume on my hand. The same cloying smell she'd left behind in my office and in Destiny's hair.

The shock of it, and the realization that I was sitting in another woman's bedroom contemplating my lover's housekeeping habits, hit me all at once.

I gagged and almost retched, but I wouldn't permit myself to throw up in Carolyn O'Keefe's house.

That's all that made me leave, or I probably would have lain in wait for her that night.

Particularly after I looked in her nightstand and found two items.

A vibrator and a photo of Destiny.

• • •

A voice sliced into my obsessive thoughts about Destiny and Carolyn. "Hey, are you sleeping?"

"No. I'm resting my eyes."

"You were breathing deep."

I yawned and stretched. "I'm fine."

"You can take a nap if you want. I'll do the scanner and the EMF by myself, just like I did when you were gone," Flax said, gulping from his plastic bucket of soda. "I won't tell Cass about that either."

As he loudly chewed his Skittles, a smacking sound accompanying each bite, I tried to sleep for a few minutes, but guilt overrode fatigue.

I had to snap out of it and stop assuming a twelve-year-old would do my job.

After I downed a can of ginger ale and a bag of Chex Mix, I took over the EMF detector duties and thermal scanner while Flax lay on the bed and fiddled with the digital camera.

Approximately five minutes into this arrangement, I said calmly, "I think I've got something."

"No way," Flax said crazily, rushing to sit up.

"The numbers on the EMF are rising."

"What about the alarm. Why didn't it—" he began, when a buzz sounded.

"Take pictures of the rocking chair," I said, my voice steady.

"Which camera?"

"The Polaroid first, then the digital," I said, as he fumbled to grab one. "Don't be scared."

His voice broke. "I'm not."

I recorded the time, temperature readings and EMF numbers on the clipboard, careful not to make any sudden movements, as Flax clicked off dozens of shots. The entire episode couldn't have lasted more than ninety seconds, yet it left both of us visibly shaken.

I paged Cass on the two-way, and she hurried down to verify our potential sighting.

She spent thirty minutes with us but couldn't capture any additional anomalies with her equipment. Nonetheless, she helped us recall and document our sensations.

I had felt a cold tingling, nothing more, whereas Flax had seen a white flash out of the corner of his eye.

Cass couldn't spot anything in the viewing window of the digital camera but assured us that was typical. Most unusual images surfaced only after enlargement and high-resolution printing. She did, however, let out a low moan when Flax produced the first Polaroid he'd taken.

There was no doubt he'd caught something on film.

A faint, white blur covered the top right corner of the photograph.

By recreating the angle and depth of his shot, we all agreed that it was unlikely the flash had inadvertently bounced off something.

Which could only mean one thing.

We'd just seen a ghost!

CHAPTER 22

I couldn't stop tingling.

Lying on top of my sleeping bag, on my back, I half-listened to Fran, Flax and Cass as they arranged their accommodations for the night. I hadn't had an ounce of caffeine all week, yet felt as if I'd downed a gallon of espresso. It was bound to be a long night.

Cass had decided we'd sleep in the reception hall, on the main floor. I suspected she'd chosen the location for its relatively clean, level floor, rather than the potential to attract visitors.

"Are you psychic?" Flax asked Cass as he munched on one of Fran's triple-chocolate brownies.

"In one sense, yes."

"There's more than one?"

"There are four major categories," Cass replied, "telepathy being one."

"Reading people's minds," Fran interjected. "Handy tool for romance."

Cass smiled. "Also, remote viewing. You can see something taking place at a different location."

"I wish I could do that," Flax said. "Then I could live in North Carolina and see my dad in Denver."

"Precognition," Cass continued. "Knowing something will happen before it actually happens."

"Useful in Vegas," Fran offered.

"Finally, micropsychokinesis, the ability of the mind to affect matter. That's the skill I have. When I was sixteen, my father entered me into a university study that measured subjects' ability to move dots on a computer screen. I tested higher than the norm."

Flax's mouth opened wide. "You can move stuff?"

"Only dots on a computer screen. I practiced every day in high school, but never managed to move anything else." Cass paused for effect. "Except . . ." She winked at me, and I snatched at the side of Flax's bag while she shouted, "A sleeping bag."

Flax jumped and yelped, "Cut it out, Kris."

I tousled his hair until his peevish frown turned into a sheepish smile.

He asked Cass, "Is every house haunted?"

"Not necessarily."

"What's the most haunted one you've been in?"

"You don't have to tell us now." I clambered into my sleeping bag and pulled the edges close to my chin.

Fran agreed. "We don't want to scare Flax. Might be a distraction, storytelling, in case we have to check the equipment, make minor adjustments."

"You're the one who's scared," Flax accused, his attention directed, thankfully, at Fran, not me.

"Am not," she retorted.

"Yes, you are. We're stuck here all night. Why can't she tell me something cool?" he persisted.

Fran and I looked at each other with resignation, and Cass said, "You two could go into another room, if it makes you uncomfortable."

Simultaneously and too loudly, we said, "No."

"Let's scoot closer together," Cass said, "I don't want to disturb any spirits who might choose to make their presence known."

We all pulled in tighter until our heads were less than a foot apart, our bodies extending out to form a cross, with Fran and Flax on one prong, and Cass and I on the other. In the middle, Fran turned up the knob on her battery-operated lantern, but Flax reached over and dimmed it.

Cass began to speak in a whisper. "The Dover Lunatic Hospital. It was built in eighteen seventy-eight to accommodate four hundred and fifty patients, six hundred if they filled the attics. It closed in nineteen ninety-two."

Fran countered Cass's quiet tone with a bellow. "Never heard of it."

"It's in Massachusetts, about twenty miles north of Boston."

"How did you get inside?" I asked.

Cass released a sneaky smile. "Which time?"

"You went more than once?" Fran said with unmistakable disdain.

"Too many to count. Asylums were my father's hobby, especially those that followed the mental health plan of the prominent psychiatrist Dr. Edward Wainright. Known as Wainrights, there are ten of these state hospitals on the East Coast, enormous castles, built on hills, with six or eight wings jutting out from the center. Wainright professed that the best cure for the mentally ill was rest and air in beautiful, private surroundings. He used a special design that ensured every room had fresh-air ventilation, ample sunlight and unobstructed views, and he had pleasure gardens planted around the property, places for rest and meditation."

"Sounds more like a spa than a loony bin," Fran observed.

"That was Wainright's plan. He meant for them to be like country retreats, a place for patients to recover their mental faculties, to rebalance their senses."

"Prozac what put 'em out of business in the 'nineties?"

"That and cost-cutting movements to release mentally ill people from institutions, which led to great numbers of them becoming homeless. Leaving the Dover, though, probably was a good thing, because in the hundred-plus years of operation, times weren't always serene. Many former patients and employees at the Dover have recounted horrid tales of neglect and abuse, most caused by overcrowding and understaffing."

"How many Wainrights have you visited?" I asked.

"Six. My father likes to sketch them. He's fascinated by the sharp angles, the turrets and spires, the high-pitched roofs, the elaborate eaves and the intricate Gothic design. He loves the blend of red brick, granite stone and copper sheeting, with ivy crawling up to the sky. He veers from accuracy on only one count. He never draws the bars on the windows. He doesn't believe they were installed in Wainright's time."

"It sounds beautiful," I said.

"And foreboding," Fran added.

"The Dover is both. My father fell in love with the structure, but I was interested in the stories. I wanted to know more about the lives of the people who spent time there. I'd go with him and traipse around the grounds with my dowsing sticks. Sometimes, a caretaker or security guard would let us inside."

"What are dowsing sticks?" Flax asked.

"They're metal L-shaped rods. When you hold two loosely, they act as psychic antennas and cross or part with every connection. They've been used for centuries, but no one knows exactly how they work."

"It sounds similar to the process used to find water for wells," I said.

"Exactly. I have a set of rods in the car. I'll go down later and get it," Cass offered.

"Can we use them tonight? Will you show me how?" Flax said, his eyes bright with anticipation.

"I'd love to."

"You visited the Dover in March, didn't you?" Fran said. "On that trip to Boston?"

"I did. You have a good memory. I went because for the first time in years they opened the grounds to the public. Prior to that, people had been sneaking in and vandalizing the property. The building is slated for demolition, and the local historic society is sponsoring tours once a month."

"They're going to tear it down?" Flax blurted, clearly offended.

"Most of it. A builder has signed a contract to spend almost a hundred million to redevelop the property into apartments and commercial space."

"Why can't they save it?" I asked.

"The brick exterior walls are mostly sodden, and the timber floors inside have fallen on top of one another, in a pancake-type collapse."

"Couldn't the developer gut it?" I suggested.

"That's what they plan to do with about one-third of the three hundred thousand square feet. They'll gut the interior of the main entrance and two adjoining wings and construct a new building within the outer shell. But the rest, the other four wings, are unworkable, thanks to Wainright's innovation. It's a web of narrow wings, with small rooms and corridors defined by bearing walls. He intentionally used a linear design, with each ward enough out of line so that it had fresh air from four sides and couldn't be seen from the other wards."

"Were you afraid, when you walked around in it?" Flax asked.

"Never. I always felt spirits were guiding me."

"When will they start demolition?" I asked.

"Not for several years."

"Good," Flax broke in. "I'm going to see the Dover next summer."

I looked at him skeptically. "How?"

"It's my turn to choose a vacation, and my sister will hate it," Flax said happily. "Everything scares her."

"Your dad must be heartbroken about the Dover," I said to Cass.

"You have no idea! He bought a digital camera and is taking thousands of shots, from every angle, in every type of light and weather, so he can sketch them the rest of his life. Until you see this castle, you can't believe the complexity of its design. The entire length of the foundation is almost a mile long, and there are two hundred and forty angles on the building."

"That'll keep your pop busy," Fran said, stifling a yawn. "Toggles the mind."

"Boggles," I corrected reflexively.

"No, toggles. I caught a memory strand there. Had an aunt who spent most of her life in mental institutions. Schizophrenia. Thought she was the Joan of Arc of Russia. Too bad Auntie never met Wainright. Things might have worked out differently."

"Wainright was a hero in his time," Cass said. "He had every detail covered. The best patients, the 'least excitable,' were to stay in upper rooms, closest to the central building. The noisiest would be the farthest away, and the feeble would reside on lower floors."

"Auntie would have been on the outer wing. Champion screamer, according to my mother."

"With an ideal occupancy of two hundred and fifty patients," Cass noted, "Wainright thought the system could cure up to eighty percent."

"Wasn't that optimistic?" I asked.

"Unheard of, but back then, society was willing to make a profound social commitment to mentally ill people. That was the best of times, around the turn of the century. By the nineteen fifties, two thousand people were warehoused at the Dover, and the mode of treatment had shifted significantly, from fresh air and rest to shock treatment and psychosurgery."

"Lobotomies?" I clarified.

When Cass nodded, Flax asked, "What's a lobotomy?"

"An operation that takes out the part of the brain that's diseased," Fran explained.

Even in the darkness, I could see the anxiety on the boy's face. "Sick! Do they still do that?"

"Only to twelve-year-old boys who misbehave," I said lightheartedly.

Flax threw a pillow at me, which I added to my stack.

"My father saw photographs from that era, with patients lying on stained concrete floors."

"Far cry from Wainright's vision," Fran said.

"By the 'seventies and 'eighties, powerful drugs had come to market, and there was a strong patient-advocacy movement to treat patients in communities, not separate them from society. In nineteen ninety-two, the Dover closed for good."

"Amen," Fran said, punctuating the thought with a long swig from her canteen.

"How many ghosts did you see there?" Flax asked after he'd wrestled his pillow from my grasp.

"Only one."

"Just one?"

"I felt the presence of other spirits and heard snippets of conversations or screams, but only one vision."

"Of an old lady or man, all hunched over and wrinkled?" Flax asked.

"No, of an eight-year-old boy. Caleb."

Flax's eyes bulged. "He told you his name?"

"He never spoke, but I named him and later matched him to a story I heard from one of the local historians."

"Someone that young was insane?" I said, dismayed.

"Probably not, but he was placed at the Dover after he pulled three false fire alarms. He only lived there six months before he fell out of one of the upper windows."

"How many times did you see his ghost?" Flax pressed.

"Almost every time I went. He was very playful. I'd usually find him in the cemetery."

Fran grimaced. "Graveyard on the grounds?"

"Almost eight hundred patients were buried around the hospital, most in numbered graves."

I swallowed hard. "How much creepier can it get? A haunted asylum on a hill, with a graveyard surrounding it."

Cass flashed a sweet smile.

"Did you see Caleb in March?" Fran asked.

"No, probably because of the crowd on the tour. Next time, I'll sneak into the grounds after dark."

"How do you get in?" Flax said.

"Through a ventilation tunnel. To keep out intruders, they've poured concrete over most of them, but one is still open. At least it was in March. I don't think the groundskeepers are aware of it. It's hidden underneath tall grasses on the south side."

Flax said wistfully, "I wish I could go inside the Dover."

"You newbies need to work your way up," Fran cautioned.

"That's true," Cass said solemnly. "You're not ready for the inside of the Dover. No one without paranormal investigating experience is. People who've slid through the iron fence have reported trauma—broken bones, memory loss, ruined relationships. It's not safe, and I don't mean physically."

"Spiritually?" Fran asked.

Cass nodded, flushed. "It's definitely the most tormented building I've encountered." I shivered when she added longingly, "This house reminds me of it."

CHAPTER 23

"May as well multitask, while those two dowse," Fran said a short time later, inclining her head toward the parlor where Cass was giving Flax instruction. "I've done some digging on our friends Carolyn O'Keefe and Shirley Bassett. You in the mood?"

"If you insist," I said, my tone lifeless.

"You want the good news or the bad news?"

"Whatever."

"We'll start with good. I put in a call to a friend who runs a nonprofit."

I yawned.

"And vetted Bassett."

"Vetted?"

"Checked out her street creds."

"Creds?"

"Wake up, Kris! Credentials."

I stretched and muffled a second yawn.

"Typical in the industry, used to screen donors. Organizations have to make sure the folks giving them big bucks don't have hidden agendas or embarrassing ties. Shirl came up clean. Gives that amount routinely."

"A hundred thousand dollars? Every day?"

"Several times a year. Proceeds come from a family trust. Supports different causes with her largesse. Mostly women's issues."

"How generous," I said flippantly.

"Seems on the up-and-up."

"That was the good news?"

"Thought so. Evidently it's open to interpretation."

"I'm hardly jumping for joy," I said, tired.

"You will be compared to the other morsels."

"Get it over with."

"Seems O'Keefe and Bassett left Phoenix abruptly. O'Keefe gave up the top post under a cloud of suspicion. Resigned from the school district because of 'politics,' but you know that's a euphemism for questionable conduct."

"Probably."

"I'm tracking down stories that would raise the hair on your neck, but I can't impart any yet."

"Keep up the good work," I said, unwilling to rise to Fran's bait. She had an irritating habit of withholding tantalizing details and making me grovel for them.

"Guess who ain't sharing the sheets no more?"

"I give up."

"I'm waiting for secondary confirmation, but it appears as if Bassett gave O'Keefe the boot. Sent her packing back to her own house, the one on Holly Street."

"Hmm," I said, displaying no emotion.

Fran eyed me with suspicion. "None of this surprises you, does it?"

I met her gaze but didn't reply.

"What have you been doing, Kris?" she said, almost with pity.

"Nothing," I mumbled.

"We had an agreement. You'd work Bert's case, I'd work over Carolyn O'Keefe. How'd you find out about the incidents in the desert."

"From a woman who sat next to me at that stupid networking meeting you forced me to attend," I said hotly. "She gossiped the whole time. What was I supposed to do?"

"The chamber lunch?"

I nodded.

"Who's the broad with the big mouth?"

"Patty Ossorio. She was friends with Shirley when she lived in Phoenix."

Fran sucked her teeth. "Interesting. The marital rift, how'd that come to your attention?"

I pulled the photo of Destiny out of my backpack. "I found this in Carolyn's nightstand." When I saw the displeasure etched on Fran's forehead, I realized too late that I should have lied.

"You came by this how?" she said in a soft, rather menacing voice.

"I stopped by Carolyn's house."

"When and for what purpose?"

"Earlier tonight. Curiosity," I said evenly.

A vein in Fran's neck throbbed. "You gained entry how?"

"I used the key she hides in the bush next to the front step."

"The key's location was detected by what means?"

"The old man next door told me where to look."

"Come again?"

"He's an idiot. He thought I was the housekeeper."

Given Fran's awareness of my steadfast refusal to pick up after anyone, that statement broke the tension. A fraction of Fran's mild temperament returned with her loud burst of laughter, but she fixed me with a harsh look. "Not wise, kiddo. You left behind a witness. Sloppy work."

"I don't care, Fran," I said, my voice splintering. "I've had it with this woman, with this situation."

"You don't trust me?"

"It's not about you."

"You don't trust Destiny?"

"It's not about her. Can't you see that Carolyn O'Keefe is pathological?"

"No argument there."

"I can't sit around and do nothing," I said desperately. "What are you doing?"

"More than you think."

"Not enough, obviously. Is Carolyn still pursuing Destiny?"

"You sure you want to know?"

"Yes," I said, reticent.

"Seems to be."

I shook my head in disgust.

"Moved up from following her to pretending to bump into her. Had two supposedly chance encounters with Destiny last week. One at Whole Foods, one at Tower Records."

"Doesn't Destiny suspect something?"

"She might. The girl ain't dumb, and at Tower, she didn't look pleased."

"Why can't she tell Carolyn to fuck off?"

"Too much at stake. Plus, yours truly has managed to shelter her from the worst."

"Which is?"

"I've snatched up a dozen business cards from your girlfriend's windshield, left there compliments of the psycho."

"What kind of business cards?"

"The 'Superintendent of Metro Denver Public Schools' variety. Complete with quaint messages on the back."

"She leaves Destiny notes?"

"Like a schoolgirl. I've taken all I could but may have missed a handful."

"What do they say?"

"Nothing too incriminating. 'Hope you had a wonderful day,' or 'Looking forward to our upcoming meeting.' I didn't memorize 'em, but that's close."

"I'm sick of this," I said, raising my voice.

"Easy there," Fran said calmly. "I've got a plan to nip this in the bud."

"How?"

"Give the mighty O'Keefe a taste of her own medicine. Hope she chokes on it."

"What are you going to do?"

"Embarrass her at a public function, but can't say more."

"Is your plan legal?"

"Last I checked. Elementary exercise in free speech," Fran said, chuckling.

• • •

Before I could badger Fran for details, Cass and Flax returned. Cass pronounced Flax a natural at dowsing, which made him grin ear to ear.

As they settled in for the night, I kept trying to catch Fran's attention, but she pointedly ignored me, and soon I heard the distinct rattle of her snores.

Damn it!

Not long after Cass's breathing deepened, I felt a tug on my sleeping bag. "This is boring."

"Leave me alone. I'm sleeping."

"No, you're not," Flax whispered. "You're talking to me."

"I was," I hissed.

"No, you weren't. I saw you blink. Want to go explore my hideout."

"Not really," I said, beyond politeness.

"It's in the basement. I made it into a dungeon."

I propped myself on one elbow and faced him. "How do you get in? Did Grandma Nell or Grandma Hazel give you a key?"

"Nope. I found a secret passage last summer."

"Through the outside cellar door?"

He shook his head. "Through Grandma Hazel's pantry."

I squinted at him in disbelief. "You come into the basement of this house through the basement of the carriage house?"

"Don't tell anyone."

"No one else knows?"

"Unh uh. Not even my dad. I asked him if he'd ever been in the carriage house basement, and he said there was no basement. But I found it."

"How?"

"One day, when I was at Grandma Hazel's, I dropped a jar of peaches. I didn't want her to know, or she would have taken it out of my step-and-fetch money. She does that when I break things. I had to move a shelf to wipe up the juice, and I found a door behind it."

"You opened it?"

"Not then," he said, animated. "I waited until Grandma Hazel's nap, when she takes out her hearing aids. I know she's almost totally deaf, because I like to sneak up and clap, and she never moves. When I whistle—"

"Enough," I said hurriedly. "Where did the door lead?"

"To some stairs and down into the basement. Then—this is the best part—to a tunnel!"

"You went through the tunnel? By yourself?"

"Sure, it was cool. Just like in my computer games."

"The tunnel led to the basement of this house?"

"Yep."

"You're sure?"

"Yes," he said stretching the word into three syllables. "I've been in this basement lots of times. My dad used to have a workshop here. He made furniture, and he'd let me build things out of the scraps, like swords."

I studied Flax. "You're telling me that if we go downstairs, into this basement, we can go through a tunnel and end up in your Grandma Hazel's basement. From there, we could walk up a flight of stairs and end up in her pantry?"

"Right next to the kitchen. Want to see?"

"Maybe. But if I go, you better wait here. Your Grandma Nell specifically said to keep you out of the basement tonight."

"She thinks there's an evil room down there, because of some séance. But me and my dad don't believe her."

"Shh," I said, alarmed at the volume of his voice. "She told you about that?"

He leaned closer. "Only ten million times. Let's go. She'll never find out. Don't tell them," he said, indicating Fran and Cass. "I don't want them to see my dungeon."

"I don't know . . ." I said, wanting to honor my promise to Nell Schwartz but not thrilled at the prospect of a lone descent.

"You'll never find the door to the tunnel," he said petulantly. "I'm the only one who knows where it is."

"You could tell me."

"Let me go." He sulked. "This is so boring."

"All right," I acquiesced, "but you have to promise you won't tell either of your grandmas."

He sat upright and hugged himself. "I won't. I swear!"

"And we can't do it tonight."

"You're just scared of the dark," he said gloomily, lying back down with a scowl.

"We'll do it in a few days."

"When?"

"Wednesday morning," I said, choosing a day at random. "Early in the morning."

That seemed to satisfy him, and within minutes, he too had nodded off.

In the next five hours, I enjoyed a total of thirty minutes of sleep, thanks to Fran's snoring, Cass's periodic equipment checks and Flax's tossing and turning.

I couldn't blame my insomnia on those three, though.

Something else disturbed me all night, something that could never be measured with a Geiger counter.

Try naked images of Carolyn O'Keefe and Destiny Greaves.

• • •

In the wee hours of Sunday morning, no more ghosts appeared at the Fielder mansion, and at first light, we packed up the equipment.

I drove Flax to his Grandma Nell's house and practically had to push him out of the car, only managing to detach by reiterating my promise that we'd visit his secret basement hideout on Wednesday.

I spent the rest of Sunday in bed, alone, catching up from Saturday's sleep deprivation.

Destiny had kissed me in the morning and again late in the evening when she returned from the office, but that was the extent of the day's contact.

Monday morning, I felt listless from the weekend's excitement, and Fran's buoyancy was like a bracing tonic . . . thrown in my face.

"Wearing myself out with all this sex," she said when I shuffled through the door at eleven.

I dropped into my chair and massaged my temples. "Tess or Roberta?"

"Both."

"You haven't chosen?"

"No need. Pros and cons with both, but I can't keep up with that woman. Went walking with her this a.m. Took a full sprint to keep up with her power stride."

"Tess?"

"Bert. Had to catch my breath at the workout stations, those mini-torture stops on the perimeter of Wash Park. When Bert did her regimen of sit-ups and pull-ups, I lay flat on my back. Ever tried to grab air from the sky? Never mind, never again. Faked a groin pull halfway through and took a shortcut to the car. That injury ought to buy me a few weeks' rest."

"You'd deceive Roberta like that?"

"You bet! Not proud of it, but have my health to consider. No sense trying to talk her out of athletic pursuits. Walks everywhere, even to work. Can't stop walking, except when she's horseback riding."

"Roberta rides?"

"Every week. Used to be a professional jockey and trick-rider."

"I would have imagined her with more intellectual pursuits—books, art, crossword puzzles."

"No shortage of those either. Devours the *Wall Street Journal* every day. Wrote six books on business law. Coauthoring a seventh. Hardly time for sex between deadlines. Gotta do it after yachting and before aerobics."

"Yachting? In a landlocked state?"

"Bert's Sunday tradition. Radio-controlled, at Lollipop Lake. Have to admit, it's a gas. Reading the wind, cornering the buoys, cruising the open water. Couldn't tear myself away."

"It sounds like you two are hitting it off. Are you getting serious?"

"Could be, but we have our differences. Take last night. Bert makes a run to Choices and grabs a spread. Grilled veggies, yams, turkey breast."

"Sounds good."

Fran cocked her head. "You tasted the takeout from that health food store?"

I nodded. "It's pretty bland."

"My point exactly. Vegetables tasted like they'd been marinated in dirt. Yams were whipped, nothing in 'em, no half-stick of butter or cup of brown sugar. Turkey, dry and dull, no gravy, no cranberries, no life. Hell, Kris, why bother eating that crap?"

"Did Roberta know you didn't like the meal?"

"She got the picture when I fed the gobbler to Uphill Shirley's cats and put the legumes and yams in the garbage disposal. Bert complained about thirty bucks down the drain. She's more concerned about money than my dietary distress."

"Food's not that important."

"Who you kidding? How'd you like it if Destiny swapped sugarless wafers for your Chewy Sprees? You 'bout tore the office apart last week looking for the roll you left at home. Can't make it through the day without three helpings of sweets."

"All right," I said curtly. "What about you and Tess?"

"Now there, we're conjoined. Breakfast, Pete's burrito, extra green chili. Lunch, Fat Boy burger and large order of onion rings. Afternoon snack, Bonnie Brae butter brickle milkshake. Dinner, Imperial sesame chicken."

"Stop! I haven't eaten yet."

"Not too late for a stack of pancakes at V.I."

"I can't go to breakfast at Village Inn. I have to type a report for our meeting with Roberta. By the way, did you say anything to her about our night in the mansion?"

"Not a word. Leaving that to the lead investigator. Fill her in this afternoon."

"Thanks," I said, unsure whether Fran meant me or Cass.

Fran leaned back in her chair, put her feet on the desk and folded her hands behind her head. From my perspective, she looked perilously close to tipping over.

"Too many women, too little time," she mused. "Hard to choose. Tess, no finesse, but lots of gumption. Good flow of saliva, but no sense of timing."

"Fran, please!" I protested feebly. "I don't want to hear this."

She rubbed her chin and said thoughtfully, "Bert, leisurely and practiced. Nothing kinky, but damn proficient at the moves she has. Decisions, decisions."

"These details," I said vehemently, "please don't tell me while Roberta Franklin's our client."

Fran shrugged. "Fair enough. Hurry and wrap it up so we can have ourselves a girl chat, would you?"

I yawned loudly. "You don't think this is dangerous—your attraction to two women at the same time?"

"What's the harm in drinking from two troughs? You, of all people, should appreciate my thirst. It's been eight months since Ruth gave me the heave-ho, and ten or twelve years since I partook of loveliness on a regular basis. Why begrudge me a little catching up?"

"Do Tess and Roberta know about each other?"

"Course they do. Full disclosure since day one. Just 'cause I'm randy doesn't mean I've lost my scruples."

"It doesn't bother either of them?"

"Tess more so than Bert. Can't blame her. Who wouldn't want a full serving of Fran Green instead of a half portion?"

CHAPTER 24

Sometimes, the office wasn't big enough to accommodate Fran Green's ego, a feeling I was about to convey when my cell phone rang. I had to settle for rolling my eyes at Fran as I scrambled to find the phone and retrieve it from my back pocket.

"Kristin Ashe?"

"Yes," I said tentatively, not recognizing the voice.

"This is Amy Mercer. Patty Ossorio asked me to call."

Amy Mercer. The French teacher who'd had an affair with Geri Cressman. The affair that had angered Carolyn O'Keefe enough to hire a pilot to fly an incendiary banner over a high school graduation ceremony.

"Right," I said anxiously. "Could you hold a minute?"

I put the phone on mute and stepped outside the office, much to Fran's puzzlement. I knew she'd harass me when I returned, but I'd deal with that later. For now, I needed privacy, and I didn't dare postpone this conversation.

I ducked into Sixth Avenue Flowers. Beth, behind the counter arranging a vase of roses, acknowledged my presence with a knowing smile. Ever since Fran had made the office her second home, I'd turned the flower shop into mine.

On Saturday, as we parted, Patty Ossorio had told me she'd contact Amy Mercer, a friend of a friend, to see if she'd be willing to share her impressions of Carolyn O'Keefe. I'd been expecting the call, but not so soon, and not from someone who sounded so young. I sat on a bench near the front of the store and said in a quiet voice, "I appreciate you calling."

"Patty said it might help with your situation in Denver."

"It might. How well do you know Carolyn O'Keefe?"

"We met once."

"But you were good friends with Geri Cressman?"

"Yes," she said simply.

"You worked at the same school?"

"Yes. Rangeview High School."

"Could you tell me about Carolyn's relationship with Geri? How did it start?"

"When Geri was in her first year as principal, Dr. O'Keefe began to request one-on-one meetings with her. She maintained that she wanted to fast-track her. She dangled the idea of curriculum development, and Geri fell for it. That was her dream, and Dr. O'Keefe manipulated her with it."

"When did Geri begin to suspect something more was going on, that Carolyn was attracted to her?"

"At an out-of-town conference they attended, toward the end of the school year. Geri thought all of the other principals from the district had been invited. When she arrived in Flagstaff, she found out it was just she and Dr. O'Keefe."

I took a deep breath. "That must have been awkward."

"Made more so when Dr. O'Keefe tried to kiss her."

A creepy feeling clung to my skin. "The kiss surprised Geri?"

"Completely."

"Had Geri given Carolyn any indication she was attracted to her?"

"No."

I let out a breath. "Was Geri receptive to Carolyn's advances?"

"Not at all."

"She must have done something . . . flirting, hints, innuendoes?"

"Nothing. The connection existed only in Dr. O'Keefe's mind."

"Did Carolyn know about your affair with Geri?" I said delicately.

Amy replied, with little emotion, "It wasn't an affair. We slept together once and realized our mistake."

"But Carolyn knew?"

"Yes. Geri told her at the conference, to stop her advances."

"How did Carolyn react?"

"She started to scream and throw things."

I bent over and put my head between my legs, but the pounding in my ears wouldn't subside. "Carolyn became violent?"

"Almost. Geri had to threaten to call hotel security before she would leave."

"How did the two of them make it through the rest of the conference?"

"They didn't. Geri left in the morning."

"How soon after the conference did Geri's lover Joan commit suicide."

"Within a few weeks."

"Did you know Joan?"

"Only to say hello at school functions."

"Do you believe Joan killed herself because of Geri's affair?"

"No," Amy said firmly. "Joan had tried to kill herself twice before she met Geri. She suffered from anxiety attacks and was taking medications to counter medications. Geri thought she could change her, but she couldn't. No one could."

"Mmm."

"Geri didn't cause Joan to take her life," Amy Mercer said, not yielding. "Nor did I."

"Did Joan know about Geri's involvement with you?"

"Yes."

"You're certain?"

"Yes. Joan confronted Geri the night before she died."

"How did Joan find out about the two of you?"

"Dr. O'Keefe had informed her."

I blinked rapidly. "What happened to Geri after the graduation ceremony, after she saw Carolyn's airplane banner?"

"She resigned the next day. Too many people in the stadium understood the meaning of the banner, and she couldn't face them. Most of the staff knew she'd been in a long-term relationship with a woman named Joan. The rest of the story, they could probably guess."

"Did you see the plane fly over?"

"No. I was inside the school, with a student who had become ill."

"After she resigned, did Geri go on to pursue her dream of writing curriculum?"

"I don't know."

"You're not in touch with her?"

"No."

"But you were in love with her?" I said levelly.

There was a long pause before she replied, "Yes."

"Do you still teach French at Rangeview?"

"No," Amy Mercer said softly. "I'm working as a receptionist for a windshield repair company."

• • •

After I left the flower shop, I took a slow walk around the block, willing myself to calm down, unwilling to let Fran Green see me upset.

By the time I returned to the office, thankfully she'd left for her bimonthly haircut.

I didn't see her again until three o'clock, when she, Roberta, Cass and I assembled at the Fielder mansion for another tour. The daytime excursion did nothing to change my opinion, or Roberta's.

I despised the Fielder mansion, and she loved it.

I'd had my fill of the dark, smelly space, and yet I had to return at least one more time—to see Flax's hideout in the basement.

Why had I agreed to that?

I had to learn to say no, at least to twelve-year-olds.

As the four of us stood on the porch, Cass presented Roberta with a twenty-page report and a packet of photographs.

Roberta scowled at the photos Flax had taken. "There's no question the house is haunted?"

"None," Cass replied calmly. "I've included electronic and photographic evidence, which is extremely rare."

"You're implying the Fielder mansion is more haunted than most?"

"It may be."

Fran added, "No reason for knee-buckling to be a deal-killer, Bert. Cass's specialty is unhaunting houses."

Cass smiled slightly. "I wouldn't put it that way. There's no foolproof way to banish ghosts, but I'd love to offer you a psychic house-clearing."

Roberta frowned. "What takes place in this so-called clearing?"

"I dislodge stagnant energy using bright lights and loud noises, and I burn incense and candles. By removing residual energy, I unblock the flow."

Roberta seemed torn. "What qualifies you to do this?"

Fran answered with pride, "Cass is prez of the Paranormal Society of Colorado."

"You believe you can conduct a successful exorcism and certify no malevolent spirits remain before I hand over a check to Hazel Middleton for five hundred thousand dollars?"

Fran, sensing Cass's agitation, butted in again, "Better not call it an exorcism."

"Why?" I said, shielding the sun from my eyes. Had I missed this nuance at the slumber party?

Cass said stiffly, "Because the term *exorcism* implies spirits are evil or dangerous, which most aren't. My function is to eliminate the dead person's corpulent energy, which has been left behind because of some type of attachment."

"How will you go about this precisely?" Roberta asked.

"Nothing I do is precise."

Fran hastily interjected, "Cass wants to burn candles in the house for a few weeks, to help dissipate the energy."

"Wouldn't that put the house at risk for fire?"

"Fran or I would be here the entire time," I assured Roberta.

"We'd do it a couple times a day," Fran elaborated. "With extinguishers in every room. Then, the Cassmeister will perform her magic."

Cass looked uncomfortable. "I'll burn sage to cleanse and purify the areas that we've identified as infected."

"Clean the slate," Fran said. "Let the new homeowners bring in their own disasters and tragedies." She laughed loudly at her own joke, but no one joined her.

After an awkward pause, Cass spoke. "I also burn sweet cedar in a smudge pot to—"

Fran interrupted, "Replace negative energy with positive."

"Positive is good," Roberta said encouragingly, although she looked slightly bewildered.

"Heck, yeah! Positive as in cash flow," Fran pointed out.

"Finally," Cass continued, "I speak to the spirits and ask them to leave."

"This works?" Roberta said mildly.

"Typically in one visit, but if necessary, I'll return."

Fran threw in, "Until they've successfully relocated."

"Where do they go?" I asked, which netted a sideways glare from Fran.

Cass looked at me thoughtfully. "I can't say there is a where. I just know they're gone. In addressing the spirits, I invite them to go wherever they need to go, but I've never presupposed where that is."

"Any recalcitrant ones?" Roberta asked.

Total silence.

Fran said eventually, "Translation, Bert?"

"Have you encountered spirits who have refused to obey?"

"A handful," Cass admitted. "But most disappear immediately after the energy shifts."

"You do this full-time?"

"Yes, for the past year."

"And before that?"

"As a hobby since I was in elementary school and as a part-time business for ten years."

Cass's work experience must have impressed Roberta, because she reached into her purse for her checkbook. "I assume you can provide references?"

"Pages," Fran said.

"I know it sounds as if I lead a weird life," Cass acknowledged, "but we have a mutual acquaintance who can vouch for my integrity. Joseph McConnell."

"As in McConnell Mortuaries?" Fran said.

Cass and Roberta nodded, and Roberta said, "Joseph is a dear friend. I've done legal work for the family for years."

"Mr. McConnell hired me to cleanse the mortuary in southwest Denver."

"The one he closed down and converted into a nightclub? He never mentioned a cleansing."

"Most people don't," Cass said. "It took a while to clear the crypt, but the other areas were straightforward. In its hundred years of operation, more than fifty thousand bodies were processed there, including some of the West's most famous outlaws."

"Doc Holliday? Buffalo Bill?" I pried.

Cass smiled patiently. "I can't divulge confidences."

"You're no fun," Fran chided.

"There were dozens of small, dark spaces laid out in labyrinth fashion. It took time because of the sheer volume of catacombs, but I restored natural balance to each area. Fortunately, most souls had been released elsewhere, at the sites of their physical deaths. I've returned once every three months as part of a follow-up program. At all six visits, I've classified the building as inactive."

"You're awfully confident," Roberta observed. "Does that certainty come with a money-back guarantee?"

"A refund wouldn't benefit either of us," Cass said coldly. "Instead, I'll warranty my performance. If necessary, I'll live in the building until every paranormal remnant has exited."

My eyes widened at the prospect.

Roberta stopped chewing on the end of her pen and removed the cap. "How much will your services cost?"

Cass backed onto the lawn and looked up at the building. "What's the square footage of the house?"

"Around eighteen thousand, including the third-floor attic."

"And the basement?"

"Twenty-four thousand total."

"And the carriage house?"

"We can't touch that," I said hastily, "or you'll be dealing with a live spirit, Hazel Middleton."

"I charge twenty cents per square foot," Cass said, returning to the porch. "Forty-eight hundred for this job."

Fran whistled. "That's a pile of coin."

"I'm moving considerable energy," Cass said, not easily intimidated. "More than a century's worth."

"We're lucky you don't charge by the decade," Roberta said wryly.

Cass looked her in the eye. "I've thought about adding a surcharge, according to the age of the building, but for now, I bid by size."

"Look at the big picture," Fran said, aware that Roberta had recapped the pen. "A year from now, you could be sitting on the second-floor balcony on the southeast corner, waving to neighbors below. Or how about some winter's night, lying in front of the marble fireplace, watching it snow through the two-story bay window." I swear Roberta winked at Fran, who continued. "Forget the plywood contraptions that pass for homes these days. You'll have one foot of solid Manitou Sandstone between you and the outside world, six-inch thick interior walls. They don't make 'em like that anymore."

"Think of the fee as a necessary line item in your one and a half million dollar budget," I added.

Roberta scratched her chin. "That's a good way of viewing it."

"With your permission," Cass said, "I'd like to come back with a team of professional investigators."

When Cass paused, Roberta said, "I'm listening."

"I meet once a month with a group of colleagues, and we visit active locations. We're scheduled for tomorrow night, and I'd be honored if we could tour the Fielder mansion. At no charge, of course."

Roberta smiled faintly. "Be my guest."

"Meantime, let's keep the dream moving forward," Fran said as she grabbed the pen, opened the checkbook and handed both back to Roberta.

Roberta Franklin wrote the check.

CHAPTER 25

Minutes after I left the Fielder mansion, Nell Schwartz reached me on my cell.

"Mother called last night to inform me that the house is inhabited. After years of ridiculing me, now she believes spirits are running amok."

I pulled over to the side of the road to concentrate. "In the carriage house?"

"In the main house. Several basement windows have been broken. Three on the north side, nearest the carriage house, are cracked."

"I was just there, with Roberta. We didn't notice anything."

"I'm sending a handyman to board them up. Mother also reports lights switching on and off in the attic window."

"But there's no electricity."

"She describes them as intense, flashing lights."

"It could be someone with a flashlight. Are you concerned your mom's at risk?"

"Only of eating crow," Nell said, and I could hear the smile in her voice.

"You're sure Hazel's telling the truth?"

"Why would she lie?"

• • •

As soon as I returned to the office, I placed a call to the district police station to find out if any reports of mischief or vandalism in the 1200 block of Pennsylvania, where the Fielder mansion was located, had been filed recently. The officer responded that the only crime statistics available to the public encompassed the entire district, a twenty-square-mile area.

Little good that did me.

Hearing the disappointment in my lukewarm thanks, she referred me to NARC, a neighborhood watch group that monitored activity in the immediate vicinity of Hazel's house.

I called NARC headquarters and left a message, and within the hour Sybil Greenwald, of Neighbors Assisting Revitalization Concerns returned my call.

A four-year-old organization, NARC had been formed to combat drug dealing in a nine-block area that included the Fielder mansion. A core group of thirty neighbors lobbied city council for stricter enforcement of existing laws, removed graffiti and trash and conducted patrols every weekend night in the company of an off-duty police officer.

To date, they'd claimed responsibility for more than 500 arrests, the elimination of "mobile bordellos" and the closure of a nightclub and liquor store, both of which regularly sold to minors.

Sybil attested that nothing was going on in the area around Hazel's house, other than garden-variety trespassing, vagrancy and urination.

She invited me to join their Friday night patrol for a "firsthand look at the challenges the neighbors face on a daily basis," an offer I declined. My own residence, less than a mile from Hazel's, often felt as if it were under siege. I didn't need any additional doses of late-night reality.

Before we disconnected, I played the "ninety-one-year-old widow living alone" card and asked Sybil to pay special attention to the Fielder mansion the next time her group passed. She agreed, and I promised to send a fifty-dollar donation.

• • •

That was about all the work I could stand for one day, and even though the clock read five-thirty, it felt like midnight.

I called Destiny at the Lesbian Community Center, only to discover that she wouldn't be breaking for dinner, so I picked up Chinese food on the way home, but I was too tired to eat it.

I went to bed at eight, slept straight through to dawn and arrived at the office by seven.

A few minutes before nine, Fran joined me. "If anyone calls, you ain't seen me for days, don't expect me for weeks," she said, glancing about furtively.

"Are you avoiding someone?" I said, not much caring.

Fran locked the door and lowered the blinds. "Tess. Gotta lose her. Created a monster. Should have seen it coming. Hard not to fall for Fran Green."

"What's wrong?"

"What's not? The girl has a pallet of Mountain Dew in her storage locker and downs a six-pack a night. Thirty hits a day on my caller ID. Crying fits in the middle of sex. Her, not me. Keeps an ax next to the bed. Again, her, not me."

"Why don't you dump her?" I said equably. "Wouldn't that be more honorable than asking me to lie for you?"

"Harder I try, more she holds on. Need a delicate approach, given the circumstances."

"Which are?"

Fran came close to me and whispered, "I'm referring to the covert op camps."

"Camps?"

"Didn't I tell you about those?" Fran said, dropping to the floor. She held a sun salutation yoga pose for a full minute before elaborating.

After she concluded, I couldn't stop shaking my head.

I think I would have remembered hearing about a woman who spent her last three vacations at covert military operation camps. Tess had completed courses on rescuing hostages, killing people in close-quarters combat and driving evasively. Surely, I wouldn't have forgotten

Tess's favorite motto, "Engage or die." Fran downplayed the severity of her paramour's interests, likening the camps to the Circus College she attended for her fiftieth birthday. Fantasy weekends, nothing more, she insisted. Except that Fran had learned how to tumble vault, and perform trapeze work. Not exactly the same as hitting vital organs with a 9mm and slashing a man's throat with his own knife.

Let me think, killing or clowning . . . assassinations or cartwheels?

Had Fran Green lost her mind?

I had little time to expand on this possibility before Fran dropped another bomb on me. "Speaking of strange, met with Shirley Bassett last night."

My heart started beating rapidly. "What? Why didn't you tell me? What happened?"

"Situation's worse than we thought."

"How?" I howled.

"Bassett knows everything. After the airplane banner stunt, she and O'Keefe moved out of Phoenix. Had to. Geri Cressman threatened to sue O'Keefe for sexual harassment. According to Bassett, O'Keefe's always been obsessed with other women. Only thing that'll kill one obsession is another obsession."

I bit my middle fingernail. "This is not good."

"Right before Destiny, O'Keefe had her sights set on an intern who worked for her. Sent her cards, letters, e-mails. Joined her gym, started shopping at her grocery store, pretended to bump into her, left business cards on her windshield. This ring a bell?"

"Even though the woman hadn't encouraged her?" I said, my voice hoarse.

"Same pattern. One night, O'Keefe filled the woman's voice mail with thirty-second messages, two hundred of 'em. Rambling, incoherent statements of love."

"How does Shirley know all of this?"

"Cops paid a visit to O'Keefe and warned her to back off."

"What happened to the intern?"

"She quit and moved out of state."

"To get away from Carolyn?"

"Seems so."

"I can't believe Shirley knows about all this and hasn't done anything to stop Carolyn," I said furiously.

"O'Keefe's high functioning fools a lot of people, including therapists."

"Carolyn's sought treatment?"

"Several times. Been diagnosed as bipolar. Takes medication, and the wacky behavior subsides. Stops because she starts feeling better and thinks she doesn't need the drugs."

"Obviously, she's not on medication now."

"Bingo. She told Bassett she's finished with talk therapy and scripted meds. No more, ever again. That's why Bassett intervened with Destiny. Soon as she saw O'Keefe's fixation, she tried to prevent an escalation. Didn't know what else to do."

"That's why Shirley gave the Lesbian Community Center the big donation?"

Fran nodded. "No other reason. She knew a large chunk of cash would give her access to Destiny. She couldn't warn Destiny directly but tried to channel Destiny's energies away from programs with O'Keefe."

"She underestimated Destiny."

"Got that right. Destiny mobilized to match the grant but insisted on following through with the teen programs, too."

"Which is why she's working twenty hours a day."

"That's what our friend Shirley discovered, belatedly."

"Why does Shirley stay with Carolyn? How could anyone's love run that deep?"

"Ain't love," Fran said calmly. "Stopped being that years ago, you ask me."

"What is it then?"

"Fear."

I looked at Fran doubtfully. "Please!"

She narrowed her eyes. "You think I'm exaggerating? That lowlife has made her lover a promise she'll never forget."

Fran's wild-eyed stare made me nervous. "Which is?"

"O'Keefe has convinced Bassett that she'll kill her if she tries to leave."

• • •

I let out a skeptical groan, which prompted Fran to say, "You don't believe me? Go talk to her yourself."

I astonished Fran by walking out of the office without another word, and in less than twenty minutes, I'd reached Shirley Bassett's investment firm in the Denver Tech Center. Ignoring the receptionist who served as gatekeeper for eight suites, I walked directly into Shirley's office and slammed the door.

She looked up, startled.

"I need to speak to you."

Shirley rose and adjusted her leaf-print, slipover shell and reached for its matching jacket. She smoothed the elastic waistband of her black cropped pants. "You look familiar. Have you come to one of the Denver Women's Chamber meetings?"

"Once, but—" I began.

"Wonderful," she said, gesturing for me to take a seat in the leather chair across from her oak desk. "You must be here for the free financial checkup. I leave coupons on every table."

"I don't need investment advice—"

"Many women feel that way, but everyone could use a tip or two, and as you can see, my passion is money."

Shirley Bassett wasn't kidding.

She'd taken a nondescript, windowless space and filled it with symbols of currency. In a freestanding, four-shelf glass case, she had a coin collection. A table behind her desk held a vintage cash register from the Old West, a ticker-tape machine, a miniature bank vault and a display of calculators and adding machines. One wall housed four clocks, set to time zones in Tokyo, Geneva, London and New York, and another was covered with framed stock certificates representing each of the thirty companies that comprised the Dow Jones Industrial Average.

"I don't care about money," I said, almost violently. "I'm here to talk about your lover, Carolyn O'Keefe."

Shirley Bassett's face lost all color. "What makes you believe we're lovers?" she said unsteadily.

"The fact that you used to spend every night together at your home on Oneida Street, even though Carolyn owns her own home in the same neighborhood, on Holly Street."

"You seem to be well-informed, which puts me at a disadvantage. I don't even know your name."

"Kristin Ashe."

"Nice to meet you," she said, force of habit.

"My lover is Destiny Greaves."

Only two strangled words came out of her mouth. "I see."

"I'm a private investigator. Twenty-seven days ago, Carolyn gave me ten thousand dollars and hired me to follow Destiny and find out everything I could. Carolyn said she was trying to decide whether to have an affair with her."

"Why did she hire you?" Shirley said, managing only a whisper.

"I don't know, but I'm sick of the games, with her and with you."

"What have I done?"

"Suddenly appeared with a hundred-thousand-dollar donation to the Lesbian Community Center."

"That contribution was confidential."

"Not anymore."

"I give large sums to a variety of organizations."

"Four days after your lover approaches me about my lover. What the hell's going on?"

Shirley sipped coffee from a NYSE mug and took forever to swallow. "I have no idea what you're talking about."

"We can do this one of two ways," I said, raising and lowering my voice to discombobulate her. "You can continue to lie, and I'll contact every business organization in this city and make the connection between your donation and your precious chamber. Are you ready for the most widespread outing of your life?"

"You wouldn't dare," she sputtered.

"You're right, I wouldn't. At least not until I've contacted the Metro Denver Public School board and played a recording of every conversation I've had with Carolyn."

Her voice faded. "You couldn't."

"I could. Happily," I lied. No such tapes existed.

"What do you want?" she said heavily.

"I want you to make Carolyn stop."

"I don't care for your tone."

"Look," I said in a placating tone. "We're on the same side. We're both about to lose our lovers. Do you want that to happen?"

"You don't know Carolyn," Shirley said, an undercurrent of fright in her voice. "She won't listen to me."

"Why do you tolerate her predatory behavior?"

"Because I love her."

I shook my head, not bothering to conceal disgust.

"You may not understand this, but Carolyn loves me, too."

"How can you delude yourself?"

"She always comes back. We may not be sexual, we haven't been in years, but we share something deeper, something none of those other women can touch."

"This is sick," I said with deep feeling.

"I left her ten years ago," Shirley said helplessly. "I stayed with my sister for a week."

I shot her a quizzical look. "Why did you leave Carolyn, and why did you go back?"

"I left because I thought I'd die if I stayed with her," Shirley said, lowering her head. "And I went back because I knew I'd die if I didn't."

CHAPTER 26

The next morning, Wednesday, I could barely drag myself out of bed. By the time I stumbled into the shower at eight, Destiny was long gone.

Lately, if it hadn't been for the frequency of my nocturnal wake-ups, I wouldn't have seen her at all. She usually joined me under the covers sometime between one and five, and we'd talk for a few minutes before she dropped off to sleep, leaving me wide awake, one of the reasons I'd hit the slumber button four times this morning.

The delay threw me off schedule, and I was a few minutes late to pick up Flax, but he didn't seem to mind.

We told his Grandma Nell we were going to a computer store to browse for a system upgrade, but as planned, we headed to the Fielder mansion.

"Here's my secret room," Flax said after we'd accessed the basement through a back stairway in the main house and walked down a narrow hallway. He switched on two battery-operated, wall-mounted lights and showed me his private fort. He'd retrieved chairs, cushions and a cooler from nearby Dumpsters and added a Harry Potter poster, a mini boom box, a stash of candy and his grandmother's collection of comic books.

While Flax practiced dowsing in the far reaches of the basement, I lounged on a beanbag chair, chewed a rope of stale red licorice and read about the adventures of Richie Rich.

Right as the plot was heating up in the comic book, Flax came running back. "I've found a ghost."

"Oh, sure," I said, prying a clump of licorice off my back molar.

"No, really, Kris. It's like something was pulling the rods out of my hand. Come see!"

"I'll wait here," I said lazily. "You do some more investigative work."

"Can I open the door of the room where I'm getting the reading?"

"Feel free," I said magnanimously.

"It's the room Grandma Nell thinks is haunted, the one they discovered at the séance. It's locked, but I'll bet I can break the lock with a hammer."

"You have a hammer?"

"A sledgehammer. I found it last summer. If Grandma Nell or Grandma Hazel finds out, will you tell them you said it was okay?"

"They'll never know. Just in case, don't do too much damage."

"Come with me, Kris. Please!"

I sighed, rose reluctantly and followed the beam of Flax's headlamp.

Brow furrowed in concentration, he delicately held the two L-shaped rods Cass had given him, one in each hand. We had passed a handful of small rooms with no results, when suddenly Flax's arms sprang into movement. The copper rods crossed and pointed downward at the threshold of the locked, allegedly haunted room.

"You're doing that to scare me," I said, my voice cracking.

"Honest, they do it on their own, like Cass said they would. I'm not moving them. Here, you try," he said, foisting the rods at me.

"I believe you," I said hurriedly, terrified of touching the metal rods that had, from all appearances, connected with energy from another world. "We should call Cass."

"We don't need her. You're just chicken."

I glared at him and, after a pause, said, "You hold the rods, and

I'll give the lock a whack." With one well-aimed blow, I knocked the padlock—hinge, screws and all—to the ground.

As Flax opened the door, it shuddered in a loud creak, which spooked us.

I instinctively took a few steps back, planning my emergency exit, but he proceeded forward toward a pile of dirt, loosely packed, in the shape of a body.

"We should leave," I said nervously.

He kicked at the mound. "I'm not scared."

I heard a gasp and the clang of two dowsing rods as they hit the dirt floor.

"There's a body in there," he said in a stage whisper, as soon as he could catch me and his breath.

"No, there isn't," I said in a little girl's voice, from my safe zone twenty feet from the room.

"Then what is it?"

"Dirt. Clear plastic," I said, relying on my split-second view before the retreat. "Candles and air fresheners."

"No way!"

"Yes way!"

"Go in and see."

"I'm not going in there," I said adamantly. "You're the one who wanted to test your dowsing skills. Let's just close the door and pretend we were never there."

Flax straightened his shoulders. "I'm going back."

"Be careful," I said as I watched his determined stride down the hall.

I'd started to return to my beanbag when Flax let out a high-pitched scream and came stumbling down the hall, his headlamp askew.

His face was pale, and I could barely understand his swollen voice. "I told you it was a body."

"Run," I shouted.

Granted, my thoughts weren't rational—dead bodies can't do much harm—but I had to get out of there.

We sprinted to the far end of the basement, up the stairs and into the alley.

In the blinding sunlight, I could see sweat cascading down Flax's face, and somewhere in our flight, he'd dropped the dowsing sticks. I took his hand and led him around the house, into the side yard farthest from the carriage house.

"What did it look like?" I asked after we'd plopped down on the grass in the shade of a large elm.

"Gross," he said, still quaking. "Do we have to call the cops? I don't want them to find my hideout."

"No, no. Let me think. It's your great-grandpa, Herman Middleton," I said dazedly. "Hazel killed him and left him there. They never did get along."

"No, sir. My dad went to his funeral."

"He told you about it?"

"A bunch of times. Plus, he makes me visit the grave. We go to the cemetery and put flowers next to a bunch of dumb relatives' headstones. His is there, with a space for Grandma Hazel when she dies."

"That doesn't mean there's a body in the plot."

"My dad saw the body," Flax said deliberately. "In the casket. That's why he wants to be cremated, because he thinks it looks fake, like you're there when you're not."

"He shared this with you?"

"We talk about everything."

I took a deep breath, uncertain of the next move. "You're sure it was a body in the basement?"

"Uh-huh. I saw a skull, with long hair."

"What color?"

"Gray. And a shirt and pants."

"What color?"

"White and light blue."

"You're sure about the color of the pants."

"I guess. I dunno."

"Wait here," I said, rising.

He blanched. "By myself?"

"Grandma Hazel's next door."

"But we're not supposed to be here."

"Then don't go get her unless it's an emergency. I'll be back in two minutes." I ran into the main house, up to the second floor and back into the yard in record time. I held up the light blue blazer I'd retrieved from the room where he and I had maintained our ghost stakeout. "Were the pants this color?"

His full-body trembling gave me the answer.

We now had a positive identification, more or less, of the body, but that merely raised more questions. If Constance Ferro was lying in the basement, who had murdered her, and why had the killer moved her or left her there?

Given that Hazel Middleton had been the last person to see her in Colorado, I knew where my next line of inquiry lay.

Understandably, I had little desire to confront a potential murderess, especially in the company of her great-grandson. To spare him the glare of the sun, I tried to talk Flax into returning to his hideout for a few minutes while I chatted with Hazel, but he wouldn't budge.

I made a quick trip to 7-Eleven and returned with fortification.

He wolfed down two candy bars and swallowed the contents of a Big Gulp before a hint of color returned to his cheeks. Assured of his health, I methodically put one foot in front of the other and crossed the grounds to Hazel Middleton's front door.

In minutes, however, I was back with Flax, mooching a roll of Smarties and cursing the fact that, in spite of the Lincoln Continental parked in the driveway, no one had answered the door.

• • •

Overriding Flax's strenuous protests, I took him home and stopped by the office to pick up the Fielder mansion file.

That might have been a mistake.

My casual "How's it going?" brought a storm of wrath from Fran Green, who was playing solitaire on the computer.

She sat up straight, drew attention to her T-shirt, "You Can't Fix Stupid," and exited the game. "Getting ridiculous. Last night, I found a videotape on my doorstep, compliments of Tess the Terrorizer."

"A tape of what?"

"Her shimmying up a giant rock near Estes Park this weekend. No equipment. Free-soloing. She's been threatening to do it since the day I met her. She scampered up without a helmet, ropes or bolts. Just a bag of chalk tied to her waist. I saw her climb at least two hundred feet. Shut it off after that. No interest in watching her attempt suicide."

"You think that's what it is?"

"Telling you, Kris, it's death in slow motion. That tape showed Tess one slip away from free-falling twenty stories."

"Who shot the footage?"

"Good question. Probably some other knucklehead climber. Don't own one brain between 'em."

"Why do you think Tess brought you the tape?"

"The note on the box claimed she wanted me to share in her amazing grace. I already knew she had vise-like fingers. Anyone who shakes her hand gets that message. Seen every muscle in her body flexed. What's she trying to prove?"

"That she's crazy?"

"Did a straight-up job of that. Cloudburst could make the rock slick. Handhold could give way. Loose stones could bonk her on the head. Any moment, she's a fraction of a second away from two hundred and six bones crushing."

"No one has that many bones," I said mildly.

"Bet me? Twenty-seven in the hand alone, fourteen in the face. Saw it last week on the Discovery Channel."

"You weren't impressed with Tess's athleticism?"

"If I go stand in the freeway, middle lane at rush hour, you gonna give me credit for good posture?"

I shrugged.

"Hell, no. You'd put me on a suicide watch at Denver Health. That girl needs help. Drugs might be in order, and you know how I feel about meds."

"That they're worthless."

"Most cases."

"What are you going to do?"

"Same as any decent human being—call her batty mom. Tell her to get out of the cave she's been living in."

"That's not very nice."

"Not joking, she's living in a cavern near Taos." Fran cleared her throat. "How'd I get into this stew?"

"Maybe you shouldn't answer any more personal ads."

"Done."

"Or have sex five times on the first date."

"Can't promise that," Fran said with a lecherous look. "Enough about me, though. What're your plans for the p.m."

"I have to go tell Hazel Middleton that Flax and I found a body in her basement, but I suspect she already knows that," I said conversationally.

"Get out!" Fran shouted.

After she recovered from the shock, I told her about Flax's dowsing and Constance's outfit.

She didn't bother to mask her delight. "Let me in on the fireworks. Love to come with you to visit Hazel."

Somehow, I didn't find as much merriment in the situation, and I suspected Hazel Middleton wouldn't either. "I'd better talk to her alone."

Fran's face fell. "Suit yourself, but give me a holler. Can't wait to hear how the lady explains away a corpse."

• • •

Hazel Middleton didn't try to explain away anything.

As soon as I confronted her with the news of Flax's discovery, she shrugged aimlessly, as if she'd been waiting years to confide in someone.

We spoke for several minutes before I confirmed, "There's no ghost in the mansion, is there?"

She smiled faintly. "None that I've seen or heard."

"You broke the windows?"

Hazel nodded, her smile still present.

"And made up the story about the lights in the attic window?"

"I told my daughter what she wanted to hear."

"Because you didn't want anyone to discover Constance?"

"I couldn't bear to be apart from her."

"How did she die?"

"From a weak heart, I presume. She collapsed and stopped breathing. It all happened quickly."

"Why were you in the basement?"

"I was walking her home. We spent almost every evening together, in her apartment or in the carriage house."

"When it was time to go home, one of you would cut through the tunnel?"

"In bad weather, yes. It saved us the trouble of bundling up. Constance didn't feel comfortable walking in the basement alone at night, but I never had such compunction. I'd escort her home and return to my place."

"Did she die in the room she's in now?"

"In the hall outside. I scooted her into the room. It wasn't difficult. She was a slip of a thing. She'd been having digestive troubles and had lost weight her last year. Truly, she was skin and bones."

"You wrapped her in the plastic?"

"I did. After a few days, when the smell became too much."

"And dug the grave?"

"Yes. Her final resting place. A few feet down, no more. I worked at it a little bit at a time, so as not to put undue stress on myself. It was difficult work."

"You held vigil with the candles?"

"Every night until I no longer could safely use the stairs."

"You never considered burying her in a cemetery?"

"Not for a moment. Constance had no family, except for an estranged niece, and I felt it was my right to decide. I couldn't have made it out to the cemetery every day, and this was more natural. We could still be together."

"You weren't worried someone would discover her?"

"Not until Roberta Franklin came along with talks of renovation. No one in my family dared go into that room."

"Are you sure the room isn't haunted?"

"My dear, you can mark my word. I often wished it were true, as I sat by Constance's side. How I craved some connection with her, but I've had to content myself with memories. Those are my only form of visitations, and the older I get, the more they fade."

"Do you believe you'll ever see Constance again?"

"I certainly hope so. It's a comfort I hold on to as I near the end of my life."

"Did Flax or Nell tell you about our experiences Saturday night?"

"They both did, yes."

"Then you know we documented what could be evidence of apparitions."

"Oh, phooey! The only people who look for ghosts are those who are too impatient to wait for their own passing or too unimaginative to dream."

I looked at Hazel curiously. "You dream of Constance?"

"Almost every day," she said, with a childlike smile. "Why do you suppose I nap in the afternoon?"

I returned her smile and pulled six photos from the Fielder mansion file. "I know you don't believe in ghosts, but you should see these."

I laid the photographs on the table, and Hazel glanced at them without leaning forward. "What am I looking at? What are these supposed to represent?"

"They show anomalies," I said, "which match up with electromagnetic changes that registered on our equipment. I won't bore you with the scientific details—Flax would be better at that."

Hazel squinted at the photographs but didn't move to touch them. "I'm to believe this white splotch is a ghost?"

"The professionals prefer the term *orb*."

"These were taken in the main house?"

"In Constance's room."

She looked stricken. "Oh, dear!"

"It might have been Constance trying to make contact," I said softly.

Hazel pursed her lips and shook her head deliberately to contradict me.

But her tender clutch of the photographs and the tears cascading down her cheeks demonstrated the heart's triumph over reason.

CHAPTER 27

That was the beauty of love . . . that it could go on forever.

Unfortunately, I was mired in the darker side of love . . . that it could go on forever.

To hell with that!

Less than forty-eight hours remained before the start of the educators conference in Steamboat Springs, and I had to do something.

Earlier in the week, by chance, I'd come across one of the business cards Carolyn O'Keefe left on Destiny's windshield. Never mind how I obtained it (all right, I stole it from the back of Fran's top desk drawer), I had the superintendent's direct line at work.

She'd handwritten the number on the back of the card, along with a peppy, "Don't get discouraged. You know we can do this."

I thought Fran would never leave the office, but she finally did around five o'clock.

The instant her taillights faded in the distance, I dialed the number, my heart pounding.

She answered on the sixth ring. "This is Dr. O'Keefe."

"Destiny Greaves is my lover."

"Kristin," she said without missing a beat, "how good of you to call."

If ten miles hadn't separated us, I would have killed her right then. "I said, Destiny is my lover."

"I'm well aware of that," came the cordial reply. "Why do you think I hired you? You certainly have no other credentials to speak of."

I bit my tongue. "How did you know about our relationship?"

"The day I met Destiny, I saw your photo in her office. I made inquiries, and it took less than two minutes to find out who you were and how to contact you. I should be a private investigator, don't you think?"

I didn't reply.

"You're not her equal," Carolyn O'Keefe said matter-of-factly.

"You think you are?"

"Certainly. Destiny and I have missions. We were meant for greatness, as individuals and as a couple. You have a pedestrian job. You were meant for nothing. I saw you watching us at the Botanic Gardens. How did it feel to know that your lover belonged to me."

"Stop contacting Destiny."

"I can't," she said pleasantly.

"You won't."

"We have a professional relationship. You must realize these youth programs could define Destiny's career."

"This isn't about programs. You're physically attracted to her, but she has no interest in you."

"I'm afraid she does. We share a passion neither of us can deny."

"It's all in your head."

"My head," Carolyn O'Keefe said with a wicked laugh. "I can assure you that's not where it resides. Every time Destiny touches me, she's in my skin, my nerves, my blood. She's a part of me, and I'm a part of her."

"You are deluded," I said furiously.

"Nothing, and no one, can separate us. I've never felt a love this strong, and neither has she."

"You thought the same about Geri Cressman, and you were wrong, weren't you? She loved Amy Mercer, not you. Nice try with the airplane banner, though."

"How dare you!"

"And Judith, she loved her consulting business, which you destroyed by shutting off her phone line."

"No, in fact—"

"And Sue, she loved plants, but you took care of that, didn't you, when strangers stripped her yard bare? You never had sex with any of the women you stalked, did you?"

I could hear a sharp intake of breath, but nothing else.

"Or any kind of meaningful relationship?"

After a long silence, Carolyn spoke in a low, ominous tone. "I didn't presume you were capable of such clever revenge."

"Me? Revenge?"

"I rather enjoyed the greeting at the elementary school I dedicated this week."

"What are you talking about?" I said, genuinely confused.

"Too bad no one else understood the meaning, but that wasn't your point, was it? You made yourself clear in two-foot tall letters. *Geri, Judith, Sue and the students and faculty of Prairie Elementary School welcome Superintendent Dr. Carolyn O'Keefe.* How much did you pay a maintenance man for that little trick?"

"I have no idea what—" I said, breaking off when I realized that this must have been Fran's idea of an elementary exercise in free speech. I smiled at my partner's ingenuity.

Apparently Carolyn didn't appreciate my denial, because when she spoke again, she amped up the aggression. "Whatever you paid, you wasted it. I went about business as usual, holding meetings and fantasizing about your lover. I also enjoyed masturbating in the faculty restroom every break, knowing at that very moment, with every stroke, Destiny was doing the same."

"How disgusting!" I spat. "Destiny does not love you. She loves me!"

"But who does she imagine when she closes her eyes and endures the tiresome motions of sex with you? Or does she bother?"

"She doesn't close her eyes. We like to—" I started to say, before catching myself. "Stay away from her!"

"How can I when we have our lovely weekend in Steamboat Springs? Has she canceled our weekend plans without my knowledge?"

"No," I muttered.

"I must ask, if what you say is true, why isn't Destiny making this call?"

"Because she thinks it's all in my head," I screamed at the top of my range, hurting my throat.

"How intriguing. Would you like details to ponder while I'm two hundred miles away, with your lover in my arms?"

"This will not happen! Destiny will not go to that conference with you!"

"Would you care to place a bet on your lover's fidelity? Let's make it charming. We won't predict the outcome of the weekend—that would spoil the fun. As an alternative, let's wager on whether Destiny arrives at the Grand Hotel in Steamboat Springs by five o'clock Friday evening, shall we?"

"You're insane!"

"If she doesn't, you win. I'll conclude my business with Destiny and withdraw from her life. You can keep the ten thousand dollars I gave you as well—"

"I don't want your money!"

"No, but you need it, don't you? I'll never tell your lover that you accepted cash to test her loyalty. Does that seem fair?"

"I can't do this," I practically whimpered.

"A more interesting conclusion involves my winning. If Destiny arrives, you agree to pack up and move out immediately. You acknowledge she belongs to me, and you leave her life for good."

"This is absurd."

"By her behavior, she'll exhibit her wishes. We're simply agreeing to honor them. I'm willing to take the chance. Are you?"

"Destiny won't come to Steamboat Springs. And if she did, she'd only come because of the GLBT programs."

"Your naïveté is almost childlike. While you're playing make-believe that you and the most beautiful woman in Denver share a precious bond, I'll be stroking her lovely hair."

"You will not—"

"As I kiss your girlfriend's lips, with a lingering tenderness she's never experienced, I'll unbutton her blouse. Slowly, teasingly, one button at a time—"

"No!"

"Swallowing her moans with my tongue, caressing them. I'll slide my hand beneath her bra and skim her hardened nipples—"

"Try touching Destiny—" I began with a garbled shout.

"Moving in aching rhythm with her subtle thrusts, I'll take her trembling hand and place it between my legs—"

"I swear, I will—"

"Where she will feel the heat of my wetness, as she lowers herself and enters me with her—"

"Kill you!"

I have no idea who disconnected first, because I'd thrown the phone across the room.

Long after the dial tone subsided, I couldn't.

Stop shaking. Stop sobbing. Stop throwing back my head. Stop gesturing wildly with my arms and legs.

I screamed into a pillow, but nothing could muffle my agony.

• • •

After the fit, I felt as if I'd run a marathon, only to have an eighteen-wheeler flatten me at the finish line.

My neck hurt, my eyes burned, and my head throbbed.

I could barely move to answer my cell phone when it rang, and my lips ached when I mumbled, "What?"

"I've been trying reach you all day," Cassandra Antonopolus said, sounding aggravated. "I keep getting a busy signal when I call the office, and I've left several messages. Don't you return calls?"

"I've been a little preoccupied."

"I've discovered something disturbing at the Fielder mansion."

"Likewise, but you go first."

"I have grave concerns."

"That's a good one," I said sarcastically.

"I'm dead serious, Kris."

I smiled sardonically. "Another one."

"We might have inadvertently stirred up something the other night."

The catch in Cass's voice finally penetrated my fractured psyche. "Pardon me?"

"I went in last night with six other investigators. The consensus is that the house is active, too active."

"What are you talking about?" I said irritably.

"I told them nothing about the history of the house, and we explored all the rooms, not including the basement. We used a grid system for our equipment, and the investigators were drawn to the room you shared with Flax."

"The one where the Dobermans died, where Constance lived and where we saw a ghost?" I said in a singsong voice, sounding to my ear drunk.

"Yes," Cass said carefully. "I had each team member fill out forms during the investigation and an hour after it was completed. They weren't allowed to share impressions while we were in the house, to prevent contagion. Yet the comments on their reports were eerily similar. They used different language, but essentially described the same feeling."

"Which was?" I said uneasily.

"Turbulence. Unrest. Violence. Unresolved conflict. Malice. Disorderly attachments."

I blew out air. "What do we do now?"

"Nothing, for the moment. I want to gather a team, people I respect from across the country. We'll do the space-clearing as soon as I can coordinate it."

I straightened up. "Can the building be saved?"

"I don't honestly know, Kris. But something has to be done, or it can't be demolished safely."

"What will I tell Roberta?"

"Do you want me to call her?"

"That would help, because I already ruined her day when Flax and I found a body in the basement this morning."

"Constance?"

"How did you know?"

"A feeling."

"Could these readings have been caused by Constance's ghost?"

"Possibly," Cass said hesitantly. "But the spirits seem more malicious. They've tilted somehow. I've seen it happen, when they'll gather in clusters, almost a pack-dog mentality."

"Roberta Franklin is *not* going to like this," I said glumly.

"This goes beyond a real-estate transaction," Cass said fiercely. "You're lucky nothing happened to you and Flax this morning. You need to stay away from the mansion until I can get this resolved. Don't let anyone go inside."

The air grew still. "What are you saying?"

"Something bad is going to happen in that house."

• • •

Something bad happened in my house when Destiny arrived home from work at midnight.

I told her everything.

I'd never seen her as livid or discouraged, and with every sentence I spoke, another bit of life drained from her. In the span of an hour, I saw her enter and exit the traditional stages of grief: denial, anger, bargaining and depression. Over and over, she circled through them, in no particular order, sometimes in the span of a breath.

I had yet to witness acceptance.

Destiny looked at me desperately. "Is it worth it? Why don't I get a regular job in a bank or a grocery store?"

"You can't do that. This is your life's work."

"I get so tired of fighting these battles by myself. When will it end?"

"What do you mean?"

"Do you think I'll ever complete the job, that the Center and lesbian activism won't be needed?"

I answered in a pessimistic monotone, "No. Not in our lifetime."

"Why do I have to do it alone. Why can't people help me?"

"Who? How?"

"Other lesbians. They've carved out their own false sense of safety, but they won't help me change the world. They'll join a chorus or a softball team. They'll catch every damned episode of Ellen's show. They'll never miss an Indigo Girls concert, but what are they doing really?"

"Writing checks to the Lesbian Community Center," I said gently.

She glared at me. "They'll take a lover to a family gathering but won't show affection. They'll whisper their secret to a few coworkers but won't fight for partner benefits. They'll blend into the suburbs but won't stand out. They'll worship at a gay splinter church but won't fight religious oppression. They'll elect gay-friendly candidates but won't press for reform." Destiny fell silent, and then in a burst yelled, "Why do I have to live for all of us? Carolyn O'Keefe pretends to help, but all she wants to do is screw me? None of this meant anything to her?"

"Probably not," I said quietly.

"Fuck it!" Destiny shouted.

Repeatedly.

She might have continued for days, but her voice gave out after a hundred or so shrieks.

I broke the eventual silence. "Forget about other lesbians, Destiny. What can I do?"

"You do it every day," she said, her voice raw, "by being in my life."

The way she looked at me, I could tell she was entering disbelief again, and it broke my heart.

"You're certain Carolyn didn't make the phone calls she promised?"

"Yes."

"She didn't clear the programs with the PTA or the district board?"

"She never tried. Fran checked," I reminded her.

Back to anger. "I'm going to show that bitch. I don't need her permission to contact people. I'll approach them on my own at the conference."

I sighed wearily. "Are you sure you want to do that?"

"I have to."

"No," I said with an anguished cry. "You don't have to go to Steamboat Springs."

"Yes, I do," Destiny said with an eerie finality. "Nothing will prevent me from checking into that hotel Friday afternoon."

CHAPTER 28

I had a way to fix this.

I spent most of Thursday preparing to take back my life. I wrote a romantic note, bought scented candles and rehearsed what I'd say.

At dusk, as I lay in wait shivering, the minutes devolving into blackness, I felt comfortable with my decision.

I'd set the stage at the Fielder mansion by leaving the front door ajar, lighting the way with candles, and promptly at eight, my prey arrived and followed the bait.

In seconds, Carolyn O'Keefe slipped onto the second-story landing, breathless.

The sight of me, crouched, stopped her cold.

Before either of us could move, however, Fran Green came bounding up the stairs, two at a time. "Hey, Kris."

Carolyn's eyes darted back and forth. "What kind of game are you two playing?"

I ignored her shrill voice and said to Fran quietly, "What are you doing here?"

"Been following you. Saw the card you put on O.K.'s windshield. Masterful."

Fran was referring to the message I'd printed on the back of one of Destiny's business cards. *I can't stop thinking about you. Why wait until Steamboat Springs? Meet me at 8:00 p.m. tonight at 1232 Pennsylvania.*

Carolyn broke in belligerently, "How dare you—"

Fran cut her off tersely. "You anxious to get yourself killed?"

While I tried to assemble my thoughts, Fran escorted Carolyn from the landing, where I remained, into Constance's room. She said to her sternly, "Wait here." Fran shut the door tightly and turned toward me, her face ashen. "What's that? A toy?"

"Very funny."

She moved toward me but pulled up when I waved the gun. "Where'd you get it?"

"From Destiny's closet."

"That the piece she bought after the death threats?"

"Yes."

Fran put her hands on her hips. "Any idea how to make it do what you want?"

"No," I said, unfazed.

"This is a bad idea, Kris. You're gonna get caught."

"I'll use the gun to make Carolyn back out of a window in the attic. Accidental death."

"What if the fall doesn't kill her?"

"Then I'll shoot her," I said stubbornly.

"Cops'll be here in no time, after Hazel sounds the alert."

"She won't call. I hid her hearing aids this afternoon, while she was napping."

Fran stared at me, nonplussed. "You've given this a lot of thought, haven't you? You feel right about it?"

"Yes."

"Then how come you're shaking?"

"Because I've never killed anyone."

"Why start now?" Fran said nonchalantly.

"What else am I supposed to do, wait for Carolyn O'Keefe to destroy our lives?"

"You given any consideration to other people?"

"Like who?"

"Me, you knucklehead. What'll I do if you're in the slammer?"

"You have a hundred friends, not to mention all the women you're dating."

"They're acquaintances. Relationships a mile wide and an inch deep. Only true friend I have is standing smack-dab in front of me."

I transferred my hardened stare from her face to the wall next to her. "I have to do this, Fran."

"Bert won't like it. This house doesn't need a murder. How's she gonna market that?"

"She can find another house."

"What about Flax? You and he bonded, high-strength resin. The kid looks up to you."

"He'll survive," I said grimly.

"And Destiny," Fran said softly. "Think of her."

"Why do you think I'm doing this?" I wailed. "Ever since Carolyn O'Keefe walked into my office, I haven't been able to think of anything else. I'm terrified of losing her."

"You won't."

"No one's ever loved me like she has."

"Vice versa."

"She's my best friend," I said, starting to cry.

"Best in the world," Fran agreed.

"I need to see her every day."

"You will."

I choked back a sob. "I miss her. I've been so lonely this past month."

"I hear you. Sit down and let me give you a slice of advice."

I lowered myself to the floor but said defiantly, "Don't try to talk me out of this."

"Have no intention of that. First tidbit, don't hold the gun in the air."

I flashed Fran a stunned look. "You're telling me how to shoot Carolyn?"

"May as well do a decent job of it. Hold the metal next to your hip, with both hands. First shot'll stop her or stand her up as she lurches. Second one'll send her back. Got that?"

I nodded weakly. "How do you know so much about guns?"

"Uphill Sherry has a side business. Designs clothes for women who pack heat."

"Are you lying to me?"

"No, ma'am. Started the biz when she couldn't find clothing that comfortably concealed a piece."

"Does she make any money?" I said, as if holding a normal conversation, not as if I were about to take a life.

"More than she used to repairing Birkenstocks. Big bucks in skirts, jackets and pants with room for a rod."

"How bizarre."

"You need any more shooting tips?"

I shrugged, losing my conviction.

"Aim for the torso, not the head."

The gun weighed forty pounds in my hand, and I felt like throwing up.

Fran crossed the room and squatted next to me. "Better yet, let me murder O'Keefe."

"Why?"

"Better me than you on a concrete bunk. I've done a lot of living, wouldn't mind resting in the joint, surrounded by women."

"You'd kill Carolyn O'Keefe for me? You're not serious?"

Fran grinned slightly. "No, but you ain't either."

"I wish I could," I said, letting out the breath I'd held for twenty-nine days.

I handed Fran the gun, and she leaned in to give me a hug, but before we could touch, a scream pierced the night.

Followed by the sound of glass shattering.

CHAPTER 29

Fran and I bolted for the bedroom door, which she reached first. She flung it open, and from the threshold, we could see the broken window.

I was paralyzed.

To Fran's credit, she approached the second-story turret window, advancing with tiny steps, waving the gun back and forth.

The twenty-foot walk seemed to take an hour.

After she put her head out the window, she turned to me, baffled. "She's gone."

• • •

Emergency medical technicians spent the better part of the night cleaning up the blood and brain matter Carolyn O'Keefe had sprayed on the building, sidewalk, yard and street.

After Fran dialed 911, she'd had the presence of mind to hide Destiny's gun in Hazel's flower wagon and to call Roberta Franklin.

The lawyer was on hand to assist when a pair of Denver police officers interviewed us, separately and together, but the questions seemed routine.

The detectives focused more attention on Fran's T-shirt, "Girls Just Wanna Love Girls," than on gathering clues. They assumed suicide, and we didn't volunteer another scenario.

As we left, I overhead one of the EMTs commenting that it seemed as if Carolyn's body had fallen from the twentieth floor, not the second floor.

It was something he couldn't explain, and neither could I.

CHAPTER 30

A month later, Hazel Middleton and I shared a pitcher of iced tea in her side yard.

"Nell's moving me into the Belleville next weekend."

"An assisted living facility? Are you okay with that?" I said, searching for a reaction.

Hazel nodded slightly. "It's a far cry from the old folks' homes of my parents' era. Happy hour every afternoon, penny poker, tai chi, although I'm not sure what that is."

"Chinese exercises."

"You don't say! I may have to forego those, but I'm looking forward to the mystery movie outings. Some Sunday, you'll have to join me for brunch. My treat. They put out a lovely spread."

"Mmm," I said noncommittally.

"Waffles, an omelet bar and six kinds of pie."

"I'm free anytime."

Hazel matched my smile before turning somber. "I didn't want to die here, with no one finding me for hours or days."

"I don't blame you," I said, responding to her note of apology.

"I've missed being around people. It will be nice to be surrounded by life again, without having to make grand plans."

"You won't have to pay Flax to step and fetch."

She let out a chuckle. "True enough. Do you suppose finding Constance's body will have a lasting effect on him?"

"He viewed it as an adventure," I said, bending the truth a bit.

"How long had he known about the passageway?"

"Since last summer. He used both basements and the tunnel as a fort, but he never went into the locked room, not until the day we found Constance."

"Ah." Hazel sighed. "It's good that you were with him. And I'm pleased Constance had a proper burial. Please thank Roberta for me, for making the arrangements."

"I will," I said succinctly, leaving out details of the markers Roberta had had to call in to get McConnell Mortuaries to bury the body.

"Everyone's been so kind," Hazel said pensively. "They're all quite concerned about my well-being."

"Will you miss the mansion?"

She gazed over at it. "A bit, I suppose."

"Roberta plans to live in one of the units, and I'm sure the other owners wouldn't mind giving you a tour."

"Oh, I won't find that necessary," Hazel Middleton said firmly. "This house and I, we've had enough of each other."

• • •

Fran Green and Tess Thompson had had enough of each other also. Fran solved the dilemma of how to remove Tess from her life by introducing her to Robyn, the insurance contracts analyst she met through her personal ad, and apparently the two of them hit it off.

Fran put the brakes on her relationship with Roberta Franklin as well. They agreed to downgrade their relationship to "sexual companions." I'd never heard of that particular definition for two senior citizens, but what did I know?

I'd donated the $10,000 Carolyn O'Keefe had paid me to the Lesbian Community Center and taken perverse satisfaction in the knowledge that it had been matched by Shirley Bassett's donation.

Destiny and I returned to normal, whatever normal was, but I did make one significant change.

I placed a photo of her on my desk at work.

No one would ever again walk into my office and not know what she meant to me.

Publications from Spinsters Ink

P.O. Box 242
Midway, Florida 32343
Phone: 800 301-6860
www.spinstersink.com

DISORDERLY ATTACHMENTS by Jennifer L. Jordan. 5th Kristin Ashe Mystery. Kris investigates whether a mansion someone wants to convert into condos is haunted.   ISBN 1-883523-74-5 $14.95

VERA'S STILL POINT by Ruth Perkinson. Vera is reminded of exactly what it is that she has been missing in life.
ISBN 1-883523-73-7 $14.95

OUTRAGEOUS by Sheila Ortiz-Taylor. Arden Benbow, a motor-cycle riding, lesbian Latina poet from LA is hired to teach poetry in a small liberal arts college in northwest Florida.
ISBN 1-883523-72-9 $14.95

UNBREAKABLE by Blayne Cooper. The bonds of love and friend-ship can be as strong as steel. But are they unbreakable?
ISBN 1-883523-76-1 $14.95

ALL BETS OFF by Jaime Clevenger. Bette Lawrence is about to find out how hard life can be for someone of low society standing in the 1900s.   ISBN 1-883523-71-0 $14.95

UNBEARABLE LOSSES by Jennifer L. Jordan. 4th in the Kristin Ashe Mystery series. Two elderly sisters have hired Kris to discover who is pilfering from their award-winning holiday display.
ISBN 1-883523-68-0 $14.95

FRENCH POSTCARDS by Jane Merchant. When Elinor moves to France with her husband and two children, she never expects that her life is about to be changed forever.

ISBN 1-883523-67-2 $14.95

EXISTING SOLUTIONS by Jennifer L. Jordan. 2nd book in the Kristin Ashe Mystery series. When Kris is hired to find an activist's biological father, things get complicated when she finds herself falling for her client.   ISBN 1-883523-69-9 $14.95

A SAFE PLACE TO SLEEP by Jennifer L. Jordan. 1st in the Kristin Ashe Mystery series. Kris is approached by well-known lesbian Destiny Greaves with an unusual request. One that will lead Kris to hunt for her own missing childhood pieces.

ISBN 1-883523-70-2 $14.95

THE SECRET KEEPING by Francine Saint Marie. The Secret Keeping is a high stakes, girl-gets-girl romance, where the moral of the story is that money can buy you love if it's invested wisely.

ISBN: 1-883523-77-X $14.95

WOMEN'S STUDIES by Julia Watts. With humor and heart, Women's Studies follows one school year in the lives of these three young women and shows that in college, one's extracurricular activities are often much more educational than what goes on in the classroom.   ISBN: 1-883523-75-3 $14.95

A POEM FOR WHAT'S HER NAME by Dani O'Connor. Professor Dani O'Connor had pretty much resigned herself to the fact that there was no such thing as a complete woman. Then out of nowhere, along comes a woman who blows Dani's theory right out of the water.   ISBN: 1-883523-78-8 $14.95